The Munich Sabbatical

The Munich Sabbatical

PAT-ANN MORGAN

MPC

First published in Great Britain 1997 by
The Malvern Publishing Company Ltd.
The Wells House, Holywell Road, Malvern Wells,
Worcestershire WR14 4LH

British Library Cataloguing in Publication Data

A catalogue record for this book is available
from the British Library

ISBN 0 947993 67 3

Printed and Bound in Great Britain

To Pastor Tietz
who gave his life fighting
the evils of Nazism.

Acknowledgements

My thanks go to Tony for allowing me the chance to publish this book; to Kate for her patient assistance in its preparation; to family and friends for their constant encouragement during its writing; and above all to my husband, Mog, for his unfailing support throughout.

Chapter One

Heino Timmermann did not want to believe a woman that good-looking could possibly do anything ugly or vicious. After all, Werner Fuchs was getting old; perhaps his legendary instincts were beginning to fail him.

He watched every move she made as she wandered through the galleries. A few times he got too close, realised in time and retreated. He was glad no-one was backing him up, seeing him make every mistake in the book.

Now she had stopped in front of a painting to which she was paying far more attention than she had to any of the others. Heino sidled around behind her to see that it was the portrait of a young man – bearded, with long, flowing hair and deep enigmatic eyes, a Christ-like figure. Abruptly, even from a distance of thirty feet, he sensed her stiffen, saw her focus on something in the adjoining gallery. Heino could not see what or who it was, until an old man appeared in the wide doorway, walking with a deliberateness caused by the limitations of his joints. Yet at the same time there was a confidence about him that only seniority and knowledge can bestow.

The woman quickly turned her gaze back to the picture in front of her. Heino could not pinpoint it, but something about her made him sure she was feeling guilty – or at least ill at ease – about her imminent encounter with the old man.

Heino had never seen him in the flesh, but he knew exactly who he was. And that seemed to confirm everything the Chief had said about the woman. Disappointed, he looked on as, almost deferentially, she took a few steps back to allow the man a view of the portrait.

When Viola had spotted him in the next gallery, she could scarcely believe that at last she was almost face to face with Professor Josef Feinstein.

"A very beautiful painting, is it not?" he said in German, as he turned to her with an eyebrow raised and a smile hovering in the corner of his mouth.

"Yes," Viola answered nervously. "Very beautiful."

Standing in front of her, Josef Feinstein was a man of diminutive proportions. Though she herself was small, he was even smaller – shrunken no doubt by age, for he looked eighty at least. He had a large shock of wiry, grey hair and an equally conspicuous nose, which more than hinted at his ethnic origin.

"Is it the painting as a work of art," he went on, "or is it primarily the beauty of the young man that we admire?"

Viola did not feel she was ready to answer this.

"You have seen the other self-portraits perhaps – in the Prado and the Louvre?" he asked, looking straight into her eyes with his own – bright, clever and piercing black.

Viola nodded. "Yes, I know them both. Hard to believe, isn't it, that this is the same man?"

"Indeed it is. And of the three, which Albrecht Dürer do you prefer? This, the most idealised, the most narcissistic, though undoubtedly the most beautiful? Or one of the others, the more unpretentious, the more – if I may say so – believable?"

Viola glanced back at the sensitive, intellectual face, the soft, brown, bottomless eyes, the full, sensuous lips. Emphatically she answered, "This one."

"We have established then, that it *is* the face of a very beautiful young man; but unfortunately perhaps, a man who is all too aware of his own superiority?"

"One should avoid over-simplistic analysis," retorted Viola. "His was a very complex character, you know."

The old man bowed politely, as best his aged bones would allow. "I stand rebuked, dear lady." He smiled, took Viola's hand and kissed it. "In future I shall endeavour to follow your advice."

Viola was flustered – not by the quaint, old-world gallantry, but by her own reluctance to tell him who she was. He sensed her unease. Again he bowed his stiff, tiny body. "Allow me to introduce myself. My name is Josef Feinstein."

"Of course!" exclaimed Viola with a convincing show of surprise. "Oh Professor Feinstein, please excuse me for not having recognised you at once. I'm Dr Addison – Viola Addison. I've written to you from London." She thought of the steady stream of letters with which she had bombarded him and looked embarrassed. "I'm afraid I left several messages at your hotel when I heard you were coming here. I hope you don't mind."

"Dr Addison, you have no need to apologise to me. It is I who should apologise to you. I have a very domineering secretary who takes it on herself to prioritise – as she puts it – my mail. I try to fight it, but," he heaved his shoulders, "I regret too many of my correspondents become victims of neglect."

Now that she had finally met Professor Feinstein, Viola was relieved that had been the case. Suddenly it seemed presumptuous of her to have entertained the notion that such a distinguished academic would be interested in her own tentative views; even though they did share the same field of expertise.

"As for your not recognising me," he was saying now, "which young lady in her right mind would take a second look at a face like mine, when she has the chance to admire one as exquisite as this?"

He looked back at the Dürer. Viola's eyes followed and for several minutes they both gazed at it in silence.

"It is to a face such as this," he then declared, "that a young lady would wish to wake up every morning. Is that not so?"

Viola smiled wistfully, without averting her attention from the painting.

"But perhaps she has already known that pleasure?" added Professor Feinstein, leaning forward to catch her expression.

"Perhaps," replied Viola, for the moment dropping her guard.

She changed the subject. She did so skillfully, well practised in the art of keeping her own counsel – and her distance. Professor Feinstein was not duped by her efforts. He had lived too long in the world for that. On the contrary, her actions only confirmed his suspicions: that the painting in question reminded this charming, young Englishwoman of her lover.

"I greatly admire your work, Professor Feinstein," Viola continued. "I was fascinated by your last book – the one on portraiture in the late Gothic period."

"Then I hope to see you at my lecture on that very subject next Tuesday evening. Perhaps you would do me the honour of being my guest?"

Viola accepted; although as far as honour was concerned, she felt it was all hers. Nor did the irony of it escape her that, after months spent trying to generate some kind of dialogue between them, she should now be receiving an invitation as his guest.

She had known Professor Feinstein was in Europe on a long-awaited and much-vaunted lecture tour. She had been annoyed at having to leave London only a day or two before he was due to speak at the Royal Academy. So when she had arrived in Munich, she had been determined not to miss his lecture there – had even gone out of her way to engineer this meeting.

Josef Feinstein had, for many decades, been the world's undisputed authority on late Gothic and early Renaissance art. Viola Addison had, for the most recent of those decades, been an unequivocal admirer of his scholarship. And she was not without discernment in this particular field; for although still not quite thirty years old, she was already well on the way towards making a name for herself as an academic art historian of meticulous care and insightful comment.

But Viola, though clever, was also modest and would have been the first to point out that she was in quite a different league from the illustrious Professor.

"You are in Munich on business?" enquired Professor Feinstein.

"I'm attending a conference."

"So your time here is limited?"

"Not really. The conference only lasts a few more days, but I shall be based here for most of the coming year. I'm on a sabbatical from my university in England."

"So – You are a linguist? Your German is excellent."

"My German is *rusty*," laughed Viola, choosing to circumvent his assumption. "It was quite good once – when I was an exchange student, here in Munich. But that was nearly ten years ago."

"Well Dr Addison, we have at least that much in common. Like me, you studied in Munich – albeit, what, half a century or more later. But unlike me, you will doubtless still have many friends here, yes?"

"No, none. There's no-one." She let out a barely discernible sigh and followed it with an even more discreet glance back at the Dürer. "I've lost touch with them all, I'm afraid. We've all gone our separate ways."

"Then I shall have no scruples about inviting you to lunch tomorrow. I shall not need to fret that, in humouring me, you will be depriving yourself of the company of some beautiful, young man." His eyes sparkled as they shot across at the portrait – but they quickly returned to hers. "You will join me, won't you, my dear Dr Addison?"

"I shall be delighted."

"Then we can discuss my latest book and your research plans. You are a Germanist, you say?"

Viola lowered her eyes, as if about to make a grave confession.

"No, an art historian."

The unexpected coincidence amused Professor Feinstein and the laughter it provoked caused his flimsy body to rock dangerously. Yet the laugh itself was strong and exuberant so that it lit up his eyes, smoothed out the deep wrinkles in his cheeks and banished the frailty from his voice.

It drew the attention of the half-dozen or so other visitors in that particular room of the gallery who, as convention dictated, were using the hushed and reverential tones normally employed in such repositories of culture. Their reactions went unnoticed by Josef Feinstein, who was too self-assured – or perhaps too old – to care. But they unsettled Viola; so much so, she was relieved that her commitments forced her to leave the galleries of the Alte Pinakothek shortly afterwards with a brief goodbye and thanks for Professor Feinstein's invitation to lunch the next day.

As it happened the afternoon's lecture was of no great interest to Viola. The subject matter might well have been – had she been prepared to give it a chance; but the speaker, pompous and patronising, was guaranteed to stifle at birth any glimmer of curiosity – at least in her. She had heard Rupert Servranckz deliver a paper before – five or six years previously. Then she had hung on his every word. In those days she had been naïve enough to assume that almost anyone knew more about almost everything than she. The intervening years had taught her to have more faith in her own opinions and less in those of others. That was why she was here in Munich after all – because she had finally come of age as regards trusting her own judgement.

She had positioned herself towards the back of the lecture theatre, both as a consequence of having arrived there somewhat late and as a conscious tactic to enable her indifference to go unnoticed. She thought of that day months ago back in London, when Professor Bryce had offered her the chance of this study leave. It had marked a turning point. After years of prevarication it had forced her into making decisions.

Her parents had advised against the move; arguing it would open up old wounds – implying hers – meaning of course their own. Still, Viola could have predicted that. Opposition from her sister, Olivia, came as no surprise either; nor did the fact that she could offer no sensible grounds for it – at any rate none Viola could find convincing. All three of them had always thought they knew what was best for her and, for as far back as she could remember, had conspired to achieve it. So what was best for her now, they had determined in a series of lengthy discussions – from which their object was naturally

12

excluded – was to settle down, to marry John, and to produce a string of babies.

John wanted that too – had done so for years. But Viola did not. Besides, how could she marry one man, when every time he made love to her she thought of another? Ambivalent she might be, but she had some integrity.

A large, bald head attached to a pair of bulky shoulders in the row directly in front of her, lolled suddenly forward and the loud snoring which followed brought the scrutiny of Dr Servranckz over to that section of the auditorium where Viola sat. She put on an appearance of interest for the brief duration of his attention. No sooner did he remove it, however, than Viola likewise withdrew hers.

She was fond of John – very fond. He was kind and gentle and he loved her. She, though, was not in love with him. She regretted having hurt him, by accepting the sabbatical. She regretted having hurt him even more, by urging him to take up the professorship he had been offered in Australia and by telling him he must go there without her. Yet she was bound to have hurt him sooner or later. She reproached herself for having left it as late as this.

Ahead of her the rhythmic snoring grew louder and more tympanic by the minute, causing something of a hiatus in the concentration of the audience around her. The wicked thought flashed through her mind that this bizarre diversion was far more entertaining than the bland, old theories being expounded from the platform. Nor was she alone in thinking so, for she noticed ripples of unrest spreading in ever wider circles throughout the scholarly assembly. Lacking any sense of the ridiculous, which now became embarrassingly clear, Dr Servranckz found it hard, if not impossible, to control his irritation. In no more than a matter of minutes and in an unmistakable fit of pique, he brought his lecture to an abrupt and premature end. No sooner done than he was forced to endure the incongruity of witnessing the architect of his ignominy awake from his slumbers and join the applause with bewildered enthusiasm.

Suddenly Viola remembered Professor Feinstein and his boyish laughter. She wondered what he would make of this fiasco. She also wondered what he would think if he knew how hard she had worked to engineer their chance encounter, and how much easier he himself had made it by opening up the conversation. But she was too excited by the prospect of being able to discuss her work with the world's leading expert in her field to feel guilty about such an innocent intrigue.

Similarly, any remnants of guilt connected with John and her family in England vanished and she knew that, in coming to Munich, she had made the right decision – for John as well as for herself.

Chapter Two

The following day, Viola kept her date with Professor Feinstein. He arrived in high spirits, congratulating himself on having escaped the clutches of his secretary two days in a row. By the time he began to evaluate his chances of making it a hat-trick – by the time, that is, the waiter came to serve them with coffee – he felt he already knew as much as he needed about Viola to form a judgement. He had breathed in the essence of the girl and had found it to his liking. She seemed to strike so perfect a balance between idealism and common sense as to make her manner entertaining, easy; but most of all, full of charm. Besides which, she was very pretty.

Viola, for her part, could find no fault with her new mentor. He had listened intently, his eyes locked on hers as she had told him her research plans for the following year. There was nothing condescending in his enquiries about why she had chosen to study the artistic heritage of King Ludwig II. He conceded it was a broad based project, to study both the art and the motives of the man who had commissioned it. Even so he made no attempt to disguise the fact he felt she should set her sights much higher.

And somehow, apart from discussing her work with the attentive old man, Viola found herself talking about other things – her year in Munich as a student and the affection she had for the place. From there, the conversation seemed to lead quite naturally onto her relationship with Lutz Ebenau.

The professor found this unanticipated openness appealing, since it seemed out of character and so must, he concluded, be taken as a compliment to himself.

It was indeed a compliment Viola paid him. Josef Feinstein was right to judge it so; for other than to Hilly, her best friend, Viola had opened her heart to no-one – ever since her student days in Munich had ended so unhappily nearly ten years before.

Viola still bore the scars from that time. The more she talked about it to Professor Feinstein, the more apparent they became. She did not try to understand why, after so long spent hiding her feelings, she should now be pouring them out to a comparative stranger. But talking to the venerable academic was like confiding in the father she never had. With her own family, there could be no such intimacies. They had seen to that when, at the end of that exchange year, they had persuaded her to give up the idea that a relationship with Lutz could be a thing of permanence.

Romantic love had much to answer for, thought Josef, as he listened to her story. How much simpler life was without it. He took another sip of the strong, black coffee and spoke.

"So my dear Viola, you have been allowing this bitterness to fester inside you all these years." He shook his head. "This is not good."

"I know it's not – but I just can't help it." Viola let out a deep sigh. "And, you know, it's not only my parents' interference I resent. I despise myself for having let them manipulate me that way."

"Have you considered – yes, I am sure you have – that what they did was for your own good – that they may have genuinely believed this Lutz was not right for you? You were, after all, very young."

"If I truly believed that, then yes, I could forgive them. But I don't. The problem was, he wasn't right for them. He was my choice, not theirs – and they think they know what's best for me. They always have."

"But now, finally, you have cut the knot." The professor's tone was triumphant. "You have broken the cycle. You have come to Munich against their advice. You are packing your John off to Australia

16

against their better judgement."

Viola's "Yes" was quiet, almost hesitant, as if she had just realised what she had done.

"And this young man, this Lutz, perhaps he is still here in Munich? Or am I to believe," he continued – the now familiar, flirtatious twinkle in his eye – "that it is purely for the purposes of academic research you are here? Purely to carry out your scholarly detective work on poor Ludwig II and his patronage of the Arts?"

Viola smiled at him. "Professor Feinstein, you're making fun of me."

"No indeed. But tell me, is he here?"

"I don't know – at least, not for certain." She felt suddenly foolish, but having started on a course of frankness, there seemed little point in stopping. "To be honest, Professor, I handled the whole situation badly when I went back to England. We should have worked out how to keep in touch before I left. But I was only twenty – I didn't want to look too keen, even if I was. Besides I just assumed I'd hear from him and that somehow we'd get back together again." She gazed for a moment into her coffee cup. "I never got so much as a post card from him. I know he went to South America, shortly after I got back home – but I can't believe he stayed there. He loved Germany too much for that. Anyway he wanted to be one of the ones to set things right – to put Germany back together again, into one country. He hated the fact it was divided."

Viola paused. Josef too fell into a thoughtful silence. The waiter approached to offer them more coffee. Viola declined. Feinstein asked for the bill.

"You were saying?" said Feinstein, as though the interruption had caused him to lose his train of thought.

"Yes, I was about to say, I think he *is* here in Munich. Certainly there's a lawyer with his name listed in the telephone directory – and he *was* studying Law. I thought of 'phoning him – but my courage failed me." She paused and took a last sip from her empty coffee cup. "I think I may have seen him, though – since I arrived back here. Actually I'm fairly sure it was him. I was afraid to look too hard in case . . ." Her voice petered out.

"In case it was not," added Josef, in an attempt to supply the missing words.

"No. In case it was."

He muttered his understanding. She smiled at him again.

"A lost cause, aren't I? I've been waiting all this time and now I'm here, look at me, I'm getting cold feet."

"So where did you see him? Or rather where do you think you saw him?"

"It was last Friday. I hadn't long arrived in Munich. I'd forgotten to pack a few things, so I needed to do some shopping. I'd been wandering along Neuhauserstraße and was just passing the Augustiner – you know, the Gaststätte in the pedestrian zone – by the Michaelskirche – with the tables outside?"

Josef nodded.

"Well, it was very busy there. It was about six – just after. People were getting together after work – all the tables were packed. Anyway, the man walking just ahead of me stopped outside and looked up and down the rows of tables – as if he were expecting to see someone he knew."

"And this man – it was Lutz?"

"No. But I *did* recognise him. It was a friend of his. Peter – Peter Lessel I think his name is. He was at university with me and Lutz. They were very close, but I never got to know him that well. Anyway, just then, out of the corner of my eye, I noticed someone waving to him. I looked around and . . ."

"And that was Lutz?"

"Yes. Well, at least I think it was. I can't be sure. I was too – oh, scared, I suppose, to look closely."

"Yes, yes. I understand."

"You have been back there since, I take it?"

"Every day. But I've seen no sign of either of them, though I'm fairly sure Peter Lessel saw me."

"So," he announced. "Tomorrow we shall begin some detective work. We shall go to the Augustiner at six o'clock and see if either one of them appears. Tomorrow," he added, emphasising the day's importance with a significant narrowing of the eyes, "it is Friday, yes?"

"Yes. But I'm afraid I'm going home for the weekend. It's my father's sixtieth birthday on Saturday. I'd never be allowed to live it down, if I missed that."

"And what time is your flight?"

"I have to be at the airport by a quarter past seven."

"So," he cried and waved his hand back and forth in a dismissive gesture, "we have time – we have time. As long as the sun shines, we shall sit and drink and chat pleasantly together. And while we wait, I shall try to persuade you to change your researches from Ludwig and his world of fantasy to Dürer and his observation of reality. Do you agree?"

Viola laughed. "I agree – to your plan that is – and thank you. As far as my research is concerned, I can't agree to change that. Besides, what more is there to say about Dürer that Panofsky and Feinstein haven't already said?"

"Now you flatter me, my dear Viola. But do not imagine such flattery will dissuade me. We shall talk more on the subject tomorrow."

When tomorrow came, though, Professor Feinstein had little opportunity to chide Viola about the subject of her forthcoming book – or anything else. It soon became apparent that he would have little chance to speak to her at all; for during the half an hour or so they spent drinking Radlermaß outside the Augustiner, in the late summer sunshine, it was Ellie Levinson, Professor Feinstein's secretary, who hogged the conversation. Viola did not mind. Ellie was a talented and witty raconteuse and, tense as Viola was that evening, she was happy just listening to her; happy just listening to English – even Ellie's colourful New York variant – after a week of using only German.

The atmosphere at the Augustiner fizzed. Surrounding their table Viola saw nothing but animated faces – all chattering, laughing, arguing – all full of vitality. In the precinct too, wherever she looked, was bustle, as Munich changed into top gear in order to drive itself headlong into the weekend.

Even Viola felt an unfamiliar sort of exhilaration – a sense of mounting anticipation. Her eyes darted to and fro, from one group to another, from one face to the next – but the only one she recognised was that of a young man she had seen talking to a guard at the Alte Pinakothek, the day she and Professor Feinstein met. Of the man she most wanted to see, Lutz Ebenau – or even his friend, Peter Lessel – there was no sign.

Josef Feinstein, it seemed, was satisfied merely to sit, taking the occasional sip from his glass, allowing the sounds of the Augustiner, the passers-by and the raucous voice of his secretary to blend together into an amiable buzz. Once or twice he lent across and squeezed Viola's hand. In her preoccupation she barely noticed – though Ellie did.

Abruptly, a single, explosive yell shattered the common mood of conviviality. All heads spun round towards it. Viola had to crane her neck to pinpoint the source of the disturbance; though when she did, she almost wished that she had not.

Two gangs of youths stood not far off, embroiled in heated argument. It was clear they had already reached the point at which violence would be the likely outcome – and the several other groups, gathering around to watch and egg them on, seemed to make it all the more inevitable.

One youth, fair-haired, short but burly, looked to be the ring-leader. He was standing at the head of his mob, spitting abuse at a slim, swarthy-skinned adversary. Such was the venom in his voice, Viola felt sick and frightened by it. Yet her fear was only to increase when he abandoned vitriol and began punching his fists into the stomach of his opponent, knocking him with such force, further and further back into the body of his gang, until finally he fell and disappeared from view.

The aggressor now, as if requiring adulation, turned full circle and as he did, Viola could see the exultation of victory burning in his eyes. He held aloft a fist and shouted some sort of primitive, barbaric war-cry; whereupon the two sides laid into each other in an uncontrolled frenzy of brutality.

Soon the ground was alive with writhing youths. Others had the blood of battle oozing from their faces. A few minutes later, the police arrived and, making use of corresponding force, broke up the mayhem and marched off those few – mainly the injured – who had not already fled the field. Viola looked about for the ring-leader, but there was no trace of him.

Then, just as suddenly as it had started, it was over. Viola turned to find Professor Feinstein ashen-faced and breathless, with Ellie fussing over him like a protective nanny. Viola mumbled her concern and when Josef raised his face to thank her, etched into it she could see fear, anger, sadness – she had not the experience to be certain which.

"Bad memories," Ellie whispered in her ear. "It's gone and brought back all those bad memories."

"Yes, yes – of course – I'm sorry," replied Viola, still half mesmerised by his expression.

"C'mon, JF," Ellie coaxed, "it's getting late. High time we were heading for the hills." She turned to Viola for support.

"Yes, you're right. It *is* getting late," she confirmed, as she helped Ellie get him to his feet. "I must be off too, or I'll miss my plane. But I *am* worried about you – you'll be all right, won't you?"

"Sure we will, won't we, JF?"

Josef Feinstein was on the point of chastising them both for treating him like a child, when a man approached to ask if they were vacating their table. One glimpse was all it needed for Josef to recognise him. This was a face he had already seen – or one very like it, even though this one was beardless and deprived of the long, waving locks of the original. He glanced across at Viola. Her look confirmed it. This was the face of Lutz Ebenau.

Whatever else Josef might have been inclined to think about this handsome young man, he knew he had no right to let his presence intrude between Viola and her former lover. Murmuring a low-key farewell, and beckoning impatiently to Ellie, he began to slip away.

21

But Viola noticed and managed to tear her attention away from the man who stood opposite her, just long enough to give the professor a dazzling smile; then he turned and melted into the bustling crowd.

Lutz Ebenau had not yet uttered a word to Viola, although the excitement in his eyes had already expressed his pleasure at seeing her again. He sat down in the chair which Josef had vacated.

"Schätzlein, how are you?" he asked, as if it had been ten days, not ten years since they had last met.

Viola felt like a teenager, kissed for the first time. She felt absurd, ashamed of herself; she tried to pull herself together. She opened her mouth to speak but, to her embarrassment, found she had to clear her throat before she could. "Lutz! I can hardly believe it's you. You haven't changed – not a bit, even without the beard." As soon as she said it, she thought how trite the words must sound.

Lutz did not seem to notice. "You have," he said in the silvery half-whisper Viola remembered so well.

"Have I?" she said, instantly assuming that she had aged, lost the bloom, the ingenuousness of the twenty-year-old she had been when he had seen her last. Nervously she put her hand up to her brow to push aside a wayward curl. At least her auburn hair, her most prized physical asset, was as luxuriant as ever – and even longer than it had been ten years before.

"Oh yes," Lutz murmured. "You are ten times more beautiful and, somehow, more alive. I can't imagine how I ever let you go."

"Nor could I, at the time," Viola laughed, almost out of control at the sensation this encounter was causing inside her.

"Why did you go?" he asked with a hint of offended pride in his voice.

"Why didn't you follow me?" she countered.

"I was going to. Do you know, I had even bought a ticket, and a map of England." He sighed. "But that day, that very day, my father died. It made me almost prepared to believe it was a sign – some kind of fatalistic message. Anyway, as a result, I had a tremendous amount to do. And you had gone. I rang a couple of times, but you were not in and you never returned my calls."

"You rang? Where?"

"Your home, of course. I spoke to a woman. Your mother; your sister?"

"But they never told me." Viola's stomach turned over at the thought.

"Then I found out that my father's interests were far wider than I had ever imagined. I had to go out to South America, to sort out some problems with the will there and that took several months. In fact I ended up taking the year out. Of course, all the time I was in America, I was hoping you would have been in touch, left some word at least. But," he shook his head in exaggerated self-pity, "there was nothing."

"Oh, Lutz," Viola stretched her hand across the table and laid it briefly on his, "I heard about your going to South America. That's when I assumed it must all be over." She withdrew her hand, clenched her fists in anger at herself. "And when I think how I let my family persuade me that you couldn't be right for me; that you were from a 'different culture'." She shook her head. "And all that time they were hiding the fact that you'd tried to get in touch with me." She swallowed hard. "I can hardly believe it."

Lutz was looking at her with motionless eyes. "Believe it; but it does not matter now. We have found each other again. What could be better?"

Viola did not trust herself to speak for a moment. That this man, who for so long had played the leading role in all her fantasies should be welcoming her back, without qualification, seemed beyond all the laws of probability.

She laughed. "Oh Lutz, it is extraordinary to see you again," she glanced at her watch, "but I've got a plane to catch." She gathered up her things. "If I don't go now I'll miss it. Will you be here next week?"

"Who knows what the future has in store?" Lutz's smile was enigmatic. "But do not go now, so soon after we have found each other again. There will be another plane; there always is."

23

Viola gazed back into the deep brown eyes that still had the power to hold her – to cast a spell on her – and slowly lowered herself back into her chair.

Chapter Three

When Heino Timmermann, the youngest detective in his department, gave his account of events at the Augustiner to his chief, Werner Fuchs was puzzled. It was becoming more difficult to predict the likely turn of events. He immediately called a meeting in his office on the top floor of Munich's Polizeipräsidium.

It was not the scuffle between rival German and Turkish gangs that worried him. Such incidents were becoming so frequent nowadays as to be almost commonplace. No, the cause for his concern was something far more worrying, something potentially far more dangerous. What bothered him was the series of encounters between Professor Josef Feinstein and the young British academic, Dr Viola Addison.

The more he thought about it, the more uneasy he became. Werner Fuchs was not a man to over-react. So on the rare occasions he did call a crisis meeting, his officers knew it to be with good cause.

As one by one they filed into his office, they saw their chief standing with his back to them, looking down on the cars manoeuvering about in Ettstraße below. The room, reflecting his taste, was simply furnished – and so sparsely that several of them had to stand, resting their backs against the filing-cabinets which lined the walls; two had the foresight to bring their own chairs with them and squeezed them in where they could. As if with the benefit of a sixth sense that told him when the team had reached full complement, Werner turned around to face them just as Tom Jablonski was closing the door.

Fuchs was not a man to waste either time or words. That he should get straight down to the heart of the matter came as no surprise to his colleagues.

"Look, I want to be sure we're all in the picture on this one. So just bear with me if you've already heard what I have to say. First – a couple of weeks ago we get a tip-off that the neo-Nazis are planning something big. To begin with we hit nothing but dead-ends. Then, earlier this week, a Professor Feinstein arrives here. He's due to give an important lecture next week on paintings, portraits, that kind of thing. But what concerns us is that the same day he arrives, we start getting phone calls – naked, unequivocal death threats against him. He's an old, distinguished Jew, here on a comparatively high-profile visit – a natural target, you could say, for our Fascist fraternity."

He looked around at his men, to see if they went along with his reading of events. They had all had to get close to the neo-Nazis at some point; they knew how their minds worked, and what they were up against.

"I suppose it's possible," said Tom Jablonski. "The public assassination of an old Jew would certainly be high profile. And Feinstein is due to be fêted by all the civic and state dignitaries while he's here; so it would create just the kind of public outrage these people thrive on."

Mohrfeld, the squad's oldest and longest serving detective, addressed their boss. "I'm not sure, Kurt. Isn't it more likely it's some old Brown Shirt, been kicking himself all these years he didn't finish Feinstein off back in the Thirties, when he had the chance? I can't believe this current bunch of bastards would bother with something like that. They're not interested in bumping off the odd old Jew."

Nods and grunts of agreement echoed around the room. Most were of the same mind as Mohrfeld. Civil disorder was what the Far Right was after. Professor Feinstein's murder was hardly going to bring that about. Werner raised his hand to prompt them to silence.

"I'll be honest with you – at first I couldn't believe it either. But . . ." He stopped for a moment to pull a cigarette from a pack in his shirt pocket, "then we had another tip-off, from what's always been a pretty good source." He picked up a large envelope from his desk and pulled out an eight by four, grainy, black-and-white telephoto shot of a woman and handed it to Mohrfeld to pass round. "Our informant tells us that this English woman, Dr Viola Addison, has been brought in to deal with Feinstein. We checked her out with the British anti-terrorist squad. They don't have anything on her, nor do any of the other agencies. Apart from a brother-in-law who has no more than fairly outspoken right-wing tendencies, there are no visible links with any Fascist organisations. She's an academic – same subject as Feinstein – and we know through his office that she's tried to contact him before. Professor Feinstein's hotel has also confirmed that she tried to speak to him on the phone as soon as he arrived there. Frankly, because she's such an unlikely proposition, I'm inclined to take this tip-off seriously."

He looked at his team for their reaction. They were non-committal as they passed around the picture of the woman. Tom Jablonski had it now. "This may not sound too scientific, but this woman's just too good-looking to be a Fascist terrorist."

Werner Fuchs grimaced impatiently. "That's what Heino said, but at least he has the excuse of youth. Anyway, we've been keeping an eye on Feinstein and Dr Addison. Heino's been doing some good work there."

All eyes shot across the office to where Heino sat, his legs dangling, on a high metal filing cabinet. He gave a self-conscious smile and dropped his eyes to avoid theirs.

"He reports," Fuchs continued, "that on Wednesday Dr Addison manages to bump into Feinstein in the Alte Pinakothek and get into conversation with him. The next day – yesterday – they meet again, for lunch."

"Oh yes. I remember reading somewhere the old man's got an eye for the ladies," came an observation from the back of the room.

"What, at his age?" exclaimed Silke Beckmeier, the only woman

27

present. "That's indecent – it's disgusting – it's . . ."

"It's normal, Silke," interjected Tom Jablonski, his voice raised to make it heard above the laughter. "What's wrong with it anyway? I know I'll still be interested when I'm that age." He grinned at her and her disgust evaporated. "Besides, wasn't even the great Goethe himself chasing young girls around when he was in his eighties?"

"Okay, Tom. Let's leave the history lesson, shall we?" said Werner, returning them to order. "So then, what have we got? – Wednesday, Feinstein meets the woman. Thursday, they have lunch together. Friday, today, they meet again – around the corner at the Augustiner – though this time he brings his secretary along. They're there roughly forty minutes, just drinking. Around a quarter to seven they're getting up to leave when another man appears and asks if he can take their table. We've established that this man is a Lutz Ebenau." Werner turned to Silke Beckmeier. "You've been checking him out. What do we know about him?"

"Quite a bit. I've personally come across him twice. Once socially." She blushed.

The men laughed. "What happened, then?" one of them asked.

"Nothing, nothing at all. He asked me for a dance, that's all. And then I think only out of politeness. We danced; I never saw him again until I met him in court. He's a lawyer. He was defending some yob on a burglary and assault charge."

"You mean he's another hungry young criminal lawyer?"

"No, as a matter of fact. He's actually very high-powered in international law. I've no idea why he was defending this oaf, unless it was out of some misguided sense of liberal justice. And he was doing it for nothing. But then he doesn't need the money. He's a very rich man in his own right."

"Ebenau Engineering, you mean?"

"That's right."

They all knew Ebenau Engineering. It was the post-war remnant of one of Germany's larger war-time weapons manufacturers; not exactly in the same league as Krupps, but the basis of a substantial fortune to succeeding generations of the founder's family. Since the late Ludwig Dieter Ebenau's death, the family trusts had sold their holdings in the original business and invested the funds across the international markets, spread so diversely now it was impossible to assess their value, although the gossip columns of *Das Bild* and other tabloids hazarded the occasional guess at its running to several hundred million D-Marks.

"Lutz Ebenau," Silke told them, "was the largest single beneficiary of the trust his father set up. He's been very effective in keeping an extremely low profile since he inherited. He's hardly ever seen at big social gatherings; he never gives interviews about anything except his work and guards his private life jealously. See how few of you had even heard of him. Yet, he's a rich man with a lot of powerful friends. But he didn't retain any holdings in the original company; he felt it would mitigate against him, outside Germany, even after all this time."

"Like it did just recently with Mick Flick, in Oxford?"

"Precisely. He is, however, a very clever lawyer – and very ambitious."

"Ambitious?" Mohrfeld let out a cynical laugh. "Ambitious for what, if he has all that money?"

"Ambitious to be well-respected in his field, I suppose," Silke said. "Making money isn't the only reason people work, you know."

"Isn't it?" grunted Mohrfeld. "I can't think of another one. What about his friends?"

"Nothing negative known." Silke shrugged. "I've only found one potentially dodgy contact: he used to be very chummy with a guy called Peter Lessel. They were at school and university together."

"And what's wrong with Lessel?"

"Again, nothing much, as far as we know, but he had some friends who were suspected members of the Network."

"So Ebenau is a friend of a friend of a friend who may be in the Network," Mohrfeld said lightly, "we can hardly condemn him for that."

"Maybe not," growled Werner. "But as this man Lessel is the only possible link we've got at the moment, however vague, I want you

29

to go on digging, Silke, through our usual snouts. See if any of them can turn up anything on him. Okay?" He nodded at Silke. "Now what are Ebenau's politics?"

"The only causes he's been known to support are generally green and liberal."

"Look, Chief," Tom Jablonski interrupted. "Why are we getting this man's life-story? All he did was take a table at the Augustiner."

"Not quite. There was something odd about that. Now listen to this – when the Professor and his secretary leave shortly after he takes that table, the Englishwoman doesn't leave with them. Ebenau sits down opposite her, and they have a long, meaningful discussion, like they've known each other for years – more than known each other, if you listen to Heino's description of the way they're gazing into each other's eyes. Is that right, Heino?"

Heino nodded.

"You reckon they're lovers, eh Heino?" Schneider laughed. "How the hell would you know?"

"Grow up, you lot. If this Englishwoman really is involved in something," Fuchs went on, "we've got to find out everything we can about her – what her relationship is to Ebenau and when and how it started. Over to you, Silke, and your friends in the gutter press. But if Heino's wrong, and they've never met before, then we've got to consider why this man should choose to strike up a conversation with this particular woman. The same woman who herself – only a day or two before – picked up Professor Feinstein, whose very public death, we're told, she's come to Munich to organise?"

Heino Timmermann interrupted. "Excuse me, Chief, but it was the other way around. She didn't pick up the Professor – it was *he* who picked up *her*."

Heino seemed eager to get things straight. Jablonski, who suspected the young man's call for accuracy was not entirely professional, laughed and teased him about his ability to tell the difference. Heino had only been with the department a couple of months and still seemed incredibly wet behind the ears. Jablonski

30

often wondered how he had managed to make it this far in the force.

As far as Werner was concerned, it was neither here nor there who had picked up whom. "Whichever way round it was, I want to know what's going on. I wanted to put a full-time guard on the old man, but he wasn't having it – said if he'd survived Hitler, he could handle a few red-necks. But I'm going to have to get as many people as I can round him at all his public appearances, and we'll have to keep a very close watch on Dr Addison. So, Tom, I'm pulling you off the Drugs Squad for a while – I need you on this one. Your work's practically finished there anyway."

It was not in Tom's nature to accept such a move without protest. Fuchs was right that the syndicate they had been working on was all but broken now – it would be no problem for someone else to take over from him and finish it off; but he was only human and, after months of hard slog, it was galling to be denied the thrill of the catch. On the other hand, getting involved in the convulsions of political extremists was a more exciting and challenging prospect than busting a relatively unsophisticated gang of drug-dealers.

He was less enthusiastic when he learned that the task Werner had in mind for him was to head up the team to investigate the woman. Tom was not a man to over-estimate his abilities, but he did know his own worth and – along with everyone else in the room – considered himself wasted in the role of routine surveillance work. He saw himself as far better suited to being out on the streets – to infiltrating one of the now omnipresent Fascist gangs – or, better still, getting associated with their bosses and uncovering the full extent of their involvement in fomenting racial unrest. Still, he could live in hope that would come as a result of the initial legwork.

Werner wisely gave him little time to brood. "I know I can count on every one of you." He looked around his office, engaging the eyes of each in an unspoken alliance of mutual loyalty. "I know you'll all want to get to the bottom of whatever's going on – just as much as I do." His eyes finally came to rest on Tom's, where they had started. "And I know we'll all want to crack it, before the smart-

31

arse spy-catchers from Bonn get to hear about it and come down to muscle in on the act."

The mumblings of accord grew louder. Werner nodded in recognition of their support – then he rubbed his hands together briskly. "Right, let's get down to business, shall we? Heino, tell us all you can about your Dr Addison."

When the meeting in Werner Fuchs's office was over, tasks had been allotted, and assignments clarified, various members of the unit drifted back to work at their desks or to go home to their beds. Finally only Fuchs, Mohrfeld and Jablonski remained.

Werner pulled his cigarettes from his pocket, put one to his lips and tossed the packet across the room to Kurt. Kurt reciprocated by extracting a lighter from his crumpled jacket and throwing it into the waiting hand of his old friend. A few seconds later the missiles made their return flights and the two older men sank back under gathering clouds of smoke. Tom rebuked them both for the damage they were inflicting on their bodies. They smiled.

"Okay. You're right. But at least we don't go throwing ourselves out of aeroplanes or hurling ourselves off the tops of mountains," laughed Kurt, "or go in for any of the other crazy activities you call fun."

Tom rocked back in his chair and chuckled. "You're just jealous because you're past it." His laughter ceased. "Anyway, it looks as if I'm going to be a bit short on action myself for a while – if I'm going to be cooped up playing Peeping Tom on this Dr Addison."

Werner felt it timely to offer a few words of consolation. "Look, Tom. I know this isn't exactly the assignment you'd have chosen for yourself – and I'll be honest with you – I wish there was someone else I could give it to. But I've a strong hunch this girl's important and I need to put someone onto her whose English is perfect – someone who's going to understand every word, every nuance of what's being said. Let's face it – you're tailor-made for the job."

There was no doubt about it – Tom's English was flawless. The product of a mixed marriage – a German mother and an American father – his whole life had been spent ferrying back and forth across the Atlantic, as one by one his family died out; so that now he was equally at home in both countries, in both cultures and in both languages. It was precisely this history that had made him the person he was today – and Werner Fuchs had few qualms about allocating his time to surveillance work in what could turn out to be a major investigation.

Chapter Four

Margaret Addison considered it symptomatic of the sort of thoughtless, selfish person her daughter had become that she should miss her flight from Munich and not arrive home until after the guests had started gathering for her husband's birthday party. It upset her to have to admit it, but Viola had long since become a disappointment to her – a disappointment all the harder to bear when she thought of what promise Viola had shown, and what expectations she had had of her.

She remembered the days when her two girls had made her the envy of all the other mothers with daughters at Bolchester High School for Girls – and she lamented. Such days were gone. Now, whenever she met those mothers – at bridge parties – at the Golf Club – at weekly visits to Eduardo, her hairdresser – it was she who envied them. All of Viola's old school friends were settled and married to suitable, professional young men; many of them had children. Nowadays, when exchanging notes, these same mothers would make polite noises about Viola – about her academic successes – about her published works on little known painters – about her several appearances in esoteric, late-night television arts programmes. But Margaret Addison knew only too well what they would be saying to each other behind her back. It would be the sort of thing she herself would be saying, if the tables were turned. Her only consolation was Olivia. At least she had one daughter for whom there was no need to make excuses.

She surveyed her elegant, eggshell blue, silk and velvet drawing room, until her eyes fell on her two children where they stood in conversation. How radiant Olivia looked. Of course, Margaret Addison thought, she always did. She glanced across at Viola. The same could not be said of her. Why, oh why, did she have to wear such sombre colours? And why did she always buy such shapeless clothes that hid her pretty figure and made her look like some sort of refugee? And her hair – that beautiful, long, thick, curly hair. What was the point of having it, if she was just going to tug it back and roll it up at her neck? Viola should go to Eduardo's. Goodness knows, she had suggested it often enough. He could transform her in no time at all.

Viola had never been the same since she went up to university. Not that Margaret Addison blamed Oxford as such – but it was there she had fallen in with the wrong sort of people – Hillary Farrell in particular. Then there had been that dreadful business in Munich. The plain truth was, Viola had been nothing but a worry to them ever since she left home. Margaret wondered how her nerves stood it.

Charles Addison grappled the foil and wire of a champagne cork. It was his view that no-one had a right to be anything but festive when such an obviously expensive beverage was being served. He glanced over at his younger daughter, noted her slightly moody air and, like his wife, felt let down.

He could not understand what had become of Viola. At school she had excelled at everything. She could have gone on to study anything she wanted: Law, Medicine, anything. He was frankly baffled that she had chosen to become an art historian. After all, what real use was it? And now, at her age, with her chances of finding a husband inevitably fading fast, he was astonished that she should so consistently reject John Bowman's proposals. He could only hope it was not at the prospect of rekindling a relationship with that German. He was prepared, reluctantly, to accept that there was such a thing as a good German, but he could never countenance his daughter's liaison with a member of the family who had been responsible for the production of so many weapons during the last war – weapons that had killed his father and his uncle.

Olivia, despite the lack of any similarity between them, felt certain she could read her sister's moods like a book. As they talked, she sensed a kind of triumphalism in Viola which suggested she had somehow overridden the family's wishes. Given that the most significant change in Viola's recent life had been the move to Munich, Olivia began to suspect it must have something to do with Lutz Ebenau; perhaps she was trying to find him again – if she had not done so already.

The time for confidences between them might have passed, but Olivia still reckoned she understood her sister better than most. She knew that in spite of that careful, almost cold exterior, inside Viola there beat a hopelessly romantic heart.

She sometimes wondered where that heart had come from. Certainly not from their parents. She herself was as unlike Viola as it was possible to be. All she had ever wanted was to build a nest and fill it with babies. University for her had simply been a means to an end; an opportunity to seek out a suitable mate – someone who could provide her with a bigger and better nest than might otherwise have been the case.

On the rare occasions she bothered to think about it, she could see herself as the logical outcome of her parents' union. Viola was not. She was a dreamer – in need of guidance in the ways of the real world. It was just such guidance that Olivia was now at pains to dispense, as they chatted together at their father's birthday luncheon. First, she had to establish the precise, current state of play.

"So, I suppose Munich must bring back some unhappy memories for you – that German who jilted you?"

The flash of anger in Viola's eyes and the moment's hesitation before she answered told Olivia that something had indeed happened.

"Actually, I've seen him."

Olivia started. "How did you find him?"

36

"I didn't. He found me; at least, we bumped into each other at the Augustiner."

"You bumped into him, after only being there a few days? That sounds like an incredible coincidence."

"It may not have been entirely coincidence. I'd seen his old friend, Peter Lessel, a few days before. And I'm pretty sure he saw me. He probably told Lutz I was around."

"Didn't Lutz tell you?"

"No, and I didn't ask."

"He always was a secretive sort of man, wasn't he?"

"He doesn't waste a lot of time talking about irrelevancies, if that's what you mean."

"But Viola, darling, are you sure it's a good idea to see him again? I mean, ten years is a long time – long enough for him to have become a different person."

"And for me, too," Viola replied.

"Yes. I suppose so. We've all changed." She thought better of this last remark. "You and I certainly have."

Viola smiled. Olivia meant well.

"But ten years, Viola. Just think – he could be married – he could have children."

"So could I."

"Yes, but you aren't – you haven't. Did you ask him?"

"Olivia, I only bumped into him yesterday evening. There wasn't time to do much talking. Look, Olly, don't worry about me – I know what I'm doing."

"But *do* you? Do you *really* think it's the right decision – starting all this up again? I mean, he didn't exactly come running after you last time, did he?"

"I was the one who left Munich, remember?" Viola said. "Anyway, he did try to contact me. He rang here, twice apparently, and left messages – which no-one ever gave me." She stared pointedly at her sister.

Olivia's eyes opened wide in innocence. "Don't blame me. That's the first I've ever heard of any phone calls."

Viola was inclined to believe her. It was more than likely their mother who had failed to pass on the messages.

"Anyway," she went on, more conciliatory. "Who says I'm starting anything up again? I haven't."

Olivia sighed. It was clear she was getting nowhere. Automatically, as her next step, she adopted the guilt-inducing tone she had learnt at her mother's knee.

"You know we only want what's best for you. All we want is your happiness. You know that, don't you darling?"

At this point it would have been easiest simply to agree – the last thing Viola ever wanted was confrontation. Besides, when it came down to it, she did not doubt Olivia's wish to see her happy. It was on how best to achieve it that they would be bound to disagree.

Fortunately for Viola, she was saved from the necessity of a response; even though her saviour did come in the unlikely guise of her brother-in-law, Rory Melhuish. He put his arm around her and kissed her full on the mouth. Viola recoiled – mentally. She was too well-mannered to let it show. She disliked Rory. He had the kind of over-familiar kiss that made her lips wet – not to mention the sort of hands that seemed to land where she least wanted them to. Viola disliked his type in general: men who thought women were there for their amusement.

Nor did she imagine for one second that this behaviour was reserved exclusively for her. She had seen him in action too often for that. She knew, just as one example, that he had tried it on with Hilly, at some reception or other in the City. It came as no surprise to Viola that her friend was afterwards taking bets against its ever happening again. Hilly could muster a rally of four letter expletives to cool any man's ardour when circumstances required it – and those particular circumstances had. Hilly was as promiscuous as they came, but she drew a line at other women's husbands.

"And how's my second favourite lady?" asked Rory, smirking first at Viola then at his wife.

"Fine, thanks."

"And how's life in the Fatherland?"

"That's fine, too."

"Having such a good time, I hear you managed to miss your plane last night."

"Oh that was just a mix-up over the departure time – my mistake." Viola was annoyed at having to make excuses – to Rory of all people. She was also annoyed at what Olivia might read into this remark. It was none of their business.

"Don't worry, little sister. I'll take you to the airport tomorrow. I'll make sure you get your flight back."

"Thank you, Rory, but there's no need. Hilly's taking me. We're meeting in town beforehand."

"Ah ha! And how is the forthright Ms Farrell? Still prowling the corridors of power – raking for sleaze?"

Viola did not answer him. She thought it unlikely he intended her to. Anyway, Olivia did not give her the chance.

"But Viola," Olivia grabbed her by the arm, "does Mother know about this? I'm sure she's expecting you to stay for tea."

"Olly, we're eating out this evening – we'll all be having breakfast together – then there'll be Sunday lunch. There's a limit to how much I can eat."

"But we'll want to hear all your news. Won't we, Rory?"

"Well there's a limit to that, too – I've only been away a week. I'll ring, I promise, when there's something to say. When I've got settled into my flat and I've got my work programme all organised – in a week or so – then I'll tell you all about it."

"Then you can tell *me* all about it – in person," threatened Rory. "No – better still – then I can see for myself. I've got to pop over to Munich some time during the next few weeks – to tie up some loose ends on a merger we're handling. But I'm sure my workload won't be so onerous I shan't be able to fit in my little sister . . . " How Viola hated the way he called her that. " . . . For dinner, perhaps."

Viola said nothing. The prospect of dinner alone with Rory, in Munich, was appalling. He had never made an outright pass at her – she hoped he had enough decency in him to save her from that – but the unpleasant innuendo and the constant touching made her

39

feel sick. It did, however, force her to think on her feet.

"Why don't you come too, Olly?" She knew she sounded uncharacteristically enthusiastic. "The boys are old enough to manage without you for a day or two. You could see my flat; we could go shopping together and I could take you to visit one of my – Ludwig's – castles."

Olivia hesitated. Viola persisted. The thought of Rory alone and let loose on her necessitated it.

"You said yourself, your new nanny is a treasure. And Mother can keep an eye on things – she does anyway."

It was one of those lucky coincidences that their mother should approach, just at the moment of Olivia's indecision. Viola's proposal was put to her. It met with her approval. It did more than that. It even went some way towards exonerating her for her late arrival at the party. Though it did not go far enough to excuse her decision to leave home early the following day and certainly not her reason for doing so. When Margaret Addison discovered that, she blanched visibly – but not for long. It was, after all, a special day, one that had been months in the planning and part of the plan was that everyone should be ecstatically happy – including her.

As if to prove the point, she threw her arms around her two daughters and hugged them in an almost hysterical show of affection. She heard the click of a camera and turned around to see her husband preserve the spectacle for posterity – record the fact that theirs was the close, loving, caring family she had always wanted it to be.

From its very inception, Margaret's acknowledged aim had been to make this party the highlight of Bolchester's social calendar. Her private objective, on the other hand, was that it should be a dual celebration – not only to mark a milestone in her dear husband's life, but more importantly to announce the engagement of her younger daughter, Viola Isabella, to Professor John Bowman. That had been her expectation. That had been her dream. It was therefore a source of bitter disappointment to her that she should have to greet John as just another guest, not as the future son-in-law she longed for him to be. Yet Margaret did not despair – especially when she saw them together. John was as in love with her daughter as ever. She could see it in his eyes. Viola's expression gave away less. But, Margaret reflected, there was always the possibility that this self-imposed separation might make Viola realise the advantages of a sound relationship with a good, reliable man. No, Margaret would not yet give up hope of organising just such another celebration as this on the occasion of their wedding.

That John was a good, reliable man Viola knew. And that at this, possibly their last meeting, there was no hint of recrimination towards her only confirmed it. It was undoubtedly his intention that day to show, by word as well as by deed, that he would always be there for her – faithful to the last. Viola was touched. So much so she felt that if Lutz had not been still a part of her life, things might have been different. But he was and with the memory of him now so fresh, so vibrant in her mind, it would be unfair to give John hope.

She suggested to him that they play in the garden with Olivia's three sons – whose only amusement up until then had been crawling in and out of the forest of legs that filled a magnificent, flower-bedecked marquee on the lawn. Her nephews adored John and he them. One day, Viola told him – as she watched them rolling around together on the grass – he would make some lucky children a wonderful father. She regretted the remark the instant she made it. It was meant as an attempt at consolation. It would probably be taken as grounds for hope.

In spite of pressing requests from both Margaret and Charles Addison, John did not stay the whole weekend. Viola was relieved. He represented an episode in her life that was over. There was nothing to be gained by prolonging it. On that much at least they were in agreement. A decision had been made, be it right or be it wrong.

Chapter Five

With no real justification, Margaret Addison persuaded her younger daughter to stay on in Bolchester an hour or two longer than planned that Sunday afternoon. This meant that Viola had to rearrange her schedule and Hilly had to drive from London out to Guildford to meet her from a later train.

Hilly took the alteration in her stride. She was used to this kind of hitch in Viola's arrangements. The manipulative tendencies of the Addison family – particularly Viola's mother – had been a vexed question between the two friends almost since the day they met – when they had found themselves occupying adjacent rooms in their Oxford college. Later, during the time they rented a flat together in Notting Hill, and until the present, when they shared the mortgage on a neat, little terraced house in Brook Green, the discussions had continued. Throughout, Hilly's view had remained unchanged – that Viola's problems were largely self-inflicted. If she simply ignored her parents' interfering or, better still, made light of it, they would soon give it up entirely. As long as she dithered, they were going to sustain their power to influence her.

Inevitably, it was the first topic to be debated as they drove along the motorway towards Heathrow. As their time together had been curtailed, this was their only chance for a chat, besides a public, somewhat staccato exchange in the café at Terminal 4. By that time, though, their conversation had moved on to other things.

"I wish they'd go away," Viola whispered, looking meaningfully at a cluster of Bangladeshi children who, while not actually interrupting their conversation, stood so close and watched and listened so intently, that Viola felt inhibited. "I can't go on telling you what happened on Friday with these listening in."

"Ignore them," said Hilly, as she attempted to shoo them off with her hand. "I don't suppose they speak English anyway."

Viola turned to the children and more politely suggested that they run off and find their parents. The response she met with was neither negative nor positive. The children just stood there, rooted to the spot, eyes agog, mouths agape. Maybe Hilly was right. Perhaps they did speak no English and it was safe to go on telling her about Lutz. She was just about to do so, when an ugly voice booming from the table behind them stopped her dead.

"Just tell 'em to sod off, sweet'eart. It's the only sort of talk them Pakis understand."

Such an attitude and such language were alien and hateful to Viola. She pretended not to have heard, then despised herself for her timidity. She smiled at the children in a bid to make amends.

"Why don't you just sod off yourself?" Hilly's voice rang out cold and uncompromising.

Silence followed.

Viola was sitting with her back to the man, so that she could not see him – but she could sense him – she could feel his hot, heavy breath against her neck. It seemed to paralyse her into total inaction. Hilly, motionless and speechless too, was not so ineffective. Her very look transmitted loathing. However loutish this bigot might be, thought Viola, surely he could not misinterpret that look.

For a few moments, the silence continued. Viola wondered who would be the first to break it. She did not have long to wait. She felt movement behind her and a man came into view.

First she saw his hand, raised in anger, swiping the air in front of the children, so that they ran off in terror. Then he stood before them, staring down at Hilly – a great mountain of a man – his tattooed arms folded across a huge chest.

"Makes you feel big, does it – frightening children?" Hilly sounded almost goading.

"It's okay for the likes of you. Your sort don't 'ave to live with them Paki bastards." The man unfolded his arms and indicated over his shoulder with his thumb. There was no need for precision. Wherever they might have cared to look, they would have seen the same dark, Asian faces. "You don't 'ave 'em taking your jobs, do you? You don't 'ave to send your kids to school with 'em. We ought to make 'em bugger off back to where they come from."

"And what if they're British?" responded Hilly calmly. "Then they have as much right as you or . . ."

She got no further – her voice drowned out by a thunder clap of laughter that shook the man's flabby body and rendered her inaudible. But in the sound he made there was no hint of mirth – only contempt.

A thin, harassed-looking woman, not much more than a girl, appeared at his side. She gripped his arm. "'Arry, don't make a fuss, please. Not now," she whined.

'Arry rounded on her. "Piss off. You keep out of it."

The woman sank back.

Viola was relieved. She pitied her.

The man had turned his attention back to Hilly, who sat unimpressed, in waiting. He lurched suddenly forward. Within an inch or two of her unblinking gaze he jabbed the emptiness between them with his forefinger. Viola noticed the letters H.A.T.E. tattooed across the knuckles of his hand and she flinched.

"Anything we can do to help, Dr Addison?"

Viola knew the voice at once. It belonged to one of her students. Even so it startled her. She jumped visibly – not only she, but Hilly as well. Their aggressor swung around towards it. And as he did, Viola caught his expression of resentment at having the confrontation interrupted. Before he had time to do anything about it, the woman started pulling him away, shrieking at him that their flight had been called. As a parting act of defiance, he prodded his index finger – already targeted at Hilly – in an obscene gesture in front of her face. He turned around and stomped off, mouthing language to match, aiming it first over his shoulder at Hilly then at the girl as she ran alongside, attempting to keep up with him.

"Poor woman," Viola muttered and mainly to herself.

"It's her choice, Flower."

Hilly did not expand. If she had to opt between discussing this disagreeable incident with Viola or chatting up a group of good-looking, well-built young men, who seemed eager to help them out of it, the latter was going to win hands down – any time.

"Having a spot of bother with the lager lout tendency, were you, Dr Addison?" asked the spokesman – or rather the only one of them known to Viola.

She smiled at him. "Just a bit, Haydn." She shook her head at the fortuitousness of his arrival. "It was lucky you spotted us. I've got a nasty feeling that awful man would still be here if you hadn't. Thank you."

"Our pleasure." He grinned at his friends. "We aim to please, don't we, gentlemen?"

"On your way back from holidays?" asked Viola, feeling that the service rendered deserved at least a minute or two of small talk.

"No, from the States. Don't you remember – I'm sure I told you – I'd be over there this month, rowing for the college?"

"Oh yes, of course I remember," lied Viola. "How did you get on?"

He catalogued a string of successes. Viola congratulated them. Hilly congratulated them – although what occupied her more was casting an expert eye over them in order to assess what she would have called their SQ. Not that she had much opportunity for anything other than a cursory look – the handsome Haydn and his fellow rowers could not stay long. After bidding them a fond farewell, Hilly rounded on Viola. "You know, Flower, I sometimes think you're mad. Why d'you even contemplate tying yourself down to one man – however much of a dish this Lutz might be – when you've got an ever-changing supply of blokes like that knocking at your door – looking for ways to improve their grades – wanting suggestions for extra-mural activities?" She all but salivated at the prospect. "Give me variety any day – every day – especially when it comes with

45

biceps like that."

"Hilly, they're scarcely more than children. Haydn, what is he? Nineteen, twenty?"

"So much the better, Dr Addison. At that age they're thirsting for knowledge – and bursting with energy."

"You're man mad, Hillary Farrell."

"Whereas you're just mad." Hilly shook her head from side to side, with all the seriousness of a doctor diagnosing insanity. "Why you persist with this hair-brained desire to mix sex and sensibility, I simply do not understand. Especially when you know it's a recipe guaranteed to break that super-sensitive, little heart of yours."

"Since when do I know that? I didn't know I did."

"Well you should do by now. God knows I've told you often enough."

"This is getting silly," declared Viola. "And it's getting us nowhere. For me, sex and love are supposed to go hand in hand – the one means next to nothing without the other. Perhaps for you they don't – but for me they do." She jumped to her feet, picked up one of her bags and began rummaging through it. "Let's leave it at that, shall we?"

Viola's wish to change the subject did not stem from irritation at her friend's nagging. The conversation was essentially light-hearted. They were covering well-trodden ground – like familiar sparring partners. They were teasing each other – in the certain knowledge that neither would take offence.

Viola hunted through her hold-all until she produced a well-worn, maroon leather Filofax. She found a fountain-pen in her shoulder-bag and wrote on a scrap of paper which she handed to Hilly.

"Right. There are three addresses here and three telephone numbers." She leant over Hilly's shoulder and ran through them. "Here at the top, that's my flat. This is the address and phone number for Lutz, and the bottom is an office at Munich University where you can leave a message if you can't reach me at either of the other numbers – just in case you've got to contact me urgently."

46

"Why should I need to do that?"

"Well you never know," replied Viola, aware that, without exception, the need for urgent contact between them had – historically at least – always stemmed from her.

"Look, Viola, everything'll be fine, just as long as you leave your rose-coloured glasses behind. Just as long as you see things for what they are – not for what you want them to be."

Hilly sounded concerned. With Viola, she came the nearest she ever did to sentimentality. She even hugged her as they said good-bye at Passport Control. "You idiot," she whispered when she saw the tears in Viola's eyes. "How the hell are you going to cope, without me around to hold your hand?"

Chapter Six

It was not surprising that a soul as romantic and sensitive as King Ludwig II of Bavaria was misunderstood by his ministers and his subjects. It was, therefore, to be expected that he should seek to avoid the Royal Residence in Munich and favour instead the refuge and seclusion of the fairy tale castles he built for himself in the far south of his domain.

The fantasy worlds he created there, using an army of architects, artists and craftsmen, were designed to be his escape from reality. What he did not foresee is that the only true means of escaping reality lies either in madness or in death. Ludwig's tragedy was that, in his case, it seems likely it led to both.

It was coincidental that Viola, coming to Munich to study what this very man had done, should find herself living only a few minutes' walk from Schloß Nymphenburg, where Ludwig had been born, around a hundred and fifty years before. And it was pure chance that the first suitable apartment she had found lay within a stone's throw of the magnificent palace gardens. The paradox of it was not lost on her – that she, Viola, could not have been more delighted with the location of her new home; while he, the ill-fated Ludwig, had spent the better part of his adult life trying to get away from it.

Viola felt that this neighbourhood would suit her needs ideally. When she was not working on her researches she could wander through the spacious grounds of the Nymphenburg or stroll through its gracious apartments and imagine what life would have been like in it – one, two or even three centuries ago.

Viola's flat was situated in a tranquil, charming crescent, bordered with lime trees which, in late August, were heavy with leaf. Its houses, like much of the surrounding suburb, dated from the third quarter of the last century. Their style was elegant, but their scale – as well as the crescent itself – was relatively small, creating an intimate, pleasant environment, which suited Viola.

The street was quiet, tucked away from busy thoroughfares. Its residents too were quiet – professional people, she guessed from their appearance, or retired – middle-class, well-mannered and private. The house which was to be her home for much of that coming year was sited halfway along the crescent. Facing south, it caught the best of the sun.

It had four storeys. The ground floor and tiny basement were occupied by the old lady who owned the building and whose income was derived from letting out that part of it which had long since become surplus to her needs. The attic rooms were poky and – other than during rare visits from her grand-niece – usually left unoccupied. But the middle storey, Viola's flat, was light and airy and Viola reckoned that, even had she been given a choice in the matter, these were the rooms she would have selected for herself.

There was a large sitting-room which overlooked the crescent below and a bedroom of roughly equal size, which afforded a view of the long, narrow jungle of a garden. Off the landing, at the head of the main staircase, one next door to the other, lay a good-sized kitchen – formerly no doubt a bedroom – and a small bathroom, with equipment and fittings so antiquated, Viola at first wondered if they would work. The character of the whole place was old-fashioned – so preferred and therefore so perpetuated by its owner. The furniture was antique – solid and comfortable – mainly Biedermeier. Heavy brocade or chenille curtains, mostly sun-faded, hung at the windows. Old oriental carpets, threadbare in places, covered the wood-blocked floors. Yet there was nothing either dilapidated in the appearance or oppressive about the atmosphere; for when the sun streamed in through the large windows, it did so through sparkling clean glass, onto highly polished wood and spotless furnishings.

Frau Doktor Menne, a title she still bore in deference to her late husband, was retiring in habit – the result of having become almost totally deaf. When Viola had first arrived, the old lady had done her best to make her new tenant feel at home; but it was clear from their first brief exchanges, that any meaningful companionship between them would be impossible. Nonetheless they smiled a good deal on the odd occasion they passed each other in the hallway – an arrangement which seemed to satisfy both.

Viola had moved into her new home the week before her father's birthday party. She had driven out to Munich in her pillar box red Mini – a present from her parents to celebrate the award of her Doctorate. The choice of gift had been her mother's – hence the colour: Margaret Addison wasted no opportunity to brighten up her daughter.

On the Monday morning after she had flown back from England, when she had to leave the flat behind and head off for the next seminar, she did so with regret. She paused some time at her front door, looking back at her sitting-room – ornamented with all the paraphernalia she had brought with her from England.

Hilly, she recalled, had laughed at her as she had crammed as much as she could into her car – had called her "Squirrel" rather than "Flower" for the rest of that day. Hilly might be able to travel light, might be able to leave memories behind her, but she could not. She needed her books, her music, her photographs, her memorabilia. Without them, somehow, she scarcely seemed to exist. Perhaps she was a nest-builder after all – like Olivia. Certainly while she busied herself unpacking, arranging and rearranging her belongings – until she had achieved an effect that pleased – that thought did more than once flit through her mind. Unlike her sister though, she would be more fastidious about the choice of a mate.

Lutz came around to her flat early that evening. After their emotional reunion at the Augustiner on Friday, Viola had dared to hope that he might have been at the airport to meet her on Sunday night. But he had been down at his old family home in Füssen, in the foothills of the Alps, and only returned to Munich that morning.

As soon as he stepped through her modest front door, a seductive smile on his face, she forgave him.

"Thank God," he said. "For two days I was afraid I had been dreaming. But you really are still very beautiful." He added in English, his smile flashing suddenly rakish, "My Viola, my instrument on which I hope to make the most beautiful music – before too long."

He stopped a few inches in front of her, put his arms around her and drew her to him. He brought his mouth down to hers and brushed his lips gently against it. The tip of his tongue eased itself inside her and snaked its way around her own. As they kissed she was conscious of nothing but the tenderness of his touch, the scent of his skin, the strength of his body. When they drew apart, Viola could not stop her craving for him. Nor did she want to.

"No, Lutz. I can't wait a moment longer. Make love to me now." Even as she said the words she was shocked by them; but at that moment she did not care. In what seemed like a single action, almost innate in its deftness, he had pinned her against the door, lifted her skirt and entered her. From then on, their bodies became as one – joined by a rhythmic, feral passion.

Viola gasped out loud at the very height of her orgasm, then slumped into Lutz's waiting arms. He held her tight against him, inside him, while she recovered, and began to think coherently again.

Later, Lutz drove her out to a restaurant in his elegant pre-war Mercedes. As they ate they found that they had little need to talk. The energy that surged between them seemed to say it all. For the first time since she was twenty Viola felt like a care-free young lover again; but while she relished the sensation, inwardly she cursed the absurdities that had kept them apart these last ten years.

Only reluctantly did Lutz speak about himself. Viola guessed, when he told her about his career, that he was being modest. He had always been the same. Being so rich, perhaps he had no need to impress people with his successes. Viola, on the other hand, was always happy to speak about her own work.

"But why have you chosen to devote so much energy and intellect to the history of art?" Lutz asked her as they sipped their coffee. "It seems such a lifeless subject for someone as physical as you."

"It's you, Lutz, who make me physical," Viola said truthfully. "In England, I'm a paid up blue-stocking."

Lutz laughed. "Blue stockings – what an exciting thought. You have not by any chance brought any with you, have you?"

"Don't tease me, Lutz. It's hard enough being taken seriously as an academic, if you look remotely feminine."

"I take you seriously. And now that we have nourished our bodies with food, Viola, we have energy to seek nourishment of another kind." He grinned at her, then nodded to the waiter to bring him the bill.

That night a mellow, honey-coloured harvest moon was casting its magic over Bavaria, over Munich and over the crescent. The path they followed to Viola's door glowed like white gold beneath their feet. When she opened the front door, the moonshine danced inside to play dreamily across the walls. As if unprepared to be excluded anywhere, it poured in too through the window of her bedroom – down onto her bed, anointing their bodies with its mystic energy – giving its heavenly blessing to their union.

They made love throughout the night. With Lutz inside her, Viola at last felt whole. For ten long years she had merely existed – in limbo – waiting for him to fill again the emptiness inside her. And now it had happened, those wasted years were as nothing. Fading as fast was all the anger, all the resentment, she had ever felt against her parents. It no longer seemed important. All that mattered was that she and Lutz were together – locked in each other's arms where they belonged.

At dawn Lutz fell asleep. Viola lay there beside him, gazing at the beauty of his face – too full of joy to think of sleep herself. Outside in the garden and scattered amongst the surrounding trees, birds started to stir and greet the day with their song, announcing a jubilation of their own at another new beginning. Viola got up and went over to the window. Quietly she lifted it.

Into the room gushed the cool, fresh air of morning, as though it had been waiting outside in readiness for her to give it entry. On it she could smell the sweet fragrance of flowers it had brought in for her from the garden. In gratitude she closed her eyes and breathed it in.

Through the open window of the attic above, Tom Jablonski breathed in the self-same scent. He heard the self-same birdsong. Though he did not do so with the self-same sensation. This was not surprising. After all, Tom Jablonski was not in love.

He felt unsettled – not that this was surprising either – not after the night he had just spent. It was the first time he had ever had to listen in to other people making love and he had not liked the experience one little bit. However much Werner Fuchs was going to try and persuade him it was all in the line of duty, he knew now – in this particular assignment – he had been handed the short straw. Even Christian, who had tailed the couple to the Augustiner, must have had a better time. At least he had been able to sink a few beers as he sat reading the sports pages in the evening sun.

Schneider, too, holed up behind a mansard on the opposite side of the street, with his 600mm lens and a clear view of the windows to Viola Addison's apartment, had scored a better job. At least he did not have to listen, and, besides, he probably enjoyed watching, if there were anything to see. But Werner had insisted, as far as monitoring the telephone and any conversations that went on in the flat, Tom was to do the lion's share; he had the English. It was, anyway, normal to assume that the greatest chance of picking up any useful talk was going to be in the target's home territory; unless the target was very cautious indeed, or already knew that she was being staked out.

Chapter Seven

Tom left as quickly as he could after Heino Timmermann arrived to relieve him. He could not get out of the building fast enough. He grunted a greeting at Heino as he went, telling him to look at his notes if he wanted to know what had gone on during the night.

Once outside the house, he ran round the corner where he had left his motor-bike the previous night. He jumped on it and rode straight back home through wisps of early morning mist. In his flat, the first thing he did was take a long shower. After he had towelled himself down, he lay on his bed, closed his eyes and tried to sleep. But, although it was nearly twenty-four hours since he last had any, sleep did not come. After fifteen minutes he stopped trying and got up.

He put water in the kettle and a CD on his stereo. He turned the volume up loud and opened wide every window in his apartment, letting the noise from the busy streets outside join in with Otis Redding and "Hard to Handle". He whistled his own, rough version of the tune as he danced backwards and forwards along his galley-kitchen, gathering en route the wherewithal for breakfast. This he laid out on the wide sill of the window that looked down onto the Sonnenstraße.

Tom's idea of breakfast consisted of coffee – the priority – followed by anything else he could lay his hands on. Just what he could lay his hands on depended mostly on what he had not eaten the evening before. In this particular case, breakfast comprised a medley of blutwurst, gherkins, yoghurt, peaches, cheese. He thought about popping down the street to the baker's shop and buying some hot rolls, but dismissed the idea almost immediately. It would involve flirting with the girls behind the counter, or being cross-examined by them as to why he was not, and he was in no mood for either. Instead he made do with what he had.

Life either speeds or dawdles along Munich's Sonnenstraße, whether it happens to come on wheels or on foot. That was the attraction for Tom in living there. Only one of his windows actually overlooked it – the one at which he breakfasted. The others fronted onto a quieter, narrow side-street with shops which catered for his day-to-day needs: the baker's, a small super-market, an off-licence and a laundry.

On this same street, directly beneath his apartment – so that his front door opened more or less inside it – was a café run by a family of Turks. In clement weather, as now, the pavement in front became an obstacle course of white, plastic chairs and tables, put there for the café's clientele – regulars in the main – men of all ages who would sit around chatting for hours on end while they drank thick, black, bitter coffee. Now and then Tom would sip a cup with them. He always enjoyed their conversation and would laugh and joke as if he were one of them himself. These days, they were the nearest he had to an extended family.

That morning – like every other when he was alone – he ate standing. Between mouthfuls he left his station at the window and made forays into the comfortable chaos of his apartment to search for items of clothing. The completion of the act of dressing having coincided with the realisation that he had eaten all he wanted, he tidied up a little, then left for work.

He walked. It was a beautiful morning – blue sky, bright sunshine – but Tom was too preoccupied to notice. And he was not in good spirits. This was unusual – Tom's disposition was almost unfailingly sunny. However, the day had started badly for him. He could not get out of his mind what he had heard during the night, though he had learned nothing that had any direct bearing on the purpose of his vigil. Once his subject and her escort had entered the flat below, hardly a word had been uttered.

He started to walk faster, so that, to maintain his pace, he had to weave in and out of the crowds on the pavement. He broke into a jog, in a subconscious attempt to escape the sounds of the night – the voice of the woman as she cried and moaned in ecstasy – her screams as, time after time, she was brought to the point of climax. Tom was glad to arrive at his desk and get down to work.

Werner Fuchs noticed him a short while later and suggested they bring forward their meeting. He could see Tom needed to get some rest. Tom declined. He wanted Heino to be there, he said; besides, he had to get back in touch with London beforehand to check a few points.

Tom had been in communication with the British police and although their anti-terrorist squad had confirmed that they had no knowledge of Viola Addison – at any rate not under that name – they had handed him over to someone in another department, who was proving to be a useful source of information. He and Tom had spoken together several times during the last couple of days. Each time they did, the developing picture came into sharper focus. By four o'clock that Tuesday afternoon, when Tom, Heino and Silke entered Werner Fuchs's office to bring him up to date with events, there was little Tom had not discovered about the young English academic – except what he most wanted to know: the precise nature of her role within the known international Fascist organisations.

Werner came quickly to the point. "At least we have some answers about the relationship between Dr Addison and Herr Ebenau." He looked down at the reports on his desk. "From what Tom heard, and what Schneider saw from his stake-out, there's more to it than politics."

"I didn't hear anything to suggest that politics come into it at all," Tom said dryly.

"It certainly didn't take them long to get to know each other, did it?" Werner nodded and turned to Silke. "What do we know about

Lutz's politics?"

"That's the strange thing," answered Silke, "He's never declared himself for any particular camp. Normally, if I were asked to guess, I'd assume he was some kind of Christian Democrat, perhaps a little to the right. But I don't know. As I mentioned to you on Friday, he has been known to undertake criminal defence for no fees. I'm trying to put together a dossier of these to see if any pattern emerges. On the face of it, though, he's a lawyer with a conscience."

"What about his sex-life?"

Silke reddened a shade. "Strangely, that's even more obscure than his politics. There's very little archive stuff on it. A couple of the hacks I spoke to think he might be a latent gay, or at least neutral, because there's just no evidence of any sexual activity."

Werner screwed up his face in thought and gazed out of his office window for a few moments. "There can't be many of you," he said quietly, "who don't know the two things that make me nervous. One is when people start acting out of character. Two is when coincidences start happening. But when coincidences start happening to people who are acting out of character – then I get *really* nervous. So why, I ask myself, is our Dr Addison making love to a man she's only just met – a man who, as far as the press knows, has never been with a woman, a man, or even a whore. Apparently this man's been made of ice. So why – when he finally melts – when the urge finally takes him – does he go for the woman who we are told – on grade one authority – is here to cause some kind of outrage involving Josef Feinstein?"

Heino shook his head in agitation. "I still don't think she's involved in the Network at all. For a start, haven't we always thought the British don't play that much of a part in it? I mean, over there it's not like here, is it? Isn't it Combat 18 and the like doing their own thing – and the Intelligentsia just talking about it?"

Werner nodded thoughtfully, glanced briefly at Tom to gauge his reaction, then gave Heino one of his indulgent smiles. "In good police work, Timmermann," Werner's tone was measured, fatherly, "we look first at the facts – or evidence. From this we draw our inferences. Finally we take the necessary action with the aim of either proving or disproving those inferences, until ultimately we are left with the truth."

Heino could not really see how this answered his doubts.

"There's quite a bit to suggest she *is* involved, Heino," Tom chipped in, in an attempt at reassurance. "Besides the tip-off we've had, fact number one – she'd been trying to make contact with Feinstein for some time, prior to coming here. Then she hangs about and catches him at the gallery and uses her bodily attributes to ensnare an old man with an eye for a young body." Tom paused. "At the same time, she's screwing Ebenau." He noticed Heino wince at the baldness of his statement. There was nothing he could do about that. It was a fact. "And as Werner says, she's acting out of character. She's certainly no whore, according to my British contacts. By the way, Chief, I didn't have a chance to include it in my report, she was an exchange student here in Munich, about ten years back."

Silke looked up sharply. "That's when Ebenau was studying law here. Maybe they knew each other then?"

Werner nodded. "That would make sense, and it's worth pursuing. Find out if they were in any political clubs, organisations, then."

"Perhaps Ebenau's involved in the Network," Tom suggested.

Werner laughed. "Now you're trying too hard, Tom. There's no way someone with his background is going to be a nationalist. His money's invested all over the world. People like that don't concern themselves with xenophobic politics. Where's their incentive?"

"I suppose you're right."

"Anyway, talk us through what you've found out about our target."

"Well, as far as our Dr Addison is concerned, it looks like her life's been pretty uneventful – academia all the way – nothing to link her with any political activity – except . . ." Tom said this last word decisively – leaning forward, elbows on knees, hands folded, his index-fingers outstretched as if pointing to something of significance, " . . . except that her oldest, closest friend is a political journalist – comes from an influential political family. Through her Addison will have had constant access to leading politicians. Then there's another thing. Her lover of the past five or six years teaches Politics. Though how much further on that gets us, I don't know. According to my source in London he's strictly middle of the road – a theorist rather than an activist."

"Any contact ever between him and the Network?" asked Fuchs, suddenly sitting to attention.

"Again, none that we're aware of. Seems he's just taken up some heavy-weight professorship in Australia. I got in touch with Sydney – soon as I knew – thought I'd better let them know what's going on."

Werner gestured his approval.

"Apparently they've been wondering how long it was going to be before their racist element started forging links with ours over here. Sounds like they've got trouble brewing too – especially now they've let in all those south-east Asians."

"You told them there's no proof the man's involved in any of this?"

"Made it crystal clear."

Again Werner indicated approbation. "What else have you got for me?"

"Nothing definite. That's the annoying part." Tom got up. He pushed his hands deep into his trouser pockets and paced backwards and forwards in front of Werner's desk – as though, by acting it out, he somehow hoped to vent his frustration. "This Addison woman's an enigma. On the surface of it she's clean."

"Of course," Werner said. "And that's precisely why she's being used for this job."

"But what about her relationship with Ebenau? How does that fit in?"

"Perhaps she has a much more basic motive for that. What about sex – good old-fashioned sex?" Werner raised an eyebrow at the younger man. "I'm surprised at you, Tom – of all people – not considering that as a possibility."

Suddenly the sounds of the previous night reverberated again around Tom's head. It required a conscious effort to force them out.

He tried to laugh. "Chief, don't think I haven't considered it, whatever the tabloid hacks might think. No-one who heard the two of them last night could fail to." He stopped pacing the office and stationed himself against the windowsill. "Anyway, there you have it. Here's a woman, with no apparent interest in politics, whose closest friends at home are positively dominated by it – friends, lovers, acquaintances."

"She's got to be mixed up in this somehow, Tom. Like I said, I don't believe in coincidences."

They both fell silent, Tom and Werner.

Heino, who until now had spoken hardly at all, took his chance. "It seems to me . . . " He paused for a second or two, plucking up the courage to go on. "It seems to me, we're in danger of only looking at the evidence that's in line with our pre-conceived ideas. You know – we want to believe that somehow or another she's involved in the Network, so we're picking out those things which imply it. There really isn't anything concrete to suggest she is, is there? – other than that she knows some people who are politically aware."

"It's a sound enough way of assessing someone's motives," suggested Tom.

"Yes I know – and I know what you're getting at. But so far we've just concentrated on people who suit our hypothesis, haven't we? Think of all the other friends she must have. People we're not mentioning now, because we don't even know they exist – people who couldn't sort out one political theory from another – and are interested even less. If we knew about *those*, then we might think differently about *her*. D'you see what I'm saying?"

Heino Timmermann was a serious, intense young man. He had joined the Police Force to fight injustice and now here, in its midst, he could see the seeds of it unwittingly starting to germinate. Perhaps other considerations did spur him on, but they were not his prime motivation. "Look, Chief – Tom – my father's got two really good friends. They all went to school together – have been big mates ever since. Dad's a teacher, the other two are both doctors. But that

60

doesn't mean, to be their friend, my father's got to be passionately or even mildly interested in medicine." Heino laughed uneasily. "As a matter of fact he thinks all doctors are quacks."

Werner smiled.

Tom laughed. "I reckon your father might have something there." He went over to Heino and slapped him on the back. "You're right, Heino. I suppose it does sound a bit as though we're jumping to conclusions." Tom turned serious, though only for a minute. "But come on now, if you're asking me to deal in the facts and nothing but the facts, then you're asking the impossible. I'm human. I'm a man, not a machine. What about intuition? How can I help hazarding the occasional, educated guess? Besides, how else am I going to sort out my ideas? Anyway, isn't that why we've got rules to follow? – and procedures – the sort the Chief was talking about earlier on. To be sure we don't make any cock-ups. Don't worry. We're not out to nail the wrong people just for the sake of nailing someone. We have a life to protect here, remember."

"The important thing," explained Werner, "as Tom will show you, is that he never relies on the premise – only on the proof. The proof is what matters. So never mind if he – you – we – do jump to all sorts of wrong conclusions on the way – just as long as we get it right in the end. I can assure you, Timmermann, I should be just as pleased for you to prove to me Dr Addison has nothing whatever to do with this bunch of Neo-Nazis, as I should be for you to prove she's their ring-leader. Just as long as you can prove it – *beyond all doubt*."

"And if it does turn out she knows nothing about the Network," added Tom, "and all she really *is* interested in is Ludwig and his castles," he winked at Heino, his face breaking afterwards into a wide grin, "let's just hope some handsome, young gallant comes riding over the horizon and pinches her from right under the nose of the rich, handsome Ebenau, who I'm sure has already had far more than he deserves. Right Heino?"

Chapter Eight

When Viola woke on the day of Josef Feinstein's lecture, she thought of what he said the first time they met, when they had both been admiring the Dürer self-portrait. "It is to a face such as this that a young lady would wish to wake up every morning."

"Absolutely," she whispered to herself as she gazed at the man sleeping beside her; the tips of his lashes shimmering gold against smooth, bronzed cheeks, which rose and fell in rhythm with his breathing.

It had been the third night she had spent with Lutz since her return to Munich. She could hardly believe that, far from diminishing, the magic was growing more intense every time they found new ways to thrill each other.

He stirred as if he sensed her eyes were on him. As his own eyes opened lazily, a telling smile parted his lips.

"Good morning, Schätzlein. My Viola," he said in his lightly accented English. "Didn't we make some beautiful music last night?"

Viola nodded and leaned down to touch his lips with hers.

He reached his arms around her and started to draw her to him.

"I have to get up, Lutz. I've got an appointment at nine."

He kissed her softly and released her. "I will savour the ache of unfulfilled longing all day. And then tonight, we go to Vienna."

"No, Lutz" Viola almost wailed. "I told you, I can't. I'm going to the lecture tonight. It's Josef Feinstein's only official engagement while he's here and he's asked me to be his guest," she added, unable to conceal her pride. "I can't possibly miss it."

Lutz opened his eyes wider. "The great Professor Josef Feinstein? No, you would not want to miss that," he said quietly. "But I shall miss you. Still, you can come another time."

"And I want to – I want to meet all the friends you've got there."

"And to go to the opera to your heart's content." He stretched, showing off his tightly muscled torso. "At least if I do not see you for two whole days, the excitement will be almost unbearable when we are together again."

Viola gave a fake sigh. "I'll try and bear it. Now," she became businesslike, "I have to get going. After my first meeting, I've got shopping to do."

"Viola, you look a million dollars. The dress – I love it."

"Thank you, Ellie. Actually it's new – I only bought it today."

Viola was taken by surprise by Ellie Levinson's remark. From the way she dressed, Viola thought it safe to assume her interest in fashion was next to non-existent. The compliment, though unexpected, was nonetheless flattering. Apart from anything it was a relief.

The garment under discussion was certainly a departure from Viola's norm: close fitting, décolleté, the colour of ripening corn. No-one could have doubted for a second that either dress or wearer did anything other than justice to the other – except Viola. But she had bought it when in a state of euphoria and had questioned her judgement ever since. For the early part of the evening she had felt conspicuous and ill at ease. Ellie's commendation changed all that. It gave her the confidence to forget what was, after all, only an item of clothing and enjoy the excitement of the evening.

Viola and Professor Feinstein had already dined, à deux, prior to meeting Ellie at the Alte Pinakothek on the grand occasion of his lecture. It was directly at Ellie's suggestion that it had happened thus. Initially Josef had been baffled by her largesse in granting him such latitude. When it later turned out that she had received a dinner invitation of her own, he understood.

For years Ellie had made much of the fact that she was on the look-out for a husband. It was a quest in pursuit of which she appeared to leave no stone unturned. Her zeal had always amused Josef – although it was all a sham and they both knew it. Neither ever seriously imagined she would desert him. However, a little flirtation, once in a while, did help to boost her morale. It allowed her to fancy that when the time finally came, there would be no shortage of admirers from which to select a spouse.

The prospective suitor, that particular evening, was not entirely unknown to Viola – or indeed to Josef Feinstein by repute. When Ellie introduced him, Viola saw by the Professor's expression, that he recognised the name. Dr Rupert Servranckz was the man – the very man whose lecture during the previous week's conference had had such soporific results on at least one member of his audience. Feinstein clearly recalled Viola's account of the incident. His eyes skipped across to hers to leave no doubt about that. Viola blushed. Josef noticed and was glad he was not yet too old to be charmed by her confusion.

Dr Servranckz had nominated himself organiser-in-chief of the evening's proceedings. That was how he and Ellie had met. Barely had the niceties of introduction been accomplished, than he whisked Professor Feinstein away to explain to him the minutiae of the forthcoming programme of events. Ellie, no stranger to organisation herself, took control of Viola, linking arms and marching her off to locate their seats.

"I guess he's no Kevin Costner," Ellie announced with a hint of apology in her voice. There was no denying the truth in what she had said. Rupert Servranckz was short, spherical and balding. "I guess he's no Lutz either. Am I right, Viola?" Viola decided it safest simply to smile. Ellie laughed good-humouredly. "Okay. Let's face it. I'm no longer young and pretty. Come to think of it – it's so long ago – I can't even remember how it is to be young. And it's for sure, I never knew how it is to be pretty." She briefly stroked Viola's cheek with the back of her hand. "Make the most of it, Viola Addison.

64

God did you quite some favour when he gave you that face. Don't waste it on a schmuck."

Viola was not sure what a "schmuck" was – but felt certain Lutz could not possibly be one.

"So? Where is he?" asked Ellie, turning her back on Viola for a moment to look at the row upon row of faces lined up behind them. She leant across and elaborated on the question in a loud stage whisper. "The love of your life – he's not here?"

"No."

"Tell me, how can you drag yourself away from him – for an entire evening?"

"He's not in Munich at the moment. He's had to go away for a few days – on business."

Viola was spared further cross-questioning by Ellie when, amid ecstatic applause, Rupert Servranckz led Professor Feinstein onto the stage. From a distance the old man looked smaller, more vulnerable than ever. He was clearly moved by his reception. From the front row where she was sitting, Viola could see tears in his eyes. He bowed to his audience then took a seat, while Dr Servranckz launched himself into a grandiloquent introduction. Ten minutes or so into it, Josef caught Viola's eye. His tears, she noted, had since been ousted by a disrespectful twinkle. And, by the time the lengthy eulogy was through and the Professor was called upon to begin his talk, it was as much as he could do to control his laughter.

Before he had chance to utter a word, the audience took to its feet to clap and cheer; as if it had collectively decided to demonstrate regard – as well perhaps as regret for all his years in exile. Josef did not attempt to stop the acclamation, but stood there – centre stage – luxuriating in it.

Given the scale of the tumult – to which she herself was adding – Viola barely heard the disturbance erupting at the rear of the hall. Had it not been for the sudden look of fear on the Professor Feinstein's face, coupled with an expression of dismay from Dr Servranckz, she might have remained in ignorance longer still. Yet just as it began to dawn on her, so did an atmosphere of alarm overwhelm the whole

assembly. The clapping ceased, allowing only the shouts of anger –
hitherto muffled by applause – to ring out unhindered, like sinister
echoes of the past: "Juden 'raus! Juden 'raus! Juden 'raus!" repeated
over and over again.

It took Viola several seconds to register the full horror of what
was happening. When at last she did look around, she saw a gang
of men – already in the throes of being ejected – still shouting their
threats, still with looks of menace on their faces. She knew that
look. It was a look she feared and hated. How, she asked herself,
could one human being be so consumed with loathing for another
simply because of his race – simply because he was a Jew? She did
not begin to understand.

The disturbance must have been anticipated – Viola was sure of
that. So many men were on hand to quash it. As they struggled to
drag the protesters – kicking, spitting, shouting – out of the hall, a
sense of deliverance lulled the entire gathering. That over, the ovation
started up again, tentatively at first; then accelerating until, running
out of control, it reached new, near hysterical heights. Only when
close to exhaustion did it settle back, where it had started, upon the
fragile figure of Professor Feinstein.

He was clearly disoriented by the experience. So much so that he
looked incapable of movement. Dr Servranckz rushed to his support
and together they walked slowly across to the podium. Once there
Servranckz waited, until satisfied that the Professor was ready. Only
then did he withdraw. Viola was sure she would never forget such
kindness. Now in position, Josef quickly regained his composure.
He raised both hands, as high above his head as he was able, in a
joint gesture of triumph and affection. Then as, little by little, a
reverential hush fell over the room, his thin, clear voice began the
lecture.

From her first reading of Professor Feinstein's book on Dürer,
Viola had admired him – more than that, she had respected, trusted,
depended upon his views. Accordingly, she had decided, this lecture
would mark a high-point in her academic life. Since she had got to
know the man – since he had, to all intents and purposes, taken her

under his wing – her presence tonight had acquired an even greater significance. She knew she would feel like a favoured, favourite disciple. It was all the more surprising then, that she should find herself unable to concentrate on his words. The fact was, she felt too fearful for his safety. Glancing into the crowd, she saw a face. She recognised it from her first meeting with Feinstein – probably some eager young academic – and instinctively she smiled at him. He smiled back.

Heino Timmermann looked quickly across the room at Tom – to check he had not witnessed the exchange. He knew he would be taken off the case forthwith if he thought there were any chance that Viola Addison had recognised him. But Heino was in luck. Tom had not seen.

If Heino had observed him longer, he would have realised that Tom had not taken his eyes off Viola since her arrival – not entirely out of dedication to duty. Certainly he was conscientious in this as in every other aspect of his work. But, as he had already pointed out to Heino the previous day, he was a man, as well as a detective.

Tom was intrigued by the idea of Viola. Right from that initial meeting in Werner's office, he had been curious as to what manner of woman could one minute arrive under suspicion of major conspiracy, then promptly turn up the next in bed with one of the most eligible young men in Bavaria; a man, by all accounts, with no recorded sex-life. As he delved deeper into her world and her relationships, he found himself ever more bewildered by the conflicting information he was uncovering. He simply could not get her out of his mind.

He had positioned himself several rows behind her and to the side, so that he had yet to see her face full on. From the mug shot they had got hold of and from Schneider's grainy surveillance shots back in the office, he had figured out she might be pretty. But somehow, he also knew, from the sound of her voice, that she would be much more than that. He felt an odd kind of excitement, at last being in her presence. It was a strange sensation – already to have learned so much about her – already to have heard her in the act of making love – and yet not to know the most fundamental thing about her, how she really looked.

Now he was there, within just a few metres of her, the first thing that grabbed his attention was her hair. It was lustrous, thick and long. He could tell that, in spite of its having been rolled up at her neck. It was curly, too. He could see that from the ringlets which hung like tendrils and now and then sprang out from the roll to brush against her skin – as if there were a wildness in there, struggling to free itself. Yet it was the colour which struck him most, which reminded him of the ripe horse-chestnuts he used to collect and polish to play with as a child: that same deep, rich earth colour – that same glowing, burnished sheen. Heino, he now remembered, had called the colour simply brown. Heino, who read poetry – much good it had done him. But Heino had simply described her as small. When, at the reception that night, he was able to see it for himself, he found that her body had a delicacy and natural grace to it, more evocative of perfect femininity than any he had ever seen. At that point, he could have envied Lutz Ebenau. But it was when finally he saw her face – as she turned around to greet Professor Feinstein, exultant from his lecture – that he truly envied him. At that moment, with sickening certainty, he knew he would have no peace – in mind as well as body – until, in the still of the night, her fragile screams of pleasure were caused by him.

Chapter Nine

Tom slept fitfully that night. The same bad dream kept recurring. He was scaling the walls of Neuschwanstein castle. It was Autumn. That he knew by the jewel-bright ochres and russets of the surrounding forests. A chill, hostile breeze, smelling of Winter, rustled through the dying leaves, groaning evil messages of foreboding – as though the encircling hills were, after all, the mighty dragon of the Nibelungen legend, awakening from its slumbers.

The climb was hazardous. Way below him, the Pöllat river – swollen, for the purposes of the nightmare, into a raging torrent – gushed down through the steep, narrow, rocky gorge. Many a time his foot lost its tenuous hold on the castle face. Yet above the moaning of the wind, the rushing of the water and the whispering of the trees, Tom could hear a woman's screams – Viola's screams. The louder they grew, so the faster he climbed; for these were cries charged with terror and the sound of them spurred him ever upward, until he reached the top.

He darted across the courtyard and slipped silently into the deserted castle. He searched for what seemed, in his dream, like hours – running wildly from room to room, up staircase upon staircase – using the screams as his guide. Finally he found himself in the Throne Hall; a towering, church-like chamber. It was unfurnished, but not empty; for there, in its very centre, were Viola and Ebenau – she, straining to free herself – he, holding her fast.

She wore a flowing, pure white, gossamer-fine gown – through which, as she fought in vain with her captor, Tom could catch intimations of her naked body. Ebenau, by contrast, arrayed like some ancient Teutonic knight, exuded harshness; his face set in a grim determination that confirmed his intention was to have her – whether she would or no. He pulled her, struggling, against him, so that the delicate fabric of her dress tore on the unforgiving chain-mail of his tunic.

She saw Tom and her eyes brimmed over with tears – tears that consumed him with passion and quickened his courage. The challenge he issued Ebenau, he yelled so loud it resounded throughout the whole castle.

Each man drew his sword. They fought hard and without mercy; each man second-guessing the next move of his enemy, battling on until exhaustion made them careless. Ebenau thrust blindly at Tom, using both hands to drive his sword at its target – but he missed Tom's chest, clipping his shoulder instead. Viola cried out in horror and when Tom looked down, he saw a deep crimson-coloured stain seeping through the rough cloth of his jerkin. Viola rushed to his side. Straightaway Tom pulled her behind him – using his body to shield hers – while the fight went on unabated.

Suddenly, with all the illogicality of a dream, it was night. Tom and Viola stood together on the balcony of the Throne Hall – while Ebenau, writhing from the pain of his wounds, lay on the floor below them. Tom took Viola's hand in his and together they jumped from the window. The breeze appeared to transport them gently downward, until they landed on the soft, grassy banks of the Alpsee. Tom whistled for his horse and it came galloping towards them. He mounted it. He pulled Viola up to sit in front of him and off they rode over the quaking ground – Viola clinging to him as if her life depended on it.

Here Tom's nightmare always reached its inconclusive end. He and Viola were fleeing on horseback, with the dragon in close pursuit – breathing flames that licked the ground under the hooves of Tom's faithful steed. The nearest they ever came to safety was the sight of the old, moated city walls of medieval Munich, way ahead of them in the distance.

That was when Tom finally woke up – to the sound of his doorbell ringing and Heino calling his name. He got out of bed and staggered across his flat to let him in.

"Sorry, Tom. Were you still in bed?"

"You'd have to be smart to work that out, Heino."

This was an unusually tetchy answer for Tom, although it was obviously a superfluous question. Tom's hair was dishevelled, his eyes half open and he had nothing on but a pair of shorts. Added to that he was yawning loudly and long.

"Sorry to get you up," apologised Heino. "You are alone, aren't you?"

Tom grunted. He pulled on a T-shirt and went across to the kitchen to boil water for coffee.

"You dashed off so quickly last night, I just wanted to ask you what you thought of her," said Heino. "You know, now you've seen her properly."

For a man who had spent the entire night rock-climbing, sword-fighting and galloping across Bavaria – all to rescue this particular distressed damsel, the last thing Tom now wanted to do was talk about her. Neither did he have any desire to hear Heino swearing his undying love for at least the third time that month. If only he would find himself a girlfriend, then he would not need to fall head over heels with every pretty face he saw. Today Tom's patience had started off a little thin.

"What the hell are you doing here, Heino? Aren't you supposed to be taking over from Max at seven o'clock?"

"It isn't even six-thirty yet," pleaded Heino.

Tom took hold of his wrist and twisted it round to check on that.

"See, I've got plenty of time," Heino protested.

"Well I haven't. I need to go for a run."

Tom sat down in an armchair and fished around under it until he produced a pair of running shoes. Heino was not deterred.

"Go on, Tom – tell me what you thought of her – just quickly."

71

"I can't," Tom replied. "I haven't made my mind up yet. We'll talk about her later, okay?" He invited Heino to make himself coffee and left.

Tom liked to run. He liked to use his body. He liked the exhilaration he felt when he put it under pressure. Normally he did not much mind where he ran. But that morning he felt it should be somewhere beautiful, so he jogged across the city centre to the Englischer Garten. It proved to be a good choice. The park looked wonderful. Until now it had not dawned on him – given the hot, dry, sunny weather they had been having – that Autumn was well on its way. The trees, he noticed, were well aware of it though and were starting to decorate themselves accordingly.

But the beauties of nature no longer distracted him, when he turned a corner and found himself jogging behind a girl. From the view he had, she looked to be every bit his type – tall, slim, athletic, with long blond hair that swished to and fro as she ran. He upped his speed and pulled alongside her. She was good-looking and – to cap it all – she had pale blue eyes, the sort you could swim in. He smiled at her. She smiled at him – the kind of come-hither smile that was generally more than enough of an invitation for Tom. He was just about to accept whatever might be on offer – when, for some unaccountable reason, Viola's image came into his mind and he ran on. Shit, he thought, this girl's really got to me.

"Tom, can I have a word?" Werner Fuchs called out, then disappeared back into his office. "Look," he began, when Tom had pulled up a chair in front of the desk. "I'm not so sure the attic surveillance work's going to be enough. And you're right – it is a waste of your talents. I think you need to get pro-active."

"You mean make contact with the Addison woman?"

"Yes, get to know her a little, her friends, what sort of person she is, try to probe some evidence out of her. We've already got the apartment – you can put on the friendly neighbour act."

"Absolutely fine by me, Chief. How far do you want me to go?"

He grinned.

Werner frowned. "I trust you, Tom – strictly no funny business, okay? I wouldn't be suggesting this sort of measure unless I thought it was essential."

Heino did not look at all happy with the change of plan.

"But Tom, you've always said – you've always impressed upon me – that you can learn just as much with careful surveillance as you can by infiltrating."

"And I still think that's true. But Werner's right – it's time to pull out the stops on this one. Surveillance is expensive and we're going to have to produce some results soon."

"But isn't it going to be tricky for you? Let's face it, you're the one co-ordinating the show. You need to look at the big picture. What about Max or Christian – why can't one of them do it?"

"It's all a question of the English, isn't it? You're just going to have to grin and bear the fact that it's going to be me."

Heino gave a dejected mumble. "I suppose you're right. It's just you always seem to get the girl, damn it – even when it's work."

"Simply one of the perks that comes with age and rank, Timmermann. Your turn will come." Tom slapped him on the back and laughed genially. "Anyway, like you say, this is work. Plus you've got to remember, under that angelic, little exterior of hers, there could well be beating a one hundred per cent nasty, neo-Nazi heart."

"No chance," snapped Heino. "She's got nothing to do with it. I know."

Tom raised an eyebrow. "Oh – and there was I under the definite impression you disapproved of mixing intuition with work," he teased. "So – you make pretty girls your exception, do you?"

"Just you remember, Jablonski – when we prove beyond all doubt she's totally innocent – I'm the one you promised could rescue her from the influence of this outrageously wealthy man."

"You wouldn't know what to do with her, even if you did. So, are we going to have this game of squash or not?"

"You want to thrash me at that too, do you?"

"D'you want me to let you win?"

"No."

"So come on. Let's see which one of us is the best man."

Chapter Ten

Tom propped himself comfortably up against the low wall that bordered Frau Doktor Menne's small front garden. He was admiring a rear view of Viola as she leaned into her car, trying to reach something on the back seat. She was dressed all in black – sweater, trousers, boots. How, Tom asked himself, could anyone so small have such long legs? He decided it must all be a question of proportion. Yes, that was it – Viola Addison was perfectly proportioned. She seemed to find what she was looking for – a book apparently – and backed out of the car.

"Hi," said Tom. "Neat car you've got there."

Viola was wary of talking to strange men, but she was disinclined to be rude. "Thank you," seemed a safe compromise.

"You're English, I guess."

"Yes."

"I'm an American." He smiled at her broadly. "But maybe you've figured that out already." Viola stared blankly at him. "Seems like we're neighbours," he added, hoping this would help things along.

"Neighbours?"

"Yeah," Tom replied. "We're going to be living in the same house for a while – 'til I can sort out some legal problems I'm having on the lease of a flat in Schwabing."

"I see."

This information came as something of a surprise to Viola. Her landlady had given her the definite impression she would be the

75

only tenant. Not that it mattered. Not that it was really any of her concern. Besides, it sounded only a temporary arrangement.

"So maybe we should introduce ourselves? I'm Tom – Tomasz Pajak Jnr to be precise."

"Viola Addison."

"Viola – that's a real pretty name."

He put out his hand and instinctively Viola offered him hers. He noticed how tiny it was. Yet her handshake was strong.

"Yes, well, it's nice to meet you, Mr Pajak Jnr, but if you'll excuse me," Viola said with a firmness Hilly would have applauded, "I'm late for an appointment." She gave a nod, sufficiently curt to discourage further conversation from this over-confident, though admittedly good-looking young man; then leaned down, locked the car and started walking down the street.

It was not long before she realised she was being followed. She turned round to recognise the Rice University base-ball jacket, the square shoulders and slim, denim-clad hips of her new neighbour.

"Hello again," he said cheerfully, and then more apologetically, "We seem to be going in the same direction. What time's your appointment? Maybe we can walk together."

Viola was about to come out with some fresh lie, before she thought better of it. "My appointment's not for another half an hour, in the Nymphenburg. But I did want to be on my own for a while." She gave him a weak smile. "Sorry," she added with a small shrug of her shoulders.

"The Nymphenburg – what a coincidence."

Viola sighed. "Don't tell me, Mr Pajak, you're going there, too."

"Would you rather I didn't?"

It was clear he assumed she would not object – or so his confident manner led Viola to suppose. She disliked pushy Americans in general and this one was doing nothing to change her mind. At times like these Viola wished she were more like Hilly.

"I'm going to meet a friend," she stated rather stiffly. It was the nearest she could bring herself to saying that she did mind. Still, surely it must have the desired effect.

"Hey, don't mind me," grinned Tom. "I'll just tag along until you tell me to get lost."

No doubt Hilly would have suggested he get lost there and then – but Viola was too well-mannered for that to be an option. Instead she gave a hollow smile and avoided his eyes.

Viola started to walk again and Tom fell in alongside her. She was due to meet Professor Feinstein at the Nymphenburg. It was a plan that had been struck the previous day. They were to wander through the palace, then afterwards sit outside the Palm House and drink coffee or, in Viola's case, indulge herself in one of the restaurant's decadent ice-creams. It was going to be their last meeting before he left for Florence and the final, official engagement of his European tour. Although thanks to a pressing invitation from Rupert Servranckz, both he and Ellie were expected to return to Munich as his guests, immediately afterwards – prior to returning home to New York.

It suited Viola well that Professor Feinstein was on the point of leaving, just as Lutz was about to come back. Her friendship with the old man seemed to have created a certain friction between them. She needed the chance to make Lutz understand it, before the two men met face to face. She very much wanted them to like each other.

"Have you lived here long?" enquired Tom, his relaxed Texan drawl ensuring the question sounded casual.

"Just a few weeks."

"All right. So maybe I can show you around. I know Munich pretty well – my grandparents lived here. I used to come visit them all the time when I was a kid."

"Thank you. But I know the city fairly well myself. I lived here for a while some years ago."

"You did?" He turned around and for a few paces walked backwards, giving himself the chance to look at her face. He clicked his fingers. "Don't tell me – I've got it. You liked the place so much, you just *had* to come back. It's got a great atmosphere, right?"

"Yes it has," she agreed, looking directly at him for the first time.

Tom wondered how he could ever have preferred blue eyes. He had to remind himself that this conversation was strictly business.

"You're going to be working here?"

"I'm on study leave – from my university."

"You're a student then."

"No. I teach."

"Say, how about that," announced Tom, looking and sounding impressed.

"And you?"

It did not escape Tom's attention, that this was the first flicker of interest she had shown in him. However small, it was a start.

"I'm a journalist – a sports journalist – with *The Houston Chronicle*. I'm going to be covering the Winter Olympics. I'm over here right now to do a series of articles on the run-up."

Viola said nothing. Sport was a topic in which she had no interest. Her expression must have shown it.

"So what d'you do for fun? Maybe we could take in a movie some time."

She gave him the sort of civilised smile that told him to keep his distance. He got the message and decided to approach from a different angle.

"I guess you know quite a few people here already?"

"A few."

"Like the friend you're going to meet?"

"Yes."

"Is that the good-looking guy with the old Mercedes?"

Viola stopped walking. She was taken aback. Suddenly, in her mind's eye, she could see this American – up in the flat above hers – overhearing while she and Lutz made love. The thought horrified her.

"He is your guy, isn't he?"

That confirmed it. Why else should he ask such a question? Why else would he even think it? Viola was overcome with embarrassment.

Tom put up his hands in a gesture of surrender and grinned.

"Sorry – I guess it's none of my business. You know what

journalists are. Just can't stop asking questions."

"Somehow I'd never thought of sports reporters as having quite the same interrogative approach as investigative journalists."

He threw back his head and laughed noisily.

"Great. That's sarcasm, right? You've got to remember, I'm not used to your British sense of humour."

They entered one of the side gates that gave access into the park of the Nymphenburg. For several minutes they walked along in silence. Viola felt uneasy – Tom, uncertain.

When he had asked her if Ebenau was her guy, instead of coming right out with it, she had acted as if she had something to hide, and that had not been the reaction he wanted to see. Maybe he was going too fast. If he wanted to win her confidence, he might have to go about it some other way. He could not decide how best to proceed, although, having introduced the subject of Lutz Ebenau, he was loathe to let it drop. But he did realise he would need to tread carefully. Viola turned onto one of the long, straight, broad paths of the large Parterre, which lead up to the grand west façade of the palace. Tom guessed he must be running out of time.

"It's just a guy likes to know where he stands. You know, he likes to check out the competition." His manner was openly flirtatious. "I guess I just want to know if I'm in there with a chance."

Although he made the statement with more than a hint of laughter in his voice, he was nonetheless aware of just how fine a line he was drawing between the requirements of the job and his self-interest. He had never been in a position like this before and he was not finding it easy.

"Viola my dear – yet *another* admirer," Josef Feinstein exclaimed, as he tottered along the path towards them. "For a young lady who, little more than one week ago, told me she knew *no-one* in Munich," he addressed this to Tom, "she certainly has a propensity for acquiring handsome young men."

"But just take a look at her," declared Tom. "How can we be expected to keep away?"

Josef nodded in approval. Viola merely noted how naturally Tom switched to using German.

Professor Feinstein took Viola's hand, kissed it, then asked to be introduced. They continued as they had started – in German. Viola and Josef always spoke it when Ellie was not around. She disliked the language. He on the other hand preferred it. Tom, Viola now discovered, spoke it fluently – far better than she.

The old man asked him to join them. Tom hesitated. He glanced across at Viola as if to seek permission. This was a sign of civility she had not expected. Perhaps he was not so brash after all. Certainly he was attentive – more than that – he was protective towards the Professor; helping him negotiate stairs; shielding him from jostling tourists. Viola liked that. It reminded her of the consideration Rupert Servranckz had shown the previous night. That also had taken her by surprise. It was plain she was no good judge of character.

Thinking about it, as she now did, she could half recognise the reason why. She was always too ready to sum people up – to categorise them. Hence Servranckz was pompous and pedantic – hence this American was pushy and self-confident – hence her mother was interfering and intolerant – and so on. As if those characteristics necessarily cancelled out the possibility of their having other, laudable qualities, such as kindness and compassion. She should stop seeing people in black and white.

"I guess I must be doing something right," Tom leant down behind her and whispered in her ear.

She glanced over her shoulder and gave him a quizzical look.

"You haven't told me to get lost yet."

Viola laughed gently. Tom grinned back. Now here was a sign he was making progress – in one area at least. To be able to make a woman laugh, he remembered telling Heino only a few days before, was as good as having one foot under her bed.

The Nymphenburg was historically the summer residence of the rulers of Bavaria. It was first conceived of in the second half of the seventeenth century when the Elector Ferdinand Maria presented the parcel of land, on which it was to stand, to his wife, Henriette of Savoy. Over the following two centuries subsequent generations of the ruling Wittelsbach family added and embellished, enlarged and aggrandised the building, so that by the time they were done, the original villa of Henriette Adelaide had metamorphosed into a vast, imposing, impersonal edifice.

The interior of the palace, due to the evolutionary nature of its development, changed much over the years; so that it now incorporates a number of styles – Baroque, Rococo, Régencé, Chinoiserie. As Professor Feinstein and his party made their slow progression through ante-rooms to chambers, along halls into galleries, that early September afternoon, Viola explained to Tom the salient features of each of those periods.

Professor Feinstein took little part in the elucidation, until they entered the South Pavilion – formerly the apartments of Queen Caroline, great-grandmother to Ludwig II – to view a set of portraits painted for her son and his grandfather, Ludwig I. Here Josef took over from Viola and himself acted as guide. He linked his arm through Tom's – to the latter's amusement – and adopted a confidential air.

"Now, my dear young man. Here we have Ludwig I's Gallery of Beauties, painted for him by Josef Stieler. You have visited the Nymphenburg many times, I am sure. So you will have admired these ladies already, yes?"

Tom ran his eye over the three dozen or so portraits that decorated the surrounding walls. He could recollect having seen them before – somewhere way back in the primordial soup of childhood memory. He had probably paid them scant attention then and would certainly do the same again. As far as Tom was concerned these women were dead and gone – and he preferred his women in the flesh. But the Professor seemed excited, so he tried his best to muster up some enthusiasm.

"My grandparents used to take me round a lot, when I was a kid," Tom admitted. "So maybe I *have* seen them, but I really can't recall."

Josef nodded. He understood. Tom would need guidance.

"Now look at them carefully and tell me – whom do you see?"

"Pretty faces . . ." began Tom.

Josef interrupted. "Not what – but whom? Do not rush – take your time."

He walked away, leaving Tom to wonder what he was expected to come up with. Had Schneider been here, he would have had a few suggestions, none of which could be voiced in polite society. As it was, Tom ran his eyes back and forth over the portraits searching for clues; though without any hint of what he was looking for, or any indication as to what conclusion he might draw if and when he found it, the task was pretty well impossible.

He could hear the Professor and Viola, across on the opposite side of the room, discussing something or other. He could not make out what. He turned to another wall, another group of paintings and began to inspect them. Again nothing special struck him.

"So Tom Pajak. What have you discovered?"

Tom glanced at Viola, hoping for help. He got none.

"I can't honestly say I've discovered a whole lot here, Professor," Tom confessed. "I have to tell you, to me these are still just a bunch of pretty faces."

"These *are* pretty faces. You are quite right. But they are not *just* pretty faces. Look how Stieler manages to take you behind their eyes. There is always much to observe beyond the superficial, is there not? The greater the artist, the wider he opens that door. A truly gifted portrait painter shows you *behind* the pretty face of which you speak and at the very least hints – at the very best lays bare – the inner life inside. You follow?"

Tom did and said as much.

"So you see, my dear young man, just as in life we must never content ourselves purely with the apparent – which can so easily mislead us. So in art we should not satisfy ourselves with paintings, which give us nothing but gloss – which offer us no hope of probing deeper."

Tom could see precisely what the old man was getting at. Even so he still had no idea how he was supposed to react. Viola, he noticed, was nodding her head in agreement. He followed suit.

"Take for example this charming girl," suggested Josef, pointing

82

to the portrait of a beautiful young woman. He lowered his spectacles and peered over their rims in order to make out the designation. "So – Amalie von Schintling. What can we learn about her? Is she pretty? – Yes. Does she have a cascade of brown curls? – Yes. Does she possess eminently kissable lips?" He grinned at Tom. "I think both you and I would agree upon that, would we not?" Josef turned to Viola. "You know, my dear Viola, I am inclined to think she looks very much like you."

If this was not flirting, Tom would like to know what was. The Professor started up again and seemed to substantiate it further.

"Yes, I think so," he mused – once more examining the portrait and then Viola. "The similarity is there beyond doubt; though facially it is little more than a similarity. It is the expression in the *eyes* that is so like hers. Young man, young man." He signalled Tom to come closer and study the painting. "Look at them carefully and explain what it is you see."

Tom had never had to do anything like this before. He was not at all sure he could. But he was prepared to have a go.

"Okay. I guess you could say she looks quite serious. I reckon she's got to be a romantic, a dreamer." He took a few paces back. "It's almost . . ."

"Carry on," encouraged Josef. "You are doing fine."

"Well it's almost as if she's on the edge of life – as if she hasn't quite become part of it yet. Maybe she's afraid of it."

"Good. Very good."

"I'll bet she wants to be, though – part of life I mean," added Tom, as though having once made a start, he was actually enjoying the experience. "Just take a look there, at her mouth. You can see how she'll love to laugh, when she finally gets to loosen up."

"Now, my dear Viola, come here." Josef took her hand and positioned her in front of Tom. "Do you agree, young man, when I say there is much similarity between the two?"

The opportunity to gaze into Viola's eyes had come quicker than Tom had bargained for. The circumstances were hardly ideal though. He, ordered to look; she, required to be looked at; the Professor looking on. As always Tom did his best.

"So? You agree?" Josef broke in, when it seemed to him he had allowed long enough for the purpose.

"I suppose," interjected Viola, before Tom had a chance to reply, "she might look a bit like me. But not *that* much."

Tom could see she was embarrassed.

"Come, come, my dear Viola. Look again at the charming Amalie," insisted Feinstein. "Do you not see yourself there, dressed for a ball?"

"Not really. And actually, since Oxford, I haven't been to a ball – although that's probably just as well. I couldn't tell a fox-trot from a rumba." She gave a dismissive shake of her head. "But *now* I'm looking forward to my ice-cream. Shall we wend our way?"

"Yes indeed, my dear. I am a little tired of walking," conceded Professor Feinstein, finally willing to allow that he had flustered her. "So Tom Pajak, if you will excuse us, we shall go to the Palm House and refresh ourselves. Besides I have shared Dr Addison with you long enough. Now I should like to have her to myself."

"Sure. I've got work to be getting on with anyway." He shook the Professor's hand. "And thanks for the lesson. Somehow, something tells me the art critic on my paper won't need to look for another job *just* yet." He laughed and the others joined in. "I'll see you around then, Viola. Oh, and if you ever want to go to that ball – or you just feel like learning to dance – it so happens this particular sports reporter from Texas also makes a great dance coach."

Chapter Eleven

No matter how often she made the journey, Viola still felt a thrill of adventure as she drove south down the Autobahn towards the Alps. It was the same sensation she used to feel as a child, when the Addison family would swoop in from the South Downs and make for the sea. There was a similar surge of excitement and promise of strange, magical things to come. She could never understand how Olivia had not felt it too, then, when they were children. And now, with the full drama of the Wettersteingebirge looming ever larger ahead of them, it astonished Viola that all her sister wanted to talk about was the inadequacy of the pillows in her hotel room, the inconvenience of having the menu written in a foreign language and other trivia. How, Viola asked herself, could two sisters turn out to be so different?

Olivia prattled on until Viola could bear it no longer and suggested they listen to some music. Rachmaninov was Viola's composer of the moment. She went through phases. She was sure any of the tapes currently in the car was likely to be one or other of his works; so she leant across Olivia to rummage around in the glove compartment until she found one. Rachmaninov it was – his second symphony. Olivia took the hint and fell silent – for the first two movements, at any rate. But just as the third started, just as

Rachmaninov reached his most ravishingly romantic, so she began again.

"How much longer, darling? We seem to have been travelling for ages."

"Not much longer now, Olly. Let's listen to the music, shall we? It'll help to pass the time."

Olivia obliged, but not for long.

"You don't seriously intend travelling all this way, every time you want to do a bit of work on one of these castles, do you? You'll be living your life in a car."

"No. I'll probably stay in Füssen when I'm working on Neuschwanstein – and Linderhof. I haven't got round to planning details yet."

"What'll you do – get a room in a little hotel?"

Viola gave up hope of listening to the music, so turned the volume down low.

"No, more than likely I'll be able to stay in a house Lutz owns, just outside the town."

"So the big romance is back on, is it?"

Viola ignored the question. She hoped if she did, it might go away. "When I'm working at Herrenchiemsee, I'll have to find an hotel though. But anyway, most of the time I'll be in Munich – I need the libraries, the archive material, all the documentation – so I'll be in my flat."

"With Lutz, I suppose?"

Viola could see there was to be no getting away from it. Sooner or later the topic would have to come up. Mother would have given Olivia explicit instructions to make sure it did. So she might as well get it over with. Besides they would both enjoy the day better once it was out of the way.

"Yes. With Lutz I suppose," said Viola. To her annoyance, the words came out sounding like a confession.

"Have you seen much of him?"

"Yes."

Olivia was relieved to have the subject so easily out into the open. She had imagined Viola would put up more of a fight to preserve her precious privacy.

"I dare say you'll spend most of your time together. I mean you've got a lot of catching up to do, haven't you?"

Viola wondered which number this was on her mother's check list of questions.

"Olly, you're in danger of sounding like the Grand Inquisitor."

"Rubbish, darling. I'm interested that's all. You *are* my baby sister."

"Well for your – and Mother's – information: yes, I'm sure we'll spend lots of time together – as much as we possibly can. But we've both got commitments, remember. I'm doing my research and Lutz takes his work very seriously. I'll be down here some of the time. Lutz has to travel abroad quite a bit."

"And he's a lawyer – that's right isn't it?"

"Yes."

"Civil or criminal?"

"Civil as far as I know."

"From what I'd always heard about him," continued Olivia, "I thought he might have gone into politics."

Viola had shut up like a clam the moment she had returned to Bolchester from Munich all that time ago. So what little Olivia had heard of Lutz had come exclusively from her parents. And she had accepted their impression of him utterly. She had never been the type to question her parents' point of view and had been happy to go along with their appraisal that, being so wealthy, Lutz was bound to be too spoilt to make a good husband. But, above all, he was simply too German to be suitable for any Addison to marry.

They had taken the view that Lutz must be a Nazi, for no apparent reason other than that he had a profound wish to see Germany reunited. Of course, people like Mr and Mrs Addison still found it difficult to believe there was such a thing as a decent German.

Viola, on the other hand, had found his passionate aspirations for his country rather touching and part of his attraction. She knew most of her parents' reasons for disapproving of Lutz inside out. Paradoxically it was those very qualities they had found alarming, that their younger daughter had found so compelling. Idealism, fervour, energy, resolve – Lutz had had them all in such abundance, Viola had never before imagined it possible for any one person to be that alive. Just being with him had charged her with vitality, with excitement. She had not shared his concern with politics, just as he had not shared her interest in art. No matter. The attraction had gone deeper. In Viola's case, it had been his person that had charmed her then. Just as the memory of it had kept her spellbound ever since.

"Didn't *you* think he'd go into politics, darling?" Olivia sounded irritated at having to repeat the question. "I thought he used to have a thing about reuniting the Fatherland."

"I haven't given it that much thought. He's patriotic, that's true. But it's German history that's his real passion. To be honest we haven't talked much about politics. I know he's pleased Germany's back to being one country. But that's understandable." Viola turned to Olivia and gave her a reassuring smile. "Anyway now that it's happened – reunification I mean – well, there's nothing left to do is there? It's all been sorted out. And like I said, he's got other commitments now."

"And he's got you."

Viola looked bashful, leant forward and turned up the music. Olivia took the hint. The audience was at an end.

Although she had agreed to this trip chiefly in order to humour Viola – shopping in Munich would have been much more up Olivia's street – she did nonetheless enjoy the day. With the interrogation out of the way and better yet, the prospect of meeting Lutz in person the following day for dinner, Olivia now felt like enjoying herself. So too did Viola for much the same reasons. And indeed it did turn out to be a memorable day.

By mid-morning, when they arrived at Neuschwanstein, the sun was midsummer hot. It was not Olivia's first view of what is arguably the most famous of Ludwig's castles. She had been there once before – years ago – when a group of sixth-formers from Bolchester High School for Girls had been chaperoned around Bavaria, Austria and

Switzerland, with the aim of broadening their minds and sharpening their sensibilities. What had chiefly stuck in Olivia's mind from that visit was the memory of the long haul from the car-park at the bottom of the mountain to the castle, perching precariously on the top.

This second visit was quite another matter. With Viola as her guide – rather than an old frump of a teacher – sight-seeing was a delightful, almost romantic experience. It seemed to Olivia there was nothing Viola did not know about the place and her knowledge of its history, her love of its decoration, her sympathy for its creator were near enough inspirational in themselves.

Future visits were talked of, such was Olivia's unexpected enthusiasm for the place. So rather than rush on that particular day, Viola proposed they leave viewing the castle at Linderhof as a project for next time. Olivia was happy to agree.

They spent what time they had left in the area driving around, enjoying the scenery; stopping when they saw a pretty church or a village full of mural painted chalets.

They ate chocolate cake oozing with cream and dotted with hazelnuts. They bought three small jackets in local, traditional style as presents for Olivia's three boys. They sent a postcard to their parents with a silly message. They laughed. They joked. They linked arms. They felt like sisters.

Chapter Twelve

Vivid as a primeval sunset, the orange-red glow from thousands of street lamps lit up the night sky above Munich as the two sisters drove towards the city. They had returned later than they should and Olivia was in a panic. A light rain, at first scarcely heavier than mist, began to fall and made the head lamps of the on-coming cars twinkle like stars in the gathering darkness. By the time they approached the outskirts, the rain had strengthened and, with the growing volume of evening traffic, curbed their progress. Olivia grew more edgy and Viola could not help catching her mood.

In the distance the whooping of sirens waxed and waned, making the tranquil pleasures of their day's excursion now seem far off. So too did the sisters' easy companionship, as Olivia became more anxious at the prospect of Rory's sexist sarcasm if she was late for the evening's cocktail party.

Several fire-engines, one after the other, went racing past. The surrounding traffic, eager to give them passage, pulled haphazardly aside, creating chaos in their wake. No sooner were they gone than Viola tried to extricate herself from the tangled mess; but with a reduction in visibility – the result of the now pouring rain – and aware of her sister's mounting agitation, it was not easy.

When the vehicles started to move again, the progress they made was slow. At ever-decreasing intervals, police cars screeched past, disappearing as quickly as they came, their drivers criss-crossing in and out of the crawling traffic like cops chasing robbers in a

Hollywood gangster movie.

Another string of fire-engines hurtled through and brought the traffic to a final, juddering halt. Men got out of their cars, looked around as best they could in the downpour and speculated with each other as to what they might be looking for. Viola and Olivia, dry and secure at least inside the Mini, also speculated and came to the conclusion that a serious accident must have happened. It was not until several minutes later, when a convoy of light-flashing, horn-blaring ambulances came wailing past that it occurred to them all this activity must be in response to a major disaster.

To Tom Jablonski, it was a personal disaster – and that at the end of a frustrating day spent chasing more leads that proved false. He had just drained a beer and was walking from the bar to his motorbike when, over his radio, he heard a general call for assistance at the scene of two unannounced explosions. In his present mood, he wanted nothing more than to ignore the plea; until he realised the explosions, and the fires they had caused, had taken place exactly where he was heading – two or three blocks along and in from the Sonnenstraße.

He had to abandon his bike quite a way from his own apartment. He was prevented from riding any nearer by a police cordon and by the ferocity of the fire that was already raging through the whole area.

A cluster of confused and terrified people – evacuated residents, many Turks – huddled behind the cordon, staring at the blazing buildings that had been their homes and their businesses. Tom made a mental note of those he knew and of those who were not there.

He walked briskly up to the policemen at the barrier and was nodded over by an officer who recognised him. He raced down Schwantalerstraße, a wall of flames lapping the rooftops above it. He turned left into his own narrower street, knowing even before he saw for himself, that his worst fears would manifest themselves. Ten feet tongues of fire, yellow-orange, darted and quivered from the shattered front window of the Turkish café where his friends, his adoptive family, used to sit and swap gossip over their peaty coffee.

More flames glowed and spurted from the windows above and from the buildings on either side. Over to his left, a knot of fire-fighters was aiming its hoses at the edifice which both looked and sounded as if on the point of collapse. He just about managed to make himself heard by one of the men at the back of the group.

"Did you get anyone out of the café?" he yelled.

"Don't know. I haven't been in there but a few people were coming out when we arrived."

"Was there an old woman?"

The fireman shook his head. "I didn't see one. I was setting up the pumps."

"Right," Tom nodded as he pulled from his pocket the balaclava he wore under his motorcycle helmet. He zipped up his leather jacket, wrapped a scarf over his mouth and, ignoring the bellows of the fireman, raced for the door of the café.

He felt no heat from the flames as he plunged in, focusing past the billowing smoke in the doorway which led to the kitchen. Within two seconds he was through it. He banged it shut behind him and took a deep breath. The air was clearer here. The fire had not yet reached the sealed room, but the noise all around was deafening, terrifying. And in the corner, perched as ever on her bentwood chair, but now rigid with fear, was the old woman he was looking for, the owner's mother.

Tom wrapped her long black shawl around her head. She was like a child when he picked her up, light and helpless. She stiffened with fear, so that he could feel her terror, when he opened the door into the furnace of the café itself. Even in the brief half minute he had been in the kitchen, the fire seemed to have worsened. But Tom was in auto-mode; reason, observation did not enter his thinking. All his actions were instinct driven. He waited only a few seconds, before a momentary but perceptible abatement of the flames gave him a passage across the thirty feet to the door leading onto the street. He plunged in, clutching his burden to him, weaving between the flaming furniture and blazing plastic dripping from the ceiling. This time, he did notice the flames as they licked over his face and he sniffed the smell of singed wool from the woman's shawl.

He could not falter for an instant, but carried on until he burst out into the open and a rush of cool evening air. He did not take in the cluster of TV news gatherers on the other side of the street, ecstatic at having caught on camera a real, live rescue from the clutches of the inferno.

Tom carried on running with the old woman, until he reached the group gathered outside the cordon. Even above the din of the fire, he heard the wail of relief from her relations, sobbing their thanks for what he had done. He established from the men in the group that there was no-one left unaccounted for from the café. So, having dealt with his own immediate connections, he found the senior police officer who was overseeing crowd control and attempting to co-ordinate the other services.

The officer, equivalent in rank to Werner Fuchs, knew Tom from his early days as a fresh-faced recruit. "Didn't you learn a bit of Turkish?" he asked.

"Yes sir."

"Well if you want to make yourself useful, get round to the ambulances. There are a lot of angry men there wanting to know what we're going to do to get the people who started this. I'm afraid this is the worst yet; there've been half a dozen fatalities so far."

Tom had seen charred corpses before, but familiarity had not lessened the impact. He fought back an urge to vomit as ambulancemen slid the recovered remains of two victims into body bags.

He tried to identify the leaders among the knot of men clustered around watching. When he thought he had, he took them round a corner, away from the sound of the fire and the sight of the bodies.

They told him that the men who had come to torch the buildings had hardly attempted to disguise themselves or what they were doing. Tom tried to get descriptions, but he did not get very far. Fear can blur the memory. And these men were afraid.

As the night wore on, the body count rose to over ten. Tom took one last fruitless foray into another burning building, before the firemen managed at last to turn the tide of the fire, dominate the flames and define the area of destruction.

Only then, when the crisis was over, did Tom begin to acknowledge fatigue, slow down and start to ponder the significance of what had happened.

Meanwhile, hours earlier, Viola had crept across Munich, growing more fearful with every yard she travelled. She fumbled with her car-radio until she found an on-the-spot description of what was going on.

Olivia, she discovered, could make the proverbial drama out of a crisis and flapped about so that the windows inside the car became steamed up and the moisture this generated ran down the glass in rivulets. Viola tried to console her, while she wiped the windscreen with the palm of her hand and negotiated the traffic.

It took them over an hour to get into the city centre. Countless policemen herded them through one diversion after another. Eventually they were directed into the Sonnenstraße and there they joined the queue of cars inching its way along in single file. At the end of a narrow side-street – somewhere in the vicinity of the Deutsches Theater – the traffic came to a standstill yet again. In her continuing struggle to clear the car of condensation, Viola wound her window right down.

They were close to the fire now, she could feel its heat – so intense it made her sweat. Acrid smoke hung in the air, clogging her nostrils. She felt the taste of it in her mouth and its texture on the back of her throat. Figures rushed about, black silhouettes against the blood-red of the blaze. Some ran to and fro with stretchers – ferrying wounded. The fire itself, as it swirled up into the night sky, made what seemed to her like the noise of the ocean heard in a conch shell – but many times louder. And above it, in order to make themselves heard, the rescue workers yelled at the top of their voices, conveying all the urgency and horror of the disaster that was unfolding in front of their eyes.

"Darling, I wish you'd stay the night," pleaded Olivia, when they finally pulled up outside the Vier Jahreszeiten Hotel.

"Thanks, Olly. But I just want to get home – away from all this. Besides, if I stayed, Rory would only want me to go to that drinks party with you – you know he would." Viola looked down at her dungarees and grinned. "And I could hardly go along looking like *this*, could I?"

"But I don't like the thought of you all alone out there – in this mayhem."

"Don't worry. I'll be all right. I'll phone as soon as I'm home. If you've already left, I'll leave a message with Reception and you can pick it up when you get back." Viola tried to sound casual. "Off you go. Rory's probably having kittens."

Olivia leant across and kissed her cheek.

"Thanks for today, darling. I really did enjoy it."

"Me too," said Viola, as she near enough pushed her sister out of the car. "Now go. You're late remember."

By the time Viola got back home she felt exhausted. Her head and her shoulders ached. Though driving away from the city centre had not been so gruelling as heading into it, it had been gruelling enough. And although after Sonnenstraße, she saw no more fires, explosions – whatever it was they were – still she could hear the intermittent sound of sirens yowling in the distance; making her ever mindful of what she had left behind. Gradually, however, even those became less audible, until in her peaceful, lime-lined crescent she could hear nothing of them at all – only the noise of rain beating on the roof of her car.

She sat outside the house for several minutes, barely able to think coherently. Yet when the front door opened and light came streaming out, she instinctively turned towards it and ran indoors.

Frau Doktor Menne greeted her in a state of agitation; not exactly panicking but certainly distraught. She asked Viola into her sitting-room – a carbon copy of the one upstairs, save for the plethora of plants which occupied every available surface. There was a bottle of wine on the table – uncorked, yet otherwise untouched – and two tall, cut-glass Hock glasses sat beside it on white, hand-crocheted doilies. Her landlady invited her to take a seat, then began to pour the wine. Viola saw how violently her hand shook and offered to take over the task.

The old lady made some reference to a television in the far corner of the room, which until now Viola had not noticed. The set was turned on. That is to say, it was transmitting pictures; but no sound came from it – though given the deafness of its owner, that in itself was not surprising. It soon became apparent that what she had been viewing was the cause of her distress and Viola could well believe it; for there on the screen – being played out in the cosy comfort of this suburban sitting-room – were the very scenes of devastation she herself had witnessed only shortly before.

"Frau Doktor," Viola asked as loudly as she could without shouting, "may I turn up the sound?"

The Frau Doktor nodded vaguely. It made no difference to her; the pictures were what mattered.

They confirmed what Viola had heard on the radio, with the added information that most of the victims were Turks. But it was only when the programme moved back into the studio that it was conjectured that the fires were the result of arson attacks, racially motivated, the work of Fascist extremists.

The prospect chilled Viola to the depths of her bones. She sat with her glass of wine, horror-struck, gazing at the television as if she were looking at some fictional horror film. She saw footage of a man rescuing an old woman, bundled in black clothing, from a blazing café. When she thought how like Tom Pajak he looked, she knew fatigue must be getting the better of her.

She finished her glass of wine and left – pleading exhaustion. This was no mere excuse. The strain of the evening's events – and above all the realisation of their cause – had clearly begun to take their toll. She went upstairs and lay on her bed for a few minutes, trying to come to terms with it. She decided that a bath might calm the thundering in her chest. She got up and went to run the water. The telephone rang. She turned off the taps and hurried to answer it. She hoped it would be Lutz. It was her mother.

"Viola, are you all right? These fires, aren't they terrible? They're not happening anywhere near you, are they? I've been worried sick."

"Yes Mother, I'm perfectly all right – and no, they're not happening anywhere near here."

"But what about Olivia? I've tried and tried the hotel, but they keep telling me she's out."

"That's because she is. She and Rory have gone to a business function."

"It won't be near all the trouble, will it? What *can* Rory be thinking of, taking her out in all that. Oh God, I don't know how my nerves stand it."

"Try to keep calm, Mother. I'm sure they'll be fine. Rory wouldn't have gone if he thought there was any danger."

"I think they'd better come home tomorrow."

"There's no need for that. Besides Rory's got meetings all day tomorrow. I know."

"Then he must cancel them. He must think of those little boys."

"I'm sure he does."

There was a moment's pause. When Margaret Addison started up again, her tone had changed.

"Viola, both your father and I think you ought to come back with Olivia and Rory. It's not safe for you out there."

"I'm quite safe, Mother. I live in a nice, respectable area. There's no sign of trouble around here. Olivia will tell you."

"But if those Germans are going to start attacking foreigners . . ."

"They're not attacking Britons – so stop worrying."

"But if they're going to start blowing up art galleries . . ."

"What do you mean?"

"Haven't you heard? There's been an explosion in a famous art gallery over there – somewhere with an unpronounceable name –

97

somewhere where Hitler used to keep his Nazi Art. I'm sure that's what they said on the News."

"Not the Haus der Kunst? Or was it one of the Pinakotheks?"

"Oh I don't know. I just can't think for worry. Viola, you really ought to come back home."

"Look, I've got to go – I've left a bath running. I'll speak to you soon, I promise."

Later on, after her bath, Viola tried to phone Hilly. She was still so wound up she had to talk to someone and she had no contact number for Lutz in Amsterdam. Hilly's voice answered, bright and bouncy as ever, but it was a recorded message. In her disappointment Viola put down the receiver without saying so much as "Hello". If John had still been in London she might even have considered calling him. He was so sensible and calm and had always helped her get things into perspective. It was just as well perhaps he was not there. But she needed to talk to someone, anyone who, unlike the Frau Doktor, could hear her.

She pulled on some clothes and went upstairs to see if her new neighbour was in. A chink of light was escaping from the only door on the attic landing, directly ahead of her, as she reached the top. She knocked softly – once, twice – then again more loudly – three, four times. There was no answer. She smiled. Why had she imagined Tom Pajak would be at home? He had hardly seemed the sort to be curled up in bed with a mug of hot milk and a good book. No doubt he was out still, boogying the night away.

Nothing could have been further from the truth. Tom Jablonski was still at the scene of the fires and remained there until shortly before the first reluctant hint of morning showed itself. He had battled all night and yet however hard he had fought, by the time the fire was extinguished, all that remained of the café and the flats above was charred and smouldering débris.

When finally he was able to clamber up through the stairs which hung like a skeleton in the gutted building, he found that his own apartment had fared little better than the ones beneath.

At first he tried to take stock of what he had lost, then found it no longer seemed important. The possessions he valued most – his health and his strength – he carried with him. Not everything had been burned, though. Some furniture was still intact, a few mementoes and trophies. As he looked around to find himself a change of clothing, he could hear the eviscerated structure groaning and creaking beneath him, as though in the final throes of death. He realised he was looking at this segment of his life for the last time. Without sentimentality, he scooped up a handful of belongings and staggered back down the shaking stairs.

As he passed her room, Tom wondered if Viola were asleep. He assumed from the presence of her car that she was there at least.

Tom himself was past sleep. Adrenalin still raced around his body. He was hungry, though, from the energy lost through all-out physical exertion. Heino had been on surveillance duty that night and had stayed on. He had, as usual, packed himself too much breakfast. Tom waded into it gratefully.

"You won't be having to do too much more of this, Heino," he said between mouthfuls.

Heino looked disappointed. "Why not?"

"I've just been talking to Fuchs. There'll be a hell of a lot to do, sussing out who's responsible for these fires, and watching over a sleeping Viola isn't going to help much, though we'll still be tailing her when she goes out. But from now on he just wants someone in twice a day to take the tapes off the machine, and for the moment that might as well be me." Heino looked up at him. "I'm moving in here, full-time. My flat's been gutted."

"The fires got that far?"

"Certainly did. They've taken out twenty buildings and about a dozen Turks."

"They? The Network?"

"I should think so. No-one's claimed it yet, but then the Network hardly ever does." Tom helped himself to another hunk of Heino's cheese and banana sandwich.

They sat for a while talking. Heino, whose nature it was to expect good of his fellow man, was shocked and saddened by what had occurred that night. Tom on the other hand had been around too long, had kept his eyes too wide open to be surprised by any kind of act one human being might be prepared to inflict upon another – but he was enraged by it nonetheless.

There was no doubt in either of their minds that the Fascist Network had been behind the attacks on the Turkish population. The fire-bomb at the Neue Pinakothek was another matter. Unlike Heino, Tom did not rule out the possibility that the two incidents were related – even if he found it hard to see how.

"But it's just too much of a coincidence, Heino. The Nazi boys choose tonight to indulge in a bout of ethnic cleansing *and* some other bunch just happens to choose it to blow up paintings?" Tom shook his head. "I can't make out the connection yet, but I'm sure there is one." Tom paused to take the mug of coffee Heino had just made him. He heaped in sugar so that the level came dangerously close to the brim. He had to lean forward to slurp some out. "Though somehow I can't see our Dr Addison being too chuffed with her fellow conspirators if they've taken it into their heads to start wrecking her precious pictures." Tom took another mouthful of the coffee. "Talking of our little suspect, what's she been up to since you came on?"

"She may be yours, Tom. But she's not mine."

Tom laughed. "D'you want to rephrase that?"

Heino ignored the comment.

"Okay," Tom said. "I know how you feel about her. I wish she weren't a suspect, too – I admit it. But we've got a job to do."

Heino looked deflated. "But Tom, I've spent hours looking at her and I reckon I know her. I know she couldn't be a part of those fires, or plan anything like killing the old Professor.

"Now, Heino, don't get yourself in such a state. She might hear." Tom squeezed his upper arm, "I understand what you're saying, but in this business, you just can't afford to go on appearances. I've seen plenty of women, just as cute as her, in my time on the job, who'd sell their own grannies at a discount if it meant they could get what they wanted." Tom squeezed his arm again. "Okay?"

Heino nodded sheepishly. "Okay, Tom," he muttered.

"Right. To business. What else happened tonight?"

Heino told him what little there was to tell.

Tom stared into space for a second or two as if trying to fathom something out. "And she didn't try to get in touch with anyone else?"

"No. Except you, I suppose. She came up here about midnight, knocked on the door a couple of times."

"Did she try the handle?" asked Tom, suddenly extra attentive.

"No. She went back downstairs – presumably to bed."

"Then it's just as well I'm moving in for real. After all, let's face it, as far as our dear Viola's concerned, I *am* supposed to be living here."

"Does the landlady know that?"

"She does, but she's a loyal citizen to the core; she thinks we're watching some secret agent in the house opposite. When we first came here and Schneider was over the road, I pointed him out to her. She said she would have guessed he was a spy – just from his face," Tom laughed. "Anyway, I'll move in and call you guys in to cover if anything really big breaks."

Chapter Thirteen

In the late twentieth century, the ripples that carry news from the epicentres of trouble to the rest of the world move very fast indeed.

While the bombs and fires in Munich happened too late in the evening for most of the next day's European newspapers, the Americans were able to run the story on all their front pages. And television stations everywhere showed it as it happened. There was no question that it was a major story.

The attacks in themselves, though shocking, were nothing new. It was well-known that a tide of violence against minority groups – both in the city and in Germany as a whole – was on the rise. Nor was this in any way a purely German phenomenon. It was widespread throughout Europe. In spite of that mitigating factor, however, when these things happened in Germany, they took on a special, sinister significance. It was inevitable. It was understandable. Old memories are the hardest to kill and take the longest to die.

Yet it was both in the scale and the ruthlessness of its execution that that night's events differed from other recent incidents. Political pundits and so-called experts in terrorist techniques agreed that this was not the work of rogue gangs of racist thugs on the rampage. They concluded that this was nothing short of war, being waged by a force that was dutifully following plans devised by intelligent, punctilious minds.

It was this, above all, that left the Security Forces in no doubt that the Network was responsible for the outrage. With deep foreboding, they speculated, privately, on what would happen next. So, publicly, did the media.

There was no question in any news editor's mind that the agonised faces of the victims of terror and the burned-out shells of their former homes made powerful copy. In contrast, what would normally have been a major story – the small fire-bomb at the Neue Pinakothek – attracted barely a mention. In certain circles, of course, the irretrievable loss of a Munch and a Schiele – together with varying degrees of damage to several other major works of art, including a Klimt – did give cause for sadness and concern.

Viola caught the news on a local station a few minutes after she woke early next morning. Professor Bryce heard it on the Today Programme on Radio 4, and telephoned Munich immediately. Unable to reach Viola in person, he left a message at the university with instructions that she should call him back with her personal assessment of the situation. Josef Feinstein picked up a brief mention of the art gallery fire on a lurid Italian television news programme. He had better luck than Professor Bryce in contacting Viola; he had her home phone number.

"Viola? Thank God," he said when she answered. "It looks like it was hell in Munich last night."

"It was – like the Inferno," Viola agreed, not feeling that this was exaggeration. She told him how near she had been to it and the sense of shock it had left in her.

"The whole thing is horrible, horrible," Feinstein muttered, with what Viola knew was heartfelt compassion. "And the Neue Pinakothek – not so bad as the loss of human life, of course, but nevertheless, it will be a considerable loss if these pictures really have been destroyed. Do you feel able to go there – to check it all out?"

Suddenly, to Viola, this seemed like the ideal antidote to the last twelve hours of nightmare. At least the activity would keep worse images away. She left as soon as she had drunk her coffee and satisfied herself that her landlady had recovered from the trauma of the previous night.

When she arrived at the Neue Pinakothek, Viola found it in a state of organised chaos. In the middle of it all stood Rupert Servranckz. She had expected to find him there – and there indeed he was, overseeing the salvage operation with all his customary thoroughness; interrupting it only long enough to grant crucial interviews to the media, when he felt that nothing short of comment from the top would do.

By the time Viola crossed paths with him a little while later, he was locked in conversation with Werner Fuchs – come in person to inspect what remained of the incendiary device responsible for the chaos the Doctor was now trying to clear up. As soon as Servranckz noticed her, he called her across and presented her to the Police Chief – as none other than the foremost British authority on German art. Viola was dumbfounded by such overblown praise. She blushed deeply. To hide her embarrassment, she backed away, muttering an unconvincing excuse for leaving. But the tactic backfired on her when she turned straight into the microphone of a lurking BBC television reporter, who had heard Servranckz's glowing introduction and now repeated it to camera for the whole of Britain to hear.

Viola blushed again as she related the incident at dinner at the Vier Jahreszeiten Hotel that same evening. She had not chosen to bring the subject up. She would have preferred to forget it, but her parents had seen the interview on the early evening news and had called the Hotel forthwith. Rory had taken the call and with it the perfect ammunition to taunt her.

"Well, little sister." Rory lolled back in his chair and eyed her under half closed lids. "I simply had no idea you were the *foremost British authority on German art*. I really am most impressed." He turned to Lutz Ebenau and Peter Lessel, whom Lutz had brought along as back-up for this momentous meeting with Viola's sister and brother-in-law, explaining to them that he had been "at a bit of a loose end that evening." "Hard to believe, isn't it, gentlemen," Rory continued, "that this pretty, little thing we see before us is such an important personage?"

104

"Is it because Viola is so small you find it difficult to believe or is it because she is so beautiful?" Lutz's tone was bland enough, though the perceptive ear might well have detected a contemptuous edge to it. "For myself, I see neither characteristic as having any bearing on her ability to be an expert in the field of painting – or any other field."

"And you are an art lover yourself, Lutz?" asked Rory, choosing to ignore the previous remark.

"No. I cannot say that I am. But I do admire anyone who has reached the top of their profession through hard work and a superior mind."

"Come, Lutz," interjected Peter. "I think what Rory was wishing to say is that beauty can often blind one to all other considerations."

This was not at all what Rory had had in mind – but it sounded good enough to put an end to the matter. Lutz, too, seemed satisfied with his old friend's interpretation. Even so, the final word he kept for himself.

"I should be the last person to deny Viola's beauty. But I hope I am sufficiently in command of my senses not to let them influence my reason. The converse of that, of course, must be my belief that my intellect will not blind me to that which is beautiful."

Lutz glanced across at Viola and gave her a look to underline the point. Viola smiled back as best she could, given that the evening was getting off to such an unpromising start. And yet perhaps it had been foolish of her to imagine it could be otherwise – when the two major players at the table were such contrary characters – and when the prejudices of both had been shaped by the preconceptions and misconceptions of a decade. But however logically she now tried to view the position, it did nothing to alter her own. She still felt like Piggy-in-the-Middle.

Viola's fears proved in the end to be over-stated; for, once they had got over their initial skirmish, Lutz and Rory seemed happy to agree to differ as, inevitably, they debated the horrific events of the previous night. Lutz's reluctance to rise to some of Rory's more outrageous statements frustrated her and she felt compelled to take up the cause herself.

"I can't believe I'm hearing this," exclaimed Viola. "From what you're saying, Rory, it sounds as though you almost sympathise with these racists."

"Well I do. I'm not ashamed to say it. I don't sympathise with their methods – torching people's homes is a touch barbaric for me – but I do with what motivates them. What's more, I can assure you, little sister, *I'm* in the majority – the *vast* majority – *you're* the one who's out of step."

Viola turned to Lutz for support.

"Viola, your brother-in-law is right. What happened last night was fairly inevitable. Sooner or later it had to happen."

"So wake up, little sister, stop dreaming about Utopia. It can't exist. Prejudices are too deep-seated. Just think of Yugoslavia. This is the real world, where Turks are Turks and Germans are Germans – and never the proverbial twain shall meet. There are bound to be tensions. When times are good, they'll just be bubbling away under the surface. But when times are bad, they'll erupt – like now. And I warn you, times are going to get a hell of a lot worse – and the violence will match it. Not just here. It'll be the same all over Europe. No doubt about it."

"But you sound so complacent – and when it's people's lives we're talking about." Again the image of the bewildered Turks gazing at their devastated homes flashed through her mind. "Surely the politicians must do something to stop it. They can't just stand by and let it happen – let mob rule take over."

"Of course, they will try to stop it," said Peter. Viola noted that he at least sounded concerned. "But their task will prove impossible. You see, Viola, many Germans have seen their living standards falling – their jobs disappearing – I'm afraid they will not take kindly to politicians asking them to support foreigners at a time when they have their own to help – the Ossies from what was the DDR."

"They were happy enough to have the Turks here to help create the Economic Miracle," stated Olivia, entering the discussion for the first time – although Rory's patronising response ensured hers was only a brief incursion.

"But that was *then*, darling, and this is *now*. You can't expect any situation to last forever. Times have changed – pure and simple. Today the Gastarbeiter are surplus to requirements. So the Germans want to weed them out. Surely that's easy enough to understand."

"To understand, yes – but not condone," Viola snapped back. "And if not condone, accept – which is what you seem prepared to do, Rory."

Lutz removed his arm from the back of Viola's chair and put it around her shoulder. "The Economic Miracle is over now. The good times are over – here and everywhere in Europe. They will not return – not for many years to come. Sadly, Rory may be right there."

From the other side of the table, Peter Lessel seemed keen to amplify what Lutz had said. "And just as a man will fight to protect his family, so those of like extraction will fight to safeguard their countries, their compatriots, their way of life. I suppose they feel it is not unreasonable."

It almost sounded convincing, the way Peter put it. But Viola knew that burning old women out of their homes could never be right – however much Peter tried to rationalise it. She reflected how, when she had known Peter ten years before, she had always sensed something insidious about him. There was nothing overt; but on the few occasions they had been in the same company he had tended to monopolise conversations – and Lutz, too. In fact, she strongly suspected it had been Lessel who had invited himself that evening.

Rory boomed on. "So Peter, are you, like me, a believer in the famous – or should I say infamous – Fortress Europe theory?" Rory butted in, the tone of his voice bullish.

"Perhaps," Peter shrugged, backing away from being cornered into a specific political stance. "Although for myself, I am inclined to think that we should use its now inevitable creation as an opportunity not to extend the European Union but to re-define it."

"I think probably the most we can hope for is a bit of damage limitation. And I'm not exactly optimistic we'll get that. I suspect the powers that be are too spineless, too weak-kneed, to do what's really needed – or won't try hard enough until it's too late – until things have started getting way out of hand."

"Perhaps they are waiting," proposed Peter, "to gauge public opinion to events such as those of last night. Perhaps they wish to ascertain the will of the masses before they act. After all, in a democracy they must always keep one eye on the next election."

"Indeed. Well," Rory raised his glass, "all any of *us* can do is wait and see – see what they come up with at the Conference in December. Though I doubt we need hold our breath – ten to one it'll be the usual vacillations."

Waiters arrived and began to serve desert. Viola no longer felt like eating and simply pushed the cheesecake around her plate in some sort of pretence of doing so.

"Schätzlein, you are not eating. You are not unwell, I hope?"

"All this talk of race riots upsets the sensibilities of women like Viola," answered Rory, feeling himself free as usual to answer on her behalf. "You know how sensitive the artistic temperament can be."

Lutz disregarded the observation. Instead he leant forward to kiss Viola's cheek. He put his lips to her ear and whispered: "I am sorry that the world can sometimes be so ugly. There is much in it that must be changed – that I would change – to make it beautiful enough for you."

He brushed his lips against her neck and at his touch, Viola felt with a surge of relief that as long as they were together, the world was beautiful enough for her just as it was. While she and Lutz retreated into private dialogue, Peter Lessel took it upon himself to change the subject, entertaining Olivia and Rory with anecdotes about Ludwig II and his castles. This was mainly in response to Olivia, who was still full of enthusiasm about her excursion the previous day. They spoke of it at length.

"Then you must certainly visit Schloß Linderhof. In my opinion it is still more beautiful – and quite different – even the location is in total contrast to that of Schloß Neuschwanstein. Take my advice – visit it in Springtime. You will then see it at its best – and with luck, without too many tourists."

"Viola, darling." Olivia lacked Peter's diplomatic touch and had no qualms about bringing her sister back into the mainstream conversation. "Did you hear that? Peter says Spring is the best time to see Linderhof. Perhaps I should arrange another visit then. What d'you say?"

"I think it's a lovely idea, Olly."

"And perhaps you would care to use my house in Füssen?" offered Lutz. "It is a beautiful, old house and has a wonderful garden – just right for little boys to explore. I speak from experience. So why not bring your sons? They would love it, I am sure. Besides, Viola has told me so much about them, I feel that I should now like to meet them."

"You'll soon change your mind if you do," cautioned Rory. "I warn you in advance – they're absolute little monsters."

"Little boys are meant to be high-spirited. That is as nature intended. Anyway, I shall enjoy them – I like children, especially little boys." He caught Viola's eye for an instant. "I look forward to the time when my own little monsters are running around the garden in Füssen."

He nodded to the waiter and asked for the bill.

That settled it. Olivia's mind was made up. She liked him. There was not one thing she could say against him. Tomorrow, when she arrived back in Bolchester, she would tell her parents they had nothing to fear. Lutz Ebenau was handsome, charming, rich, hospitable, very much in love with her sister – and wanted to be a family man. As far as Olivia was concerned the visit as a whole – and above all the evening's dinner – had been an out and out success.

That, to a greater or lesser extent, was the judgement of the whole party. If any one of them had misgivings, it would have been Viola – and the few she had disappeared that night as she lay in Lutz's arms. And as they made love, even the vision of the old woman – the ghost that had haunted her throughout the day – faded by degrees into nothing.

109

Chapter Fourteen

"Well Tom, have you fucked her yet – this Viola Addison?" Tom glanced at Heino, then smiled sweetly at the man who had delivered the question.

"Give me a chance, Schneider," Tom laughed. "There's the not insubstantial problem of the rich and handsome Lutz between us, remember. But I'm working on it."

"That's what I like to hear," said Schneider, giving him a slap on the back. "Just make sure you get a move on. You've only got a few more weeks to get in there – or I'm going to be kissing a couple of hundred marks goodbye."

As he sauntered off Tom looked to Heino for enlightenment.

"They're taking bets that you'll have slept with her by the end of the Oktoberfest."

Tom threw back his head and laughed out loud. "Heino, Heino – just about the last thing in my mind when I think about Viola Addison is sleep. Now shall we go to this meeting?"

As they walked towards Werner Fuchs's office, Schneider pulled Tom a little aside. He put his arm around his shoulder and lowered his voice to a confidential pitch.

"By the way, if you need inspiration – you know, getting it up – come over to my desk after the meeting and take a look at the pictures I've got of her and Ebenau. I went back after that first night and managed to get some when they didn't have those curtains in

110

the way. Believe me, Jablonski, they're sexier than any of the stuff the porn squad comes back with." He dropped his voice still further. "Seems this girl does anything he asks. And remember, here's a man catching up on ten years of fantasies."

"You're a sad old man, Schneider." This time there was a harder edge to Tom's voice.

Werner Fuchs looked tired. This was a bad sign. When things were going well, it did not matter how much he deprived himself of sleep, he seemed to thrive on activity. When an operation was fouling up, he could age a decade in a week.

"Okay, it's sixty hours since the fires started, and what have we got?" It was not a question looking for an answer. Everyone in the room was depressingly aware that they did not have any answers to offer. "I'll tell you what we've got," Werner went on, "an absolute Zero."

"That's not right, surely, Chief," Heino started tentatively. "We've identified one of them."

"And how far do you think he'll get us?" Fuchs sighed. "One bull head, as stubborn as a mule and half as intelligent. We could put him on the rack and he wouldn't talk. He never has, whenever we've picked him up." He gazed at the half-dozen men in his office, one by one, as if he were looking to them for inspiration.

Werner did not often let his state of mind get in the way of his work; he considered that totally unprofessional. But the lack of progress was beginning to make him feel inadequate. As Werner sucked moodily on a cigarette, an air of gloom settled over the room and although any one of them would have liked to lift it, no-one was sure how it could be done. Mohrfeld was prepared to try; even if the only way he could think of getting started was with yet another re-run of what they already knew only too well. Though he did carry on to produce a rallying cry of sorts.

"The press are getting it right for once. What we're dealing with here is an army – trained to carry out orders, to the letter. And they're not making any mistakes – not at the moment at any rate.

But sooner or later one of them is going to trip up. Someone, somewhere along the line, is going to make the big error – and when that happens, we'll be there to nab them. What we've got to make damned sure of is that we *are* there. We can't allow ourselves to be caught sleeping on the job." Heino glanced at Tom. "Am I right, Chief?"

Werner was grateful to him and was not slow to show it. "You're right, Kurt – and thank you for summing things up so well." He looked around at the rest of his men. "I'm sure you're all aware how vital it is we keep on our toes on this case. Like Kurt said – we've got to be sure we're in a position to take advantage if they put so much as a foot wrong. But in the meantime we're going to identify any possible areas of weakness – they're bound to have them – and concentrate our efforts on those. For instance, it's my hunch one of their weakest spots is Dr Addison."

"Someone remind us of her movements that day," Mohrfeld said.

"She'd been out of town all day," said Max, "looking at castles with her sister. I had quite a relaxing day there, in fact – the scenery's wonderful." Fuchs shot a warning glance at him. Max took note and adopted a more serious tone. "The fires were already well on their way when she came back."

"Did she go near them?"

"She drove by, along Sonnenstraße. She didn't have a lot of choice about where to go, though. The traffic boys were sending them all round the houses. She dropped her sister at her hotel and drove home."

"Then what?"

Heino chipped in. "It's in my report, Chief. She came in, ran a bath, spoke to her mother on the phone and went to bed."

"Alone?"

"Yes."

"Where was loverboy Lutz, then?"

"He was in Amsterdam, on some case, I think. He didn't get back until the following afternoon. Then he, Viola, her sister, Rory Melhuish and Peter Lessel met up at the Vier Jahreszeiten Hotel. Unfortunately

112

the restaurant was full and we couldn't get a handle on what they met up about."

"Peter Lessel, eh?" Werner raised an eyebrow. "So the whole family's becoming chummy now."

"You know, Chief," interrupted Tom. "I'm beginning to agree with Heino. She hasn't got anything to do with the fires, or the Network. If she really did, she'd have killed off old Feinstein by now – before he went off to Italy. She had her chances. Why wait 'til he gets back? Plus," he added, thinking back to his visit to the Nymphenburg, "she really seems to like the old man."

Werner shook his head. "It's possible the Network is playing a long game here. I have a feeling it's going to be like a jigsaw puzzle, where we won't see the whole picture until the final piece is inserted. When I met her at the Neue Pinakothek, there's no doubt about it, she looked shifty as hell. And when she found out who *I* was, she couldn't get away fast enough. Now that's precisely why I say she's a weak link. She's simply not as hard as the bosses in the Network. She hasn't got their nerve. Sooner or later she'll give the game away, you mark my words. So, Tom, it's back to you. I want to know what she's doing – what she's saying – every single minute of the day and night. I want to know *everything* she gets up to."

"All sounds pretty fair to me," added Schneider, as he gave Tom a look that said it all.

"I'm not saying she's *not* involved," persisted Tom, not ready to let Fuchs proceed onto the next item on his agenda without having had his final word on this. "All I'm saying is, it just doesn't hang together, and I'm getting pissed off listening to screwing or snoring all night. It's just a bloody waste of time." Tom stopped abruptly. He knew he had gone further than he should.

Werner Fuchs took a deep breath and looked at Tom for a moment before he answered. "I decide what is or isn't a waste of time. There's a connection between this woman and the Network – I can *smell* it; and my nose has never let me down. Look, you chose to move in there – rent free – so earn your keep."

"But, boss," Tom persevered, despite the remonstration, "If she *is* in the Network, how does that square with them blowing up paintings? Her being an art expert, I mean."

Mohrfeld looked surprised. "I didn't know we'd established a connection between the Network and the gallery fire." He looked at Werner for clarification.

"We haven't. And Tom, stop looking for one. These people are quite logical and what logic would there be in destroying paintings – when it's Turks they want to get rid of? Why would they waste their resources? What would be the point?"

"Like you said yourself, Chief, the Network is playing a long game. And I wonder," Tom expanded, "if last week was just a warning shot. You know, a signal to Bonn – that if it doesn't do what the Network wants – begin repatriating immigrants that is – then they'll widen the net. They'll start attacking other things. Things, it has to be said, a lot of influential people we know would make a lot more fuss about than a group of displaced Turks."

"But if that *is* the case – if it *is* going to be a form of blackmail," asked Kurt, "why don't they start making demands – threats? Why leave us in the dark?"

"They'd lose their advantage," explained Tom, making up his theory as he went along. "This way they're keeping us all guessing."

"So what do the rest of you think?" sighed Fuchs, throwing it open to the floor, resigned to the fact that between them – for one reason or another – Tom and Heino were determined to clear Dr Viola Addison, when – for the time being at least – she was his only hope for a breakthrough. He received only blank looks in reply.

A few minutes later, when anything that could be usefully said had been, the meeting broke up. As the others filed out, Werner asked Tom to stay behind for a moment.

"What is it, Chief?"

"Close the door, Tom. I don't want Schneider listening in on this."

Tom sensed what was coming.

"Did you see Schneider's surveillance shots?"

"Not yet."

"I decided not to show them at the meeting; I didn't want it degenerating into a peep-show." His voice hardened abruptly. "Look, I know what kind of a mind Schneider's got, and I'll be hauling him in here later today to give him a verbal warning. But I want to hear it from your mouth. Tell me you're keeping it on a – " he coughed, "business footing with Viola Addison."

Tom sighed, then looked Werner in the eye. "I've only managed to get one meeting with her so far, Chief. And we didn't even get to first base." He grinned.

Werner pursed his lips. "Tom, you might have noticed my sense of humour has rather waned recently. I don't want these rumours to get out of hand – or out of this station. You're one of my best detectives, and you know it. And for that reason, you also know if you try to screw a suspect, you'll end up in very deep shit. I agreed to your moving into the building with her, but if I find any substance in the rumours, I won't hesitate to pull you off this case. Got that?"

"Got it, Chief." He grinned again, thinking honesty was his best policy at this point. "Anyway, what chance would I have? You've seen from Schneider's shots how intimate she is with Ebenau."

Several hours after the meeting Tom made his way slowly across the office to see Schneider, stopping to discuss this or that with a few others on the way. When at last he reached his destination, he parked himself on the edge of an empty, adjacent desk and held out his hand.

Schneider looked up and gave him a knowing smile. He rummaged about through the pile of papers that cluttered his workspace until, from somewhere near the bottom, he produced a brown manila envelope which he handed over to Tom. Tom noticed the letters E/A pencilled in the top right hand corner. Slowly, hesitantly, Tom opened the envelope and took out its contents.

Now in his hands he held a dozen or so large, glossy, black and white photographs. On the top – the first he saw – was an image of Viola. She was completely naked and lying diagonally across the bed. Both her hands and her arms were stretched out in front of her in a gesture of entreaty – and although she was alone in the picture, it was not difficult to deduce to whom – or for what – she was entreating. One of her legs was outstretched and to the side – the other bent at the knee and dropped down onto the bed, causing her back to arch slightly and her breasts to tilt upwards – yet these were barely visible through the mass of shining, waving, curling hair which fell around her body like a waterfall. Never had Tom seen anything so erotic.

He was aware of Schneider's voice urging him to go on, to look at the rest of the photographs. He could hear the lecherous joking and sniggering of other men as they gathered around to peer over his shoulder. Yet the sound of their voices seemed distant – from another world, on another plane – not there in the picture with him.

"I was wrong about you, Schneider," he said finally, "you're not just sad, you're a bloody degenerate." He kept his tone light, pretending to joke along with the others – pretending to be one of the boys; perhaps because he was one of the boys – or rather, had been until that point. But at that point everything altered. Notwithstanding Fuchs's warning, he now knew he did not merely want to have Viola Addison. He realised he was in love with her.

He put the photographs back in the envelope and dropped it on Schneider's desk. Then he walked off to his locker, as casually as he could, and changed into his shorts and trainers. Thank God it was the end of the shift, he thought, and he could go for a run.

The first thing he noticed – the first thing he looked for whenever he turned into the crescent – was Viola's car. Although there was no longer any real need for secrecy, on that particular evening Tom chose to use the back staircase. It led from the cellar straight up to the attic – their clandestine means of coming and going – used of late by Heino and himself. It ended up at a door opening directly into what they called their "office" – a box-room in which they kept the bulk of their monitoring equipment.

He found Heino in there checking the tapes. For a moment he wondered what he was up to; but then he remembered he had

116

asked Heino to pick them up and take them back to Fuchs so he could have the evening off, forget work and catch up with some kip. He smiled to himself. He was tired enough to have forgotten this, although now he had absolutely no desire to sleep.

Heino put the tapes in his case, but hovered around the desk.

"Something the matter?" asked Tom.

"No, I was just listening to the music down there. Richard Strauß – 'I'm Abendrot' – it's a setting of the Eichendorff poem. D'you know it?"

Tom nodded. His mother had read it constantly in the few months that separated his father's death from her own. He said nothing.

"Oh, there was a phone call a moment ago – from Ebenau's secretary – to say he be around later."

Tom sighed. He would hardly be able to forget the investigation now. Heino seemed eager to say something else.

"Tom – you know what you were saying earlier – to Schneider? I mean, about working on getting Viola Addison into bed."

Tom brushed it off.

"We were just fooling, Heino. You know what a joker Schneider is."

Tom wandered across to the window and looked down onto the garden. Through the gloom he could see Frau Doktor Menne struggling to cut back a stand of over-grown bushes. The job was clearly too much for her. He opened the window and called down that she should leave it for him to do. She did not hear.

"But if she came to you willingly – because she wanted to . . ."

Tom noted Heino's embarrassment. "What d'you want me to say, Heino? That I'd put in a good word for you?" He picked up Heino's case and handed it to him. "Now go on back to work. forget it – forget her – she's Lutz Ebenau's woman and our suspect. That's all."

Heino seemed to accept that there was no point in pursuing his favourite topic. "Yes, you're right. I'll see you tomorrow." And he left.

Not long after Tom saw him slip out of the back garden gate, he heard Lutz Ebenau arrive in the flat below. He steeled himself for yet another night of someone else's passion. But Viola snatched the bitter-sweet pleasure from under his nose.

"Lutz, darling," she said – between kisses, Tom guessed – "I've been slaving away all afternoon. I need to get out."

"Of course we can go out," Ebenau murmured, "after we have made love."

"No, I'm too wound up. I need to get out."

Tom listened, holding his breath.

"Very well, Schätzlein, if that is what you want."

"Yes, I do. Just a walk and a drink and some evening air."

Thank God for that, thought Tom, and dialled Heino's mobile number to call him back to tail her. They might be going somewhere significant, although he doubted it. He for one was going to have a night off. His men could continue this futile investigation of Dr Viola Addison.

Viola was not sure herself why she did not want Lutz inside her, as he had been every evening they had been together since her return to Munich. Maybe it genuinely was the intensity of her work. She had set her mind on getting down to it at last, and now she found it was taking a while to unwind. She wanted to drink, to laugh, even to dance – something she would normally never even contemplate. And when she thought of dancing, she thought of Tom Pajak and how he had offered to teach her.

Lutz followed her down the stairs and outside. With a display of good grace, he opened the door of the sleek old Mercedes. They drove to the Augustiner, where, to Lutz's annoyance, they met a group of his friends engaged in a drinking contest. How he hated the Oktoberfest.

Quite out of character, Viola was ready to join in the fun – the kind of fun that, at any other time, she would have despised. She did not seem to notice either just how drunk she was getting, which was when Lutz decided it was time for them to leave.

"Let's walk a bit first, Lutz," Viola giggled. "Look." She pointed at the narrow entrance of a jazz club she had often noticed, but never even considered entering. The moan of a saxophone was easing an escape out of the smoky confines of the cellar and came wafting up into the warm Bavarian evening air. It was a sensuous, beguiling sound, especially after too many cocktails.

"Come on, let's go down and dance."

"You cannot really want to go into a place like that?"

"Tonight I do." Viola sounded determined. "I've never been in a place like that, let alone danced in one. Perhaps it's time I did."

She deliberately ignored the tight-lipped look of disapproval on his face, and marched across the street to the open door.

Lutz followed her and on down the narrow stairs into the dimly-lit interior. Smoke, scent and the haunting sound of the saxophone mingled together in an atmosphere, clammy with exhilarated people.

On a low stage, sparsely spotlit, a trio of black musicians were seducing their audience with music. Viola turned to Lutz, her eyes bright with this new discovery. "Isn't this music great? It's so moody. These guys are fantastic."

"It is not really my taste," Lutz replied tightly.

"Well, just make an effort. Come on, let's dance."

Viola was still feeling exuberant when they left two hours later and drove home. Lutz had decided to put as good a face on the evening as he could, and Viola appreciated that in him. But she was still impatient with his refusal at least to try to understand the music they had been listening to.

"I mean," she said, all at once an expert, "This music has its roots in Africa, in slavery. You can almost hear the endless struggle for freedom in it."

"Those people looked pretty free to me. And I am sure you do not need to worry about how much money they earn – more than enough to smoke cannabis and blow their horns all night."

Lutz had just parked the Mercedes in the crescent. He leaned over to kiss Viola. He slid his hand up her skirt to probe between her legs. "So are you in the mood now?" he muttered.

119

Tom woke from the half sleep into which he had drifted. He caught the sound of them clambering up the stairs, more noisily than usual. Maybe Ebenau was drunk. That would be a first. To begin with, Tom had been impressed by Lutz's steely restraint. Despite all the talk of his riches and how spoilt he must be, he seemed to have no shortage of self-control. And Tom was someone who valued that gift highly; although in Lutz Ebenau he was starting to resent it.

As he listened, he wished Viola could have possessed a little more. Within minutes, Tom could hear again the sounds he dreaded. To distract himself he got out of bed, took up his briefcase and rooted around in it for some information he had sent for – about enrolling with the Houston Police Department. He knew it was in there somewhere. He started to pull out a likely looking envelope; but in place of a postmark in the top right hand corner, what he saw were the initials E/A.

"Schneider, you bastard," he muttered.

From then on his hands, his eyes, his whole body seemed to work independently of his brain. Almost against his will, he took out the photographs and looked at them again. He knelt down on the floor and laid them out around him in a wide semi-circle – in sequence – allowing his imagination to fill in the gaps between each shot; his powers of invention aided by the noises emanating from Viola's bedroom beneath.

And the longer he looked, the deeper grew his envy of Ebenau. And the louder Viola cried, the more urgent became his need to win her from him – not in this flimsy, illusory world inside his head – but in reality where he understood how to function.

Beside himself with frustration, he stuffed the photographs back into their envelope and went across to the office to kill the sound.

The silence was a relief. Paradoxically, though, had he continued to listen in, Tom would have gained something more than relief. He would have gained encouragement in his pursuit of Viola. For in the hush of the small hours, when the love-making was over, the first faint notes of discord were struck between the lovers.

Angry words were whispered. Not such angry words, perhaps,

but enough to cause them both distress. In short, Viola had asked Lutz to go with her to a reception for Professor Feinstein – had made it plain how much it mattered to her – but he had declined, citing an unspecified prior engagement. Viola had been disappointed. Worse than that, she had felt badly let down. Lutz knew it. He expressed regret. For the time being, though, it was left at that.

But, upstairs, Tom dozed in and out of sleep, until long after Lutz Ebenau had slipped from Viola's bed and out into the frosty Autumn morning.

Chapter Fifteen

When Viola woke later that morning, she remembered with a twinge of hurt that Lutz had gone, pleading an early plane to Paris.

As soon as she thought Hilly would be awake, she dialled her number in London and got the answerphone. She left a message asking her to ring the following afternoon, around three. There had been no direct contact between them since Viola's arrival back in Munich. Hilly had not been at home whenever she had tried to phone and, curiously for someone who lived by the pen, demonstrated an infuriating, pathological aversion to the writing of letters. Still, Viola wanted to know what she had been up to and above all needed to tell her what was happening here. So she persevered.

She looked out of the window and saw that in the night there had been a sharp frost. She had quite forgotten how early and suddenly wintry weather came to Bavaria. Her car looked as though it had been glazed with icing-sugar and the passers-by in the crescent below were wrapped up snugly against the early morning cold. But the sun shone out brightly enticing and the sky was blue and clear, right to infinity. Viola pulled on woollen leggings under her skirt, a huge, thick Arran sweater over her shirt and went off to the Nymphenburg for a walk.

She had half forgotten last night's tiff with Lutz until – while she stood feeding the wildfowl on the edge of the Badenburg lake – it was brought back to her when she noticed Tom jogging towards her. She was not surprised to see him. He looked the type to exercise – and what better place could there be to do it?

Viola waved to him. Tom waved back and ran around the lake to where she stood.

"Some guys get all the luck," he said by way of a greeting – pointing to the medley of ducks that waddled around her feet, pecking up crumbs. "How come they get to be fed breakfast by someone as gorgeous as you?"

At least this time she seemed to recognise the accolade, even if she did seem to shy away from it. The way she behaved made Tom think of the phrase "shrinking violet". At the moment it struck him as appropriate.

"Are you named after the flower – or the instrument?"

"Neither. Why do you ask?"

"Oh, just wondering that's all. I kind of thought it must be the flower." He stood back and pointedly looked her up and down. "Let's face it, as far as musical instruments go, you're more of a violin than a viola."

"I'm not sure how I'm supposed to take that."

"As a compliment I hope – like it was meant."

He smiled at her. She smiled at him. She was no longer offended by his comments about her size. It was easy to be touchy, but it did no good.

"If you really want to know, I'm named after a character in a Shakespeare play. It's a bit of a long story. My mother once played the part of Olivia in a school production of *Twelfth Night*. I think it went to her head – being cast as the beautiful, aloof countess. Anyway, she fell in love with the name – thought it sounded aristocratic. So when my sister was born, she became Olivia. Then when I came along, I just got tagged with the name of another – in fact the main character in the play. Hence Viola."

"Well, it sure is a pretty name. It suits you."

"But it's a good thing I was a girl," added Viola. "Or just think, there might be some poor, unfortunate *Orsino* Addison around now, ruing the day he was born."

"Even that might be better than being Tom. Every fifth guy in the entire universe is called Tom."

"But it's a lovely name," protested Viola. "It's uncomplicated, strong, manly."

She stopped abruptly – felt awkward – without fully realising why. She brought her hands up to her face. Her fingers were starting to feel numb with cold, so she made them into a cup and blew into it vigorously.

"You're frozen," said Tom, taking her hands and rubbing them in his. "Here, let me warm you up."

"You're the one who should be feeling cold," countered Viola, referring to the fact that all Tom had between him and the elements were shorts and a T-shirt.

"Don't worry about me; I'm tough enough."

"Well I can't believe it's doing you any good, standing around in this weather with next to nothing on."

Tom laughed. "Is this your polite, English way of telling me to beat it again?"

"No, not at all," cried Viola, alarmed at having given that impression. "Actually, I'm glad I've bumped into you. I've got an invitation to pass on."

Tom was intrigued and suggested they walk – pointing out that, even if he was the one with next to nothing on, she was the one shivering from cold.

"You remember Professor Feinstein?"

"Yep," said Tom, wondering what was coming next. "In fact I doubt I'll forget him. He was quite a character for such an old-timer."

She smiled. "There's a reception in his honour at the Haus der Kunst on Friday evening. I thought you might like to come along with me."

Tom was curious. He knew about Feinstein's imminent return to Munich and he knew all about the reception. The opportunities to carry out the death threat were diminishing, and he and Fuchs had discussed a whole string of possibilities. Using the Haus der Kunst – built to symbolise Nazi domination over the art world – was bound to provoke trouble. Anyway, they would be mobilising a hell of a lot of extra manpower for Feinstein's protection that night. But what interested Tom more was why she was inviting him, not Lutz. He had not thought he had scored that much of a hit at the art gallery last week. He decided he might as well come out with it and ask.

"So will that guy of yours be there? Don't say I'm finally going to get to meet him."

Viola stiffened. "No. I'm afraid he can't make it. He has to work late that evening."

"Then I guess that has to make me second best," he said with a grin.

She looked flustered, saying quickly, "Oh, don't think that – please. Professor Feinstein really liked you. I'm sure he'd want you to be there."

"Hey, don't mind me. I was just fooling. What's the matter anyway? Trouble with your boyfriend?"

Viola looked at him sharply. Inside her, she was still smarting from last night and the conclusion she could no longer escape – that Lutz had no real interest in her work or in any of her intellectual aspirations. This feeling had not come out of the blue. Despite the aching passion she still felt every time they made love, she had begun to ask herself if there ought not to be more to their relationship than mere physical fulfilment – however desirable that might be. Hence the outing last night.

"No, not really," she said. "It's just that I'd been hoping he'd be able to make it."

"Listen, there's no way *I'm* going to miss that old guy's party. Dr Addison, you've got yourself a date." He put his arm around her.

Apart from their initial handshake, they had only touched for the first time that day – when he had rubbed her hands – and although later her reaction to it was to strike her as strangely powerful, at the time the intimacy of this present gesture seemed to her to be totally appropriate. So much so that, without faltering, she slipped her arm around Tom's waist. It felt like the natural thing to do.

It did not feel natural to Tom. For the hundred yards or so they walked along that way, he felt the very opposite of comfortable. He half expected Heino or, even worse, Schneider or Fuchs, to appear at any moment, declaring "We knew what you were up to all along." And so when, after a short lull in the conversation, Viola re-opened it with an enquiry as to how his articles were coming on, for a moment he did not know what she was talking about. His expression made her think he had not heard the question, so she repeated it.

"Oh, the articles." He laughed a little self-consciously. "Sure, they're doing fine. Seems like my editor's happy enough anyway." He was determined to shift the emphasis away from himself. "So how about you? I reckon that book of yours must be running into its second volume by now. You *never* stop working."

Viola managed to smile and look serious at one and the same time.

"If only that were true. But I'm afraid it's not. As a matter of fact, at the moment I seem to have come to a complete standstill. I'm going down to Füssen before long though, to do some – for want of a better word – fieldwork."

Tom interrupted her. "Are you trying to tell me you're deserting *me* – in favour of Mad Ludwig?"

She removed her arm from his waist and herself from his grip.

"Tell me – why is it everyone always assumes he was mad?"

"How about because he was?"

"Well, I don't see why. All he did – all people base that assumption on – was to try to alter his life. He didn't much like the one he had – so he set about creating another."

"And another – and another. I mean, wasn't that the point of building all those castles?"

"But was that really so terrible?"

"Viola, you can't hide from reality. No-one can – not even kings."

"But you don't have to accept it. What I'm saying is, you don't have to put up with things the way they are. You can at least try to change them. If you think they're adversely affecting the quality of your life, that is."

"You've also got to remember," warned Tom – the customary mirth in his voice suddenly noticeably absent, "that one man's dream can pretty soon become another man's nightmare. Your old friend, the Professor, could tell you all about that for sure."

"Yes," said Viola, barely louder than a whisper. "That's true I know. It's important always to be aware of the repercussions of one's actions – and of one's responsibilities to society." She raised her head, looked Tom straight in the eye and smiled sadly. "So perhaps what poor Ludwig did wasn't so terrible after all. At the end of the day, the only person to fall foul of his dream fulfilment was himself."

When they got back to the house Viola was going to ask Tom in for coffee, but when she heard her telephone start to ring, she did not. She simply said goodbye and he carried on up to the attic. He did not listen in on her conversation. There was plenty of time for that later.

A mountain of paper work awaited him on his desk at work, but the meeting with Viola had unsettled him. The run had woken him up and he needed to do something physical. He remembered his offer to Frau Doktor Menne to help out in the garden, and decided he could spare her half an hour or so. Werner Fuchs had told him to do his "friendly neighbour act", after all.

As Viola lent across her desk – positioned as it was under the bedroom window to take advantage of the good north light – she looked down onto the garden and saw Tom working there. Quite unconsciously she chose to sit on the desk – rather than at it – and watch him, while she chatted on the telephone.

It was Hilly on the line – by coincidence as it emerged – she had yet to get Viola's message. So this was a chance call – or rather it was by chance she had been prompted to make it. The previous night, Hilly said, while waiting in the foyer of the Wyndham's Theatre for her latest man, she had found herself standing alongside Olivia and Rory. From them had come confirmation of what Viola herself had recently written – that Lutz had received their seal of approval and was therefore poised on the brink of acceptance into the bosom of the Addison family. Though baffled by the fact, Hilly was well aware that her family's good opinion was important to Viola. Thus, the purpose of making contact now was to offer her – for want of a better word – congratulations.

Yet while before their conversation everything had appeared set fair for her friend's future happiness – five minutes into it Hilly caught sight of storm clouds gathering on the horizon over Professor Feinstein's reception.

"Flower, has it ever occurred to you Lutz might be like most other men – totally self-centred? He wants to be the centre of your world – like you want to be the centre of his. And he doesn't like you being distracted by some octogenarian."

"I wouldn't mind if he just sometimes took an interest in my work," Viola complained.

"You should have learned by now – reluctant though I am to deal in clichés – that your Lutz is probably your standard chauvinist. I expect he's just as jealous as hell of any man you look at. And who can blame him? But the best thing, Flower, is to have it out with him – that's my advice anyway."

To Hilly this seemed the obvious solution – get things out in the open – clear the air. That was her style – always had been. But she knew it was not Viola's; hers was to agonise about anything and everything. Hilly's tone softened still further.

"You are all right, aren't you? I mean, I don't need to worry about you – do I?"

"I'm fine," replied Viola, managing a laugh of sorts. "So you don't have to give me a second thought. You're not indispensable, you know – there's no shortage of spare shoulders over here. Quite apart from Lutz, there's Professor Feinstein, there's Ellie, there's Tom Pajak . . ."

"Ah yes – your Texan. Tell me about him." Hilly was relieved to have something flippant to talk about. "I want to know everything. You're onto my favourite subject now, remember. I have to say it though, I *am* surprised at you. A sports reporter sounds a highly improbable sort of chum for you to be playing with. So what's he like?"

"He's very nice."

"Oh God, spare me the platitudes – *please.*"

"Well he is. And he's fun. He makes me laugh."

"Is he good-looking?"

"Yes – very," answered Viola slowly. "Not in the beautiful way Lutz is, but in a . . . in a . . . virile, physical sort of way."

"You mean he's a bit macho?" Hilly perked up audibly. "This is getting better by the minute."

"No, I don't mean that."

"Okay, okay, you don't mean macho. Carry on – how about the all-important SQ? Where does he score on that?"

"You know I don't go in for all that rubbish."

"Don't talk crap, Flower. This is me – Hilly Farrell – life-long friend and confidante. You find men sexy, just like the rest of us girls. Come on now, spit it out. How does this he-man you keep up in your attic score in the fanciability stakes?"

Viola paused. She gazed down into the garden – to where Tom was working. He was chopping at what remained of a large, old tree-trunk which the border clearance had revealed. Frau Doktor Menne – standing well clear to allow him space to swing the axe – was looking on. So too did Viola from her window – captivated by the rhythmic movement, by the effortless power of his body. He stopped. The old lady had spoken to him and he broke off to answer her. Then just as he was about to resume, he happened to look up at Viola's window. He noticed her and winked. She smiled back.

"Well?" badgered Hilly.

"Yes. I suppose he *is* fanciable. There, I've said it. *Now* are you satisfied?"

"Well, well, Viola Isabella Addison. I'm glad to hear you admit it. There might be hope for you yet."

Chapter Sixteen

Over the next few days Tom saw little of Viola. They collided a few times on the stairs – no more than that. The lack of progress on the case meant he found himself being dragged back into his previous investigation, which involved a heavy workload. The routine was leaving him tired and irritable. He hated it when he found himself sitting up in bed listening to Viola and Ebenau making love. At one point he even asked Werner to release him from the job – to terminate the monitoring on the grounds that there was no mileage in it and it was just costing too much. He presented him with a dossier of Viola's comments, particularly to Hilly, as evidence of her attitudes and therefore of the impossibility of her being involved in any extreme organisation like the Network.

But Werner kept on like a dog with a bone. "Come on, Tom, if you were engaged in her sort of mission, wouldn't you want to confuse the media? The woman she was talking to is a high profile political journalist, for God's sake!"

"But she's one of her closest friends."

"People in that business don't have close friends," Werner had said. "No, Tom, even if she's not a member of the Network, as you keep insisting, there had to be some reason why she was pin-pointed, why she was chosen to give a dead lead. And nothing you lot have thrown up so far has contradicted that. Let's at least wait until this reception and see what happens then."

Tom left it at that. Fuchs did have a point and recently he had

had to ask himself some awkward questions. Had Viola invited him because she was innocent and, as far as she was concerned, nothing was going to happen? It seemed to him that if she were planning to be party to some public outrage, she would not want him in the way while she made last minute contacts, arrangements, phone calls.

Or would he make a very useful alibi to her, especially if she already knew he was a police officer? Somehow he doubted this was a possibility. Meanwhile, playing Peeping Tom was making him feel guilty. At the very least it was a violation of Viola's privacy – and then there was what it was doing to him. In fact, he was experiencing a feeling close to dejection; although, as always, the deepest of deep emotions defied definition.

When Viola temporarily decamped for a couple of nights to Lutz's magnificent apartment in Lehel, Tom hoped for some respite, however brief, from the whole business. It was not to be. Instead he had to endure detailed reports about her from Schneider and his men, who took a vicarious delight in keeping him informed of the state of play between the two. Despite the disagreement which Tom had sensed between the lovers over the invitation to Feinstein's reception, relations between them seemed as strong as ever. Tom could not dispute this. Schneider had given him copies of tapes and photographs to prove it.

On the evening of the reception Tom had arranged to meet with Viola at a bar in the Amalienpassage. Tom got there first. He made a point of it. He had taken clothes for the occasion into work with him that morning, so that he could get changed at the Polizeipräsidium – to be sure there was no possibility of his being late – although he very nearly was, having been called back to check out some last-minute security measures for the event.

As Tom made his way to the bar, he was aware of two colleagues mingling among the crowds on the pavement outside the entrance. Suddenly full of guilt, he tried to reconcile the job he had to do with his emotions.

Inside the bar, he searched out a corner table that allowed him a clear view through to the entrance. He sat down and ordered a beer. He took out a copy of *Der Spiegel* he had picked up on the way; but almost as soon as he opened it, he folded it up again and stuffed it back into the pocket of his overcoat – without even reading a word. His beer arrived and as he sipped it, his eyes darted methodically back and forth between his watch and the door. After the sixth or seventh instance of checking the time – all within the space of ten minutes – he caught onto the fact that he was nervous and unashamedly smiled at himself.

It was five minutes past the time they had agreed to meet when Tom started to wonder what had gone wrong. He told himself to stop thinking like a nervous teenager, then it occurred to the optimist in him that Viola might already have been in the bar when he arrived.

He stood up and gazed around the room. When he saw Viola, he felt a nasty jolt in the pit of his stomach. She was sitting at a table, profile to him, opposite another man. She was smiling and relaxed. Tom reminded himself that there was no reason why she should not have other friends, and that not every man she knew would be a lover; especially when Ebenau had been keeping her so busy.

As he looked, she glanced up, saw him and waved. Tom watched her explaining to the man that she had to go. Then she threaded her way through the tables towards Tom. To him, she came like a vision out of a dream – fragile, romantic – wrapped in a serape of fine, black velvet and satin which accentuated the impression of other-worldliness. Though when she reached the table and let the wrap slip from her shoulders, she revealed a figure that was far from illusory. She was wearing the same dress she had worn the first time he had seen her; a dress which left no doubt that she was every inch a woman.

Suddenly he felt awkward and shy. "Viola, hi." He winced at the clumsiness of the greeting as he bent down and, for the first time, allowed his lips to touch her cheek in greeting.

"Hello, Tom. Have you been here long?"

"I got here a little early. I was just catching up with the local news. What would you like to drink?"

"I think I'll have a coffee, please. I expect we'll have to guzzle champagne all evening at the Professor's party."

"How terrible!" laughed Tom.

He looked at her with undisguised warmth. He had known a lot of attractive women in his adult life, but Viola was unlike any of them. All the other beautiful girls he had met knew they were beautiful and, without exception, had exploited their sexual advantage. They had flaunted, flirted, flitted from one admirer to the next like butterflies that flutter from blossom to blossom, searching out the tastiest nectar.

But, Tom thought, Viola did not think of herself in those terms at all. That was her charm and what gave her an aura of innocence. He could understand why even a man like Lutz Ebenau – super-rich, good-looking, probably with the pick of Europe's beautiful women available to him – had been more than ready to fall in love with her again, after a gap of ten years.

"So what's the story behind this reception?" he asked.

"It's Rupert Servranckz's idea, I suspect. Partly in recognition of Professor Feinstein's scholarship and the fundamental changes he's made to thinking on late Renaissance art. And, I suppose, tacitly to make up for his having been driven out of Munich before the war."

"Thank God," Tom said, wearing for a moment his professional hat, "there are Germans who think like that." He watched her reaction carefully, and as dispassionately as he could.

"Yes," she murmured with heartfelt agreement. "I just find it terrifying there are still some people around who want to go back to all that."

Inwardly, Tom sighed with relief. He had detected nothing disingenuous in her manner.

He ordered her coffee and another beer for himself. "Who was that you were talking to?" he asked as lightly as he could.

"Oh, that was a man called Peter Lessel."

Tom's ears pricked up. She had been seen with Lessel at the Hotel only a few days ago, he remembered. So far they had not managed to find out much about him either.

Viola, unaware of Tom's discomfort, went on. "I used to know

133

him a bit when I was at the university here. He was reading politics then and took life very seriously. Still does, I think."

"Oh." Tom was determined not to let her see his interest.

"Yes," Viola went on. "He's become pretty humourless; I don't suppose being gay helps much – at least that's what Lutz says. I think they lost track of each other for a few years but now Lutz can't seem to get rid of him."

"He's gay, is he?" Tom was surprised Silke had failed to dig that one up. At least the fact removed one reason for his unease.

The conversation flowed freely while they finished their drinks. As for Viola she was happy simply to be entertained. She found Tom easy to be with – and uncomplicated. With him – as with Hilly – she felt she knew precisely where she stood. And when she next checked her watch, she could scarcely believe how the time had flown.

Outside, they could feel at once that the hour just gone had seen a change in the weather. A breeze – light enough, yet freezing – had begun to blow in from the Alps. On it occasional snowflakes, presaging Winter, hung in suspension – doing their utmost to defy gravity – coming reluctantly to rest only when they collided with an obstruction. Tom was the first to notice them as several in quick succession landed on Viola's shoulders; like tiny star-shaped sequins against the night-black velvet of her serape. He recommended they quicken their pace. This was no weather for strolling.

Viola started to shiver. Secretly she wished she had opted for practicality rather than effect and worn a coat. Tom read her thoughts, took off his overcoat and draped it over her shoulders. They both laughed out loud at the spectacle it made of her. Though when they emerged from the underpass by the Englischer Garten, their laughter petered out.

A smallish crowd of men, predominantly young men, youths – forty, possibly fifty strong – was gathered outside the Haus der Kunst, jostling against a make-shift cordon of uniformed police officers. They were shouting a monotonous, though nonetheless belligerent incantation which Viola had difficulty in making out. They were stamping too, up and down on the pavement; possibly a measure to combat the cold – more likely as means of adding undertones of menace to their chants. Either way, the sound they made thundered out like a grim reminder of another past, but not forgotten era. Some held banners on which were written anti-Jewish threats, targeted – Viola read as they got nearer – specifically at Josef Feinstein.

As they came level with the protest Tom instinctively took Viola's arm, giving her no chance to slacken her pace – so that she almost had to run to keep up with him. He marched her straight on past the group and around to the main entrance; whereupon they themselves became the object of the mob's derision, as it interrupted its chanting to launch abuse directed openly at them. Viola looked hard into their faces – for confirmation – for explanation – for some reason or other that made sense of what was happening. But the threats, flaring out at her from their eyes, frightened her and she quickly turned away – no wiser.

Inside the building was a different world: warm, bright, civilised. A string quartet – engaged to entertain the guests upon arrival – aided the atmosphere of refinement. And the company itself had clearly come prepared to play its part – the ladies in their rainbow-hued silks and taffetas – the gentlemen in their obligatory black and white. From an inner room they could hear the drone of polished voices, competing with the elegant trills and cadenzas of Haydn and Mozart. As they walked on, the contrasting sounds underwent a reversal of consequence; so that by the time they reached the reception proper, the music was barely audible above the hum of cultured conversation.

Whether by luck or because he had been keeping one eye permanently on the door, Josef Feinstein picked out Viola and Tom the very moment they entered the room. He despatched Ellie forthwith to gather them up and bring them to him. Tom could tell from the look on the old man's face that he was nothing short of elated at seeing his protégé again. He acted like a man infatuated – holding her hand as though afraid to let it go. Tom could not help thinking that, had the Professor been a little more robust – or Viola

135

a little less eager for sexual excitement – Lutz Ebenau might have had another rival on his hands.

Tom and Viola saw little of each other during the evening. Rather, they talked little to one another. There was no opportunity to do so; Professor Feinstein monopolised Viola, while Ellie Levinson made a beeline for Tom. Once or twice during the course of the evening Viola's eyes met Tom's – Tom gave her his customary wink and she gave him her now familiar smile.

When the time came for Josef Feinstein to leave, it was suggested he do so by a side door to avoid the demonstration. It seemed a common sense precaution. In spite of the fact that nearly everyone – and most vociferously the indomitable Ms Levinson – recommended it, Feinstein rejected the advice outright. Perhaps Viola encouraging him to make the stand and show the Fascists what he thought of them, or perhaps the imbibing of generous quantities of champagne had some bearing on it. Perhaps he had simply decided himself to deny this current bunch of hooligans the satisfaction of hounding him out of Munich for a second time in his life. Whatever his motivation, the outcome was the same. He and his coterie were to leave by the front door – not slink away like cowards. Professor Feinstein insisted upon it.

It must have been nearing midnight when they finally appeared at the main entrance to the Haus der Kunst. Their host, the Minister-President, along with a delegation of more minor state officials, came out to bid them farewell at the door. To Tom's relief, the mob now seemed less daunting than it had done earlier. He turned to Viola at his side.

"This gang seems quieter now. Maybe the cold has numbed their fighting spirit."

"Yes, thank God," Viola agreed. "They don't look anything like as angry as they did when we arrived – not as threatening."

The two of them stood a little aside – delayed while Feinstein finished shaking hands with his effusive hosts. Ellie and Rupert respectively bustled and fidgeted around the Professor – to such an extent he began to show signs of irritation. He looked about for Viola and beckoned her to join him. Tom followed.

While waiting for Professor Feinstein to conclude the niceties of leave-taking, Tom kept a careful watch on the demonstrators. This closer scrutiny confirmed his first impression: that they no longer outnumbered the police presence, but were themselves outnumbered by it.

Among the officers restraining the crowd Tom could spot old friends and colleagues from his early days in uniform. He picked out more familiar faces amid the several small bands of on-lookers, who had gathered a short way off in expectation of some dramatic episode. There were Heino and Silke, doing their studied best to blend in with neighbouring by-standers. There were Kurt and Max, making a more convincing job of it. Not that Tom offered any one of them the slightest token of recognition – nor they him. He simply marked them in passing, as his eyes ranged to and fro over the scene. Their being there produced in him a mixed reaction. It was reassuring. Then again, seeing so many of them did make him wonder if they had not over-manned for the event. Kurt Mohrfeld, older and obviously wiser, had – he could see it now – hit the nail on the head ages ago, when he had been so sure that taking out the "odd old Jew" would be of next to no interest to the Network.

Eventually, after what seemed to Viola like an over-indulgence of goodbyes and thank yous, Professor Feinstein was ready to leave. He turned around and faced the demonstrators head on for the first time that night. As though this in itself were an act of provocation – or else had been the very sign for which they had been waiting – they now let out a deafening cacophony of shouts, threats, taunts and like invective. At the sound the old man started with fright and reeled backwards. Viola was at his side and tried to catch him, but the unexpectedness of the tirade had shaken her nearly as much as it had Feinstein and she could not.

Ellie could. She possessed the strength Viola lacked. She also had courage – and the determination to use it; to defy anyone who might mean harm to her dearest JF. Tom watched her body language.

It was loaded with undisguised aggression. He noted her eyes, glowering with scorn. At that moment he was filled with admiration for her – quite apart from the more mundane reaction of being relieved that they were both on the same side.

Suddenly, like a bolt from the blue, from somewhere in the middle of the disturbance, an object whistled through the air, heading straight in their direction. It landed on the steps, a little ahead of them – a stone – not large, but large enough to have caused damage had it met its mark. Tom decided the time had come to put himself between Professor Feinstein and the mob.

It was then – as Tom tried to hurry Feinstein and the others towards the waiting car – that it happened.

Tom identified the noise instantly, even above the din. The crack of gunfire – the sound of bullets from an automatic hand-gun. All within the space of that same split second, Tom knew intuitively where it had come from. Not from those Nazi yobs they had all been watching with such assiduous attention – but from thirty or forty metres to their right – from one of the spectators – from a man standing somewhere just behind Silke and Heino. Tom picked him out as soon as he turned and ran. Using him as the starting point Tom's eyes instinctively retraced the bullet's trajectory, until they fell upon its target – its victims – two of them. For what he saw was not only, without doubt, its intended target – the old man, Josef Feinstein – lying inert on the pavement; but also Ellie.

He could tell at first sight that she was dead – or very close to it. The wounds to her head were too severe for even the strongest human being to survive. Feinstein's injuries were not at once apparent – but Tom was in no mood to wait and find out what they might be. Seconds after the shots had been fired, he was off, after the man who had carried out this act of barbarity.

Now he had to battle his way through the throng. Its ghoulish curiosity had been whetted and it pressed relentlessly forward – blocking his progress at every turn. Once past the on-lookers he caught sight of the man again – way up in front – haring across Prinzregentenstraße. It looked – as far as Tom could tell – as though he intended sticking to the road. Tom asked himself why? He should have side-tracked off into the Englischer Garten – or bolted down a side street. There seemed no logic in staying out in the open – in full view. If it was because he was confident of being able to out-run any opponent, then he had better think again. Maybe he had not bargained on having someone so quickly on his tail.

Tom was sure he had the speed to catch this man. And on a level playing-field that would have been the case. But in this instance he was at a disadvantage. The killer had come ready for the race; kitted out for running – whereas he was handicapped by the clothes he was wearing – more by the leather soles of his shoes which, rather than grip the snow-dusted pavement, made him slip every few metres.

Only a minute or two later a car came screeching to a halt, snatched the man up, then sped away, just as Tom was sure he as good as had him within his grasp.

Now Tom had no choice but to resign himself to the escape. He made a mental note of the details of the car as it sped off – though he doubted it would do much good. In all probability it would be stolen. He took a deep breath and then another – more as an antidote to frustration than because he was short on air. After that he turned around and began to jog back to the Haus der Kunst, passing a couple of other officers who had followed him in pursuit of the assassin. He shook his head, and they turned back with him.

Glaring, dazzling bright, the lights from a squad of ambulances and police vehicles flashed nervously on and off to demarcate the scene of the killing. By the time Tom reached it, Ellie's body had already been stowed away in one of them. All that remained of her presence was a pool of blood; still so warm that the snowflakes – which had once again begun to fall – melted when they touched its surface.

Josef Feinstein was lying on a stretcher, being transported towards an ambulance parked close at hand. A whole team of paramedics was at work around him. A drip was being fixed into his arm and an oxygen mask had been attached to his face. At least all the frantic effort meant he was still alive. Although when, as Tom drew level with the stretcher, he looked into the old man's face, it was a glimpse of death itself he caught – empty, skeletal, final.

He had a search on his hands to find Viola. The whole place was in turmoil – people being sectioned off here and there – some being questioned, others arrested – anyone and everyone being shuffled this way and that, so that the ambulances could get clear. When at length he found her, she was gazing, as if paralysed by the spectacle being played out all around her. The moment she saw him, her face lightened and she ran towards him, crying with relief. He began to move her away from the chaos. It was a slow job. Whichever way they turned, they were pushed and shoved.

They came up against a queue of protesters, being manhandled into line, ready for interrogation by a group of police detectives. Tom started to turn her back to look for another, better escape route, when all at once Viola stopped, as if frozen to the spot. "What's wrong?" he asked. She did not answer so instead he followed the direction of her stare. It led him across to the line-up of thugs – to one specific face.

Tom knew that face – he had perused the folders of mug-shots of Network suspects many times – and it worried him that Viola seemed to know it; it worried him a lot.

But right then, all Tom wanted was to get her away. He put his arm round her, propelled her bodily towards a quieter street and hailed a taxi.

In the car, he questioned her tentatively.

"Something scared you there. What was it?"

"The whole thing," Viola muttered, still not fully in control. "It was horrible. I've never seen anything like that before in my life, and to the Professor . . . to Ellie . . . I just can't believe it's happened."

"But there was something else, just before we left . . ." Tom prompted gently.

"There was a man – I'd seen him before. It doesn't matter; it probably doesn't mean anything. Poor Josef," she shuddered.

Her answer had neither confirmed nor denied Tom's niggling doubts. One thing was certain, if she knew the man whose face had so obviously upset her, there was another connection with the Network of which Werner Fuchs was so certain.

Ebenau was waiting for them when they arrived back home. Tom recognised his Mercedes as soon as they pulled into the crescent. As Tom helped Viola out of the car, he came across to meet them. Viola introduced them, explaining that Tom was her neighbour. Though Tom felt for her embarrassment, he could not deny that the message it gave caused him a slight thrill.

Ebenau could see that Viola was upset. "What is it, Schätzlein? What has happened?"

"Haven't you heard what happened tonight?" Tom asked.

Ebenau shrugged. "I heard something on the car radio, driving back from the airport – some demo? A shooting, maybe?"

"Viola was there, right behind the man and woman who were shot."

"My God!" Ebenau was appalled. "Why must you be with people who are in this sort of danger? Are you all right?"

"She's shocked," Tom answered for her. "Look after her."

Ebenau did not demean himself by answering this exhortation from a potential rival. There simply followed a kind of hand-over – Tom giving – Ebenau receiving. Tom did not delude himself that Viola went unwillingly. He had only to watch her to see how eager she was to get into his car. And as Ebenau drove off, she did not give him so much as a second look.

What remained of that night Tom spent in the small flat above Viola's. He telephoned the hospital and heard that Feinstein had suffered a heart attack; he was still alive – but only just. Tom lay on his bed, wide awake, listening to Otis Redding – the same track over and over again. And each time the earth-rich, yearning voice sang the words, "*Come to me – Forget the past*", the ache in his body grew as hard to bear as the hurt in his heart.

Chapter Seventeen

A fine decanter of forty-year-old Armagnac was circulating around the dining table at Lutz Ebenau's home in Füssen.

"Well, Ebenau, I must say it's a rare and wholly unanticipated treat you've given us this time."

Lutz's guests all nodded or muttered their agreement. Viola was the only one of them at the table to be unaware that the treat referred to was none other than herself. Nick Bingham edged his chair a little closer to hers and elaborated his point to ensure she got it.

"As you can see, Viola, we're strictly a men only little clique as a rule. So to be able to sit next to a beautiful and intelligent woman – especially a contemporary of mine at Oxford – is an unexpected bonus."

"*Oui, bien sûr.* We are accustomed when we visit Lutz here in Füssen, to the excellent food and fine wines but we seldom have the good fortune to entertain such a charming companion."

Serge Duvergier caught Viola's eye and raised his glass. Viola blushed and looked embarrassed.

"I think I'm the lucky one," she said, anxious to divert anything as mortifying as a toast to herself. "I can't remember the last time I met so many and such enthusiastic art lovers. You must all positively haunt the major galleries of Europe, to be so knowledgeable about them."

"I understand, Viola, that you will be staying on in Füssen," commented Duvergier, "to carry out your study of Ludwig's wonderful castles."

"That was my plan, yes. Originally I'd arranged to be here for several weeks – but unfortunately a friend of mine is very ill in hospital in Munich, so naturally I want to be there. Like you, this time I'm just here for the weekend. I'll be leaving when Lutz goes back on Sunday evening."

This reference to Professor Feinstein was unavoidable, though Viola did her best to make it as brief and low-key as possible. Even so she was hurt to notice that Lutz should choose that very moment to remove his hand from hers – ostensibly to pour himself another glass of wine. She got up to leave the table.

"Well, if you'll all excuse me, I have a pile of notes to plough through before I go to Linderhof tomorrow morning. Besides, I'm quite sure you've got plenty of things you'd rather be discussing than art. I happen to know, for instance, it's a subject that bores Lutz stiff. So thank you all for indulging me."

"Take no notice of Ebenau, Viola," advised Nick, still laughing. "Hasn't it dawned on you yet, he only likes to talk about the things he knows more about than the rest of us?"

Peter jumped quickly to his feet to lead the chorus in wishing her goodnight. Lutz too got up and kissed her cheek. She left them with the feeling that, while she had amused them for a time, they had much more important, masculine things to discuss. Unaccountably annoyed, she went up to her room.

The following morning Viola got up early – even before Lutz was awake, before it was fully light. She went down and found breakfast already laid by unseen staff. She had not intended to eat any, but it looked too inviting. A maid came in – a local girl, by the look of her, and brought coffee.

Viola had just finished and was preparing to go when Peter Lessel appeared.

"Good morning," he said in his precise English. "You are going straight to the Linderhof?"

"Yes, I've got so much to do, I thought I'd better make an early start."

"How are you getting there?"

"I was going to walk into town and find a taxi."

"For goodness' sake, I shall take you."

"Oh no, there's no need."

"But I should be delighted."

Viola could not very well tell Peter that she felt uncomfortable in his company. She was still unsure why that was herself. She hoped she was not being a bigot about his homosexuality. No, she felt certain it was something else, something she had not yet identified. As it was, she accepted his offer as gracefully as she could, and twenty minutes later was dropped at the great gates of the extraordinary castle. She got out of the car, relieved to be on her own again.

As she wandered around Linderhof, the darkness of that terrible night in Munich began to leave her. There was a lightness of touch about the place that was enchanting. Ludwig had conceived the small palace and its grounds in such a way as to indulge his longing to escape into the fantasy world inside his head. And nowhere in Linderhof did Viola feel that longing and his presence more strongly than in the grotto created on the mountainside above the palace.

Its most striking feature is the waterfall, which comes gushing out from high among rocks fashioned out of canvas, cement and lustrous stibnite, then plunges down into an underground lake beneath – artificially lit, like the roof above it, by a wonder of early electrical engineering. The effect achieved is both magical and moving – or so Viola always found.

General access to the grotto was restricted; though a guide unlocked the entrance to it at allotted times each day and led through groups of tourists, pointing out interesting features, filling in historical information, as well as answering questions. In high season such tours were fairly frequent – in winter, as now, less so. Viola preferred it that way. She liked to be in there alone. It was then that she was best able to get inside Ludwig.

After a cup of coffee and a short chat with the curator, Viola set off, key in hand, to let herself into the grotto. It was a freezing cold day and the steep path approach was slippery. Viola was weighed down with paraphernalia: briefcase, folding stool, hurricane lamp – so took it slowly. When she arrived at the gate, she noticed the next tour was not due for another couple of hours. That was good. It would give her a head start.

Entering the grotto that November morning was like going into a subterranean freezer. Viola could not remember ever feeling that cold. The beam from her torch fidgeted nervously across the cave-like walls, keeping time with the frenzied shivering of her hands. Once inside she fumbled around, until she found the light switch and turned it on. The illumination thus provided, though barely adequate for the purposes of her work, did produce the more immediate psychological effect of warming her up. She set up her stool, took out her notebook, sketchbook and pencil-case, removed her gloves and got down to her work – and quickly forgot that she was cold.

It was not until she heard the metal gates being unlocked, creaking open, then slamming shut again, that she realised she could do with a break. She looked down at her watch. It was another half-hour before the tour was due to start. She looked up again and that was when, out of the corner of her eye, she noticed a shadow – large and amorphous – ghosting across the rocky wall-face beside her. At first it barely registered – her senses reacted sooner than her brain. By the time she had noted it a second, then a third time, her body was already on its guard. Someone was watching her.

There was nothing in Viola's past that could have prepared her for this moment – or anything that could have taught her how to deal with it when it occurred. So perhaps it is just as well that even among the most civilised, most passive human beings, instinct is never far away – lying in wait, just below the surface. For it was on that, that Viola had now to rely.

In motion so slow it seemed to take forever, she reached down towards her briefcase, lying on the floor beside her stool. Silently she slid her hand inside and searched around for the big iron key she needed to unlock the entrance gates. Once she had located it – and was sure she had it firmly in her grasp – just as gradually she straightened up. Then, with one mammoth effort, she leapt to her feet and made a dash for it towards the door. And it was as she made that bid for freedom – though for the life of her she could not tell how it happened – that somehow she managed to drop the key. The noise it made as it hit the stony floor resonated round and round inside the grotto like the clanking slam of a cell door.

She fell onto her knees and groped helplessly about her on the floor, blinded by panic, yet desperate to find the key. She saw it. But the relief that overcame her when she did, vanished as fast; for just as she stretched out her hand towards it, another, larger, stronger hand made a fist around it, clenching it tight.

At that moment what little courage she had mustered, deserted her – all except for a preparedness to know her fate. She looked up. Even in the dim, now suddenly eerie light of the grotto she recognised the face. Its features were stamped indelibly on her mind. It was the youth – the fair-haired, burly youth – she had first seen weeks before, leading the fight outside the Augustiner, and, more recently, on the night the Fascists had tried to shoot Professor Feinstein – the night this brute had warned her, simply with his stare, that she was next.

Viola could move only her eyes and with them she watched his every step – transfixed – as if controlled by some overpowering force. He moved slowly, taking her eyes with his, boring his message of menace deep into her consciousness. He said nothing – nor did he attempt to touch her. He simply took up the key and with it sauntered over to the gate. He stood there for several moments – his back leaning nonchalantly against the wall; throwing the key repeatedly way above his head, then snatching it out of the air with his fist. Finally, as if bored with a game he no longer felt like playing, he turned his back on her, unlocked the gates and left.

Abruptly, and quite without warning – though coming as no real surprise – Viola's stomach turned over and she felt horribly giddy and sick. She started to retch violently but could bring nothing up, despite her body's prolonged attempts to do so. She thought of Professor Feinstein, lying unconscious in hospital on the verge of death; and she thought of Ellie, stretched out in the snow, blood oozing out of what little had remained of her face. She retched again – again it came to nothing. Then she lurched over to her stool and sat down. The peace that Linderhof had brought her earlier this morning, had vanished to be replaced by deep, uncontrollable fear.

Chapter Eighteen

Apart from Hilly, Viola told no-one about the incident in the grotto at Linderhof. She nearly told Tom, when he asked her again if she knew the demonstrator who had frightened her that night outside the Haus der Kunst. But it sounded so feeble, to be afraid of someone's stare, that, as before, she brushed it off and told him nothing.

Hilly, however, had sounded as worried as she was when she explained it over the phone.

" . . . and are you absolutely sure it was the same bloke?" she repeated. "I mean, there was quite a gap between that fight at the Augustiner and them killing poor Ellie What's-her-name. And let's face it, both times you must have been pretty bloody panicky – so it is possible your memory might have been playing tricks on you."

"Hilly, I know what I saw."

"Well then, Flower, if you're one hundred per cent convinced, I really think you ought to go to the police."

"And tell them what? That there's a young man somewhere out there who makes horrid faces at me? They'd think I was some kind of neurotic."

Hilly was silent.

"You don't think that, do you, Hilly – that I'm being neurotic – that I'm imagining it all?"

Hilly laughed. "No, idiot. Of course I don't. But I *do* want it put on record, I think you're making a big mistake by not going to the

Polizei. I mean, if this man really *is* one of those neo-Nazis – and all you say suggests he is – I think you've *got* to tell someone – someone who's in a position to do something about it."

Viola said nothing.

"Look, Flower, these are seriously nasty people – who do seriously nasty things."

"I know."

"These characters don't think twice about hurting people – killing people – maiming people. They're bloody bastards, Viola. Only yesterday, for Christ's sake – you must have heard about it, you live in Munich – they sent one of those letter bombs, they're so disgustingly fond of, to their Chief of Police. Took three of his fingers off. And that's exactly what I'm saying – they're savages."

"But Hilly, what's happened to me hasn't got anything to do with any of that. And after all, he didn't even try to touch me."

"Well just promise me you'll go to the police, if you so much as *see* him again."

"I promise."

"And are you certain it's *just* him who's worrying you?"

Viola did not respond – which, as far as Hilly was concerned, meant someone else was.

"A simple yes or no is called for, Viola. Is it just him?"

"Well, there is another man – about the same age. Not that I've ever seen the two of them together – so I don't think there can be any connection. But this other one's been cropping up ever since I got here. He was there when I met Professor Feinstein – he was at the next table the first time I met Lutz – then I saw him again at the Professor's talk – and again the night Ellie was killed."

"And you say you've never seen them together?"

"Never. And he's not like the yob. He's a totally different type – more like a student. Sometimes he seems quite nice – he even smiles at me. Then at other times it's – well – it's almost as if he's pretending he hasn't seen me."

"Has he ever spoken to you?"

"No, not a word."

"Viola, I *really* think you ought to tell someone else about all this. I mean, I'm no bloody good to you, am I? – over here in London. Who cares if they think you're a nut – just as long as you're safe. Tell Lutz. Tell your Texan. Best of all, tell the Police. I don't like the sound of this at all."

Kurt Mohrfeld did not much like what he heard, either, particularly the reference to Heino Timmermann. In Werner Fuchs's absence in hospital after the assault by post, he was convening the morning meeting. Schneider, Silke and Heino had all turned up – Heino, to his mortification, with the incriminating tape. Tom was late.

"We're going to have to pull you out, Heino," Mohrfeld said when he had switched off the tape. "How could you screw up like that? Didn't they teach you anything about keeping your head down when you're on surveillance?" Heino wished the ground would swallow him up. He was expecting Mohrfeld to take him off the case altogether, so it came as a surprise when the next thing he said was, "Okay, Heino, don't ask me why, but I'm going to give you a chance to redeem yourself. You can check out that idea you had about hacking into the Network's bulletin board, and put your pretty boy looks to good use by cruising the gay bars. I've been thinking, if Peter Lessel *really is* gay like Tom said, you may find a lead there. Silke still hasn't turned up much about him; but he may well have opened up to someone – revealed something he shouldn't." Heino relaxed, thinking he was off the hook. "But just tell me this – what the hell did you think you were playing at? Making eyes at her? Good God, this isn't a dating agency we're running."

"What's this, Heino? Been a naughty boy?" laughed Tom, as he arrived just in time to pick up on the tail end of the ticking off. "Sorry I'm late, Kurt," he apologised. "I got held up in traffic on my way back from the hospital. By the way, the Chief *says* he feels fine – *says* he intends to be back at his desk tomorrow. But I warn you, he *looks* awful. And the latest on Feinstein is that they now seem to think he might pull through. Apparently the old devil's been asking to see Viola Addison, which suggests he's feeling better." He rubbed

150

his hands together. "Okay – what are we discussing?"

"This new development, this phone call between Addison and her friend in London, the journalist." Kurt looked across at Heino. "Will Tom have heard it?"

"No," answered Heino, still looking sheepish. "Not yet."

"Right. Let's play it through one more time." He signalled to Tom to take a seat and for the rest of them to keep quiet.

As he listened to the revelations, Tom gave away nothing – except to raise an eyebrow at Viola's not unexpected reference to Heino.

"So what do you make of it, Tom?" Mohrfeld asked when the tape had stopped.

"Yet more proof that Viola can't be in the Network?"

Kurt Mohrfeld shook his head from side to side. He was a chip off the old Fuchs block. "I'm surprised Werner's let you stay on this case. You and Heino are as bad as each other. For a start, she was talking to this journalist in London; and she wouldn't be the world's first practitioner of disinformation. It's more likely she's worried that the contact she's made with this man is going to get back to someone – to us, maybe, if she already knows she's being watched. It would help if we knew who the hell he was."

"Sorry, Chief," said Schneider. "We had to wait outside. The only one we saw her with was Lessel when he dropped her off there."

"I know who it is," Tom said, "I was with her when she saw him in the line up after Feinstein's secretary was shot. We've even got him on file: he's been hauled in here a few times for various scuffles: Volker Metzger. A known member of the Network, but we've never managed to pin much on him." He picked up the phone and punched a couple of numbers. "Anke, bring in the red file on top of my desk, will you."

A few moments later, Anke appeared in the doorway with the file. Tom took it from her, and withdrew the photograph and description. Then he handed it round. "If you ask me, this bloke doesn't look the type to be working on his own on this. From the sound of that tape, someone paid him to give Addison a scare."

"Well, if we go with your theory –" began Mohrfeld, "but I'm still

151

not convinced she's innocent – Lessel was the one who dropped her there that day."

"We're still clutching at straws, but yes," said Tom, "he is a possibility. He could have given Metzger the tip-off."

"Over to you then, Heino, and your trip to the gay bars. Fill Tom in – you'd better not screw this one up."

Schneider chuckled. "Of course the other theory is that Addison's fucking Ebenau because it gives her the chance to see Lessel without overtly consorting with him."

"That's a possibility, too," Mohrfeld said.

"No way," said Tom and Heino in unison.

"Do you think Ebenau suspects?" Silke said.

"I doubt it. These people don't even tell their own mothers, not yet, not until the glorious establishment of the Fourth Reich. And you keep saying Lessel's come up clean so far, so he's nothing if not discreet."

"You may be right," Tom conceded. "But the more I think about it, the more I get an uneasy feeling that by pinning so many of our theories on Viola Addison we're running the risk of missing something bigger, something far more significant."

"So where do you suggest we go from here?" Mohrfeld sounded uninspired.

"Well, if she's genuine and follows her friend's advice," Tom said. "She'll either talk to Lutz about Metzger – or else to me. Either way I reckon, we'll soon know what's going on."

"Okay, but in the meantime we've still got a lot of work to do on these arson attacks if we're ever going to pin them on the Fascists. Now, I want to go through your reports, one by one to identify any cross-references."

That evening Tom was checking the tapes in the makeshift attic office when he heard Viola and Ebenau come in.

Tom knew at once, by the tone of Viola's voice, that something was bothering her. She was on edge – building up to something – waiting for the moment to be right for it. He thought of Hilly's advice to her that morning and wondered if she was about to take it. So when she did – only a matter of minutes later – it came as no particular surprise.

She told Lutz what had happened at Linderhof much as she had to Hilly. Doing it was evidently an effort for her. It was hard to judge why. Was she ashamed of herself for how she felt about Metzger? Or did she think Lutz might not believe her? Or was it really some story she had concocted? And if so, why?

When she had finished, there was a moment's silence before Lutz started laughing. It was not an unkind or mocking laugh, but a laugh which completely contradicted her fears.

"Schätzlein, what are you thinking about? A man helps you find the key after you have dropped it and unlocks the door for you? This sounds like the act of a polite and helpful person. You have been under so much stress lately. How could it have been the same man? – you say he was in a line-up, why then the police will be holding him. It is more likely it was someone like him – after all, from your description, he sounds like an average German."

"Lutz," Viola said coolly, "I'm absolutely certain it was the same man."

Tom could almost hear Lutz shrug his shoulders. "Maybe he saw you and was a little besotted with you, like me. Who can blame him? And he obviously did not wish you any harm."

"People don't look at you the way he did and not mean you harm."

There was a pause in which Tom heard them kiss.

"Schätzlein, how much I love you. You are so sweet and sensitive. If you see this man again, you tell me. If he really is a villain, I have contacts in the office who can identify him and I shall have something done about him, I promise."

There was a further – longer – pause. Tom heard them kiss again.

"Schätzlein," Lutz murmured after a while, "I think it is high time you took a rest from your work, it is too much for you. You must move in with me and we must be married."

Viola dreamt that night. She was running through a tunnel, deep down below the ground. Now and then distant rays of sunlight, from openings high above her, came flooding onto the rocky passageway. It was during one of those spasmodic spates of illumination that she first realised she was being followed. When she was next able to look back, she could just about distinguish two figures; both, she noted, already having gained ground on her.

The passage twisted and turned, so that on top of the exhaustion already racking her body, she began to feel dizzy. Eventually she was able only to stagger. She started to stumble every few paces and when she turned yet another corner and found herself confronted by a gigantic boulder, blocking her path, she flung herself to the ground in front of it and wept.

Her pursuers now slackened their pace. The end was decided. They had their quarry. There was no urgency to catch it. As they approached, Viola could see it was a couple – a man and a woman – he striding forward, she having to run to keep up with him. Viola's eyes were smarting from the salt of her tears, yet even so she could manage to make them out. The man she had expected to be blond and burly; but, when he came close enough, Viola saw it was the man from the airport; the one who had confronted Hilly. She looked across at his companion, being half dragged along beside him. Her head was bowed – it seemed to Viola as if in shame. Then – as she got nearer – as the woman lifted her head to look into her eyes – the face Viola saw was her own.

Chapter Nineteen

The pricking of the public conscience caused by the bid to assassinate Josef Feinstein lasted all the longer as a result of its very failure. Had it been brought off, the ordinary people of Munich would doubtless have felt shocked; in some cases perhaps, even outraged. No one was more conscious than the Germans themselves that the public assassination in Germany of a Jew of international reputation and prominence in his field, would be a source of intense embarrassment to their government, indeed to their nation.

The whole episode was performed under the inevitable spotlight of the media which undoubtedly gave it extra impetus, and was currently fixed on Josef Feinstein's dogged determination to cling onto his existence. A small band of sympathisers had been firmly ensconced outside the hospital for days, along with a selection of banners – some denouncing the crimes and malefactions of the neo-Nazis; others pledging sympathy and support for the victims.

When Viola arrived at the hospital to make the first visit she was being allowed to pay Professor Feinstein since his admission, this same small group was deep in consultation with a television-crew: reporter, cameraman, sound recordist. As Viola drew nearer, she noticed they were from the BBC. This did not surprise her. She had already thought the interviewer looked familiar and now remembered it was the same man who had hauled her in front of the cameras the day after the firebomb attack at the Neue Pinakothek. As she passed, he happened to glance in her direction. She saw a flicker of recognition pass across his face – but it was no more than that. This time it was she who had the advantage over him.

Security surrounding Professor Feinstein was strict. In spite of the fact that her visit had been sanctioned by the powers that be, even Viola was subjected to its protracted scrutiny. When she was finally allowed in to see the invalid, she was unexpectedly reassured by what she found. She had prepared herself for the worst; but his cheeks were a glowing pink, there was a liveliness in his expression and a twinkling in his eye. Here was hardly the face of an old man close to death. Here was someone still radiating a curiosity about life.

As soon as he saw Viola enter the room, he tried to prop himself up in order to greet her, but a nurse who was sitting to attention nearby jumped to her feet and ordered him to lie back against his pillows. Viola chided gently and reminded him she would be made to leave if he got over-excited. He smiled at her and promised to behave.

Viola had brought him lilies. She knew they were his favourite. She held them close to his face so that he could smell their scent. She had brought him Strudel too, though she doubted he would be able to eat very much of it.

The nurse busied herself with the flowers, until Josef told her to leave them for Viola to arrange. While she did so, he watched her in silence. Next she fed him a morsel or two of Strudel, but it was clear he could swallow it only with difficulty – so she put it to one side and suggested they talk instead. At first that too seemed an effort, but such was the old man's interest in his young visitor, it was an effort he was more than happy to make.

He very soon detected something was bothering Viola and he could think of only one thing that it might be. He ought, he knew, to lead into it tactfully. But when time is short – and he was well aware that his now was – good manners can often seem an ill-affordable indulgence. He plunged in.

"And so, my dear Viola, you and your young man are to be

156

married, yes?"

She dropped her eyes onto her lap.

"Perhaps."

"Has he yet to propose to you, then?"

Viola knew how persistent Josef Feinstein could be at times. If this was one of them, there would be little point in deferring the inevitable.

"He has asked me to marry him. Yes."

"And have you not accepted?"

"No, not yet – not in so many words."

"But, my dear Viola, is this not precisely what you have been hoping for? Has this not been your dream over all these years – to be the wife of this young man, this Lutz?"

"Yes." She let out a brief, nervous laugh. "It's exactly what I've been dreaming of." She fell silent.

"So. I see. Am I then to understand that there is something which is stopping you from making that dream a reality? There is perhaps something not quite as it should be in this relationship – something which troubles you?"

He reached out his hand towards hers. She offered it to him. He moved his head an inch or two further in her direction and tried to drop his voice – though in fact it was only the tone he was able to alter.

"Or do I become too personal? Stop me if that is so."

"No. Not at all. Anyway you're right."

"Tell me – of course only if you wish it – does it feel wrong when he makes love to you?"

"I'm not sure. I know he excites me."

She could scarcely believe what she heard herself saying. She wondered what ability he possessed, that he could extract such confidences. There seemed nothing she was able to keep from him.

"So, if as a lover he is succeeding already, then it must be as a friend that he is failing. Is it therefore when you converse that you feel something is amiss?"

"Yes. I suppose it is."

"It is then imperative," concluded Josef, "that you do *not* marry this man. If you do not feel comfortable or at ease with him, he will not suit. Many men can make passionate lovers but that alone is no foundation for marriage. No. Above all your husband *must* be your friend. He will be your home and you must feel at home with him. I am right, am I not?"

Viola held his hand a little tighter.

"You are right, Professor."

"Josef."

"You are right, Josef."

"Ah, my dear Viola. If only I were younger."

His eyes looked into hers. She noticed the sparkle had left them – as though a gauze-like film had dropped down over their surface, allowing him to peer out, but preventing her from seeing in.

"But there speaks a foolish old man." He tried to laugh, but found it too painful. "What nonsense am I saying? At my age, I should know better than to start building castles in the air."

"Oh, it's only human to do that. I should know; I'm more guilty of doing it than anyone I know."

"Except your King Ludwig."

"Yes. Except perhaps for poor Ludwig."

He tried to laugh again, but the effort proved more than his small body could take and he began to fight for breath. She looked around and saw that the nurse was already on her feet and ringing for help. Viola got up to leave, but Josef clung onto her.

"Come again," he rasped, "tomorrow." He released her hand and let her go, just as a team of medics came rushing in.

Viola was much affected by the visit. So much so that all she wanted was to get back to her flat to think over what he had said. She did not wait for the lift to take her down into the hospital foyer. Somehow she felt the need to keep on the move. She ran down the stairs instead.

"Oh, Dr Addison – Dr Addison."

It required the repetition to make her notice. She looked around. When she heard her name a third time, she homed in on the voice calling it. It belonged to the BBC reporter, running to catch up with her. At first she kept on walking – the last thing she wanted was to give an interview. But when he called her name a fourth time it was clear that, short of being rude, there could be no escape. She stopped and turned around to face him.

"Good afternoon," she said stiffly. "Did you want to speak to me?"

He held out his hand.

"Morton Voller – from the BBC. D'you remember, we met just after the neo-Nazis tried to blow up the art gallery here? You were good enough to give us your reactions to that business."

"Yes. I remember."

Viola noticed his colleagues had caught up with him and that their camera was already targeted at her.

"I understand you've been in to see Professor Feinstein. His first visitor, I believe, since he came out of intensive care."

"You're well informed, Mr . . ."

"Voller. Morton Voller," he repeated briskly. "And how did you find the Professor, Dr Addison? D'you reckon he's going to pull through?"

"You'll have to rely on the medical bulletins for that information, Mr Voller. I'm afraid I can't help you there."

"But what were your impressions of him?"

"He seemed to have as lively an interest in things as ever."

"Is he afraid of another attempt on his life?"

"We didn't discuss it."

"Do *you* think the neo-Nazis will try it again?"

"I really have no idea. I sincerely hope not."

"And do you think they'll be making any more attacks on art galleries?"

"Mr Voller! How can *I* be expected to answer that question – other than by offering as wild a guess as you."

"But you have heard nothing of any plans? Nothing from any of your influential friends in Munich for example?"

"No. I've heard nothing."

159

"I understand, Dr Addison, that you are a friend of Peter Lessel?"

"If you'll excuse me, Mr Voller. I'm late for an appointment. Good afternoon."

As Viola drove home, she ran through the afternoon's events again and again – not just her conversation with Professor Feinstein, but also the interview with Morton Voller. Oddly enough, it was the latter that played on her mind more. It had left her feeling unsettled, confused – wondering why he should have brought Lessel into it, when it had started out as a straightforward enquiry about the Professor's recovery.

When she got home, she made herself a cup of tea. She sat with it at her desk and took out a letter she had received from Australia that morning – from John. She read it through again. It was a long letter – all about his new home, new friends, new job – a detailed description of the university, his department and the art history department which, he happened to mention, was looking for a new professor. He missed her. He did not shrink from saying so. But there was no mawkishness in the expression of his feelings – no attempt at making her feel guilty about the past.

It left her feeling better. John was a friend, a good friend – and always would be. She opened the drawer of her desk, took out some writing paper to begin a reply – and tried to blank everything else out of her mind.

Chapter Twenty

Snow fell all that night, its myriad flakes fluttering delicately out of the vastness of the sky to lay a coverlet, like opulent ermine, over the dormant city. In the morning, the soft, thick blanket, that had been put down did its best to hold back the demands of time – muffling those sounds of civilisation which stir the sleeping from their slumbers. And, as if to add to the conspiracy of Nature wanting Munich for itself, it had chosen a Sunday for this, the first real snowfall of that Winter; the one morning of the week when alarm clocks are switched off and city dwellers rely upon the rhythms of the Earth to tell them when the time has come to rise.

When Viola finally awoke, she simply lay in her bed, swaddled in eiderdown, watching the bright, clear light of day peeping in on either side of her blinds; listening to the hush outside in the surrounding crescent gardens; floating through the memory-banks of her mind, until she hit upon the combination of past sensations that told her it must have snowed.

She jumped out of bed and ran over to the window. Up went the blinds and into her bedroom burst that unrivalled brilliance of sunshine glistening on pure, perfect whiteness. It almost blinded her. She rubbed her eyes. Then once they had become accustomed to the light, she looked again – out onto the snow enveloped garden. And when she did, she chuckled; for there among the trees and bushes, looking sorry for themselves under the weight of their unfamiliar burden, stood a snowman – larger than life-size – smiling up at her window, his coal-black eyes beaming directly into hers. And then, from behind the snowman, emerged Tom, which came as no great surprise. Viola opened up her window and shouted down at him.

"Tom! How old did you say you are?"

He looked up and grinned. "Thirty-three – thirty-four next Spring."

"Well, if you're absolutely sure about that, don't you think it's about time you started growing up?"

Tom laughed instead of answering and vanished again behind his frozen giant of a friend. When he re-emerged a second or two later, he held in his hand a large snowball. On his face he had a broad, mischievous smirk. He raised his hand above his shoulder, pulled it right back and – all within the same expert action – threw. She had no time to duck. The snowball was already hurtling at her; not exactly hitting her – Tom's aim was true – but smashing against the wall within inches of her window. As it atomised into thousands of tiny, freezing droplets, Viola caught some of the spray on her face and body.

"Just so you know how much I really care," shouted Tom, laughing at her as she made a fist at him.

She quickly shut her window tight, before he felt the urge to send along another token of his esteem. But he threw no more snowballs. Instead he blew her a long, exaggerated kiss – while she, like the flirtatious little schoolgirl she had never been, poked out her tongue at him from behind the safety of her window panes and retired into her room.

Shortly afterwards, her mother phoned, as she did every Sunday. It was a weekly ritual. The content of this call, also, was easy to predict: which one of Viola's old school friends had most recently reproduced, who had said what to whom at the latest Bridge party, and numerous tales about Olivia's little boys – although Viola was always pleased to hear these. It seemed there was currently much excitement in the Melhuish household. Edward, Viola's eldest nephew, had been chosen to play one of the Three Wise Men in his school's Nativity Play and his younger brother, James, was to be a lamb. Henry, not yet old enough to be a pupil at that same school, had nonetheless landed himself the equally prestigious role of the Star of Bethlehem in his Kindergarten's Christmas offering.

"Darling, as soon as the dates are fixed, I'll let you know," said Margaret Addison, having discussed the matter at great length, as though it were some grand opening night in the West End. "I told the boys, I was sure their Aunty Viola would be there."

"I'll do my best, Mother. But I can't promise. I *do* wish you hadn't built up their hopes like that."

Viola's subtle criticism was ignored.

"Now, Viola – about Christmas. Your father, Olivia and I have been discussing it . . ."

"Mother, Christmas is weeks away."

This reproof was granted as little consideration as the last. Viola could tell she was about to be informed of ready-made arrangements.

"We *all* think it would be rather nice, if we invited Lutz to join us."

Viola could not help smiling at the irony of the proposition.

"After all, Christmas is a time for families and I know he has little of his own. Olivia asked him."

"Well I'm not sure, Mother. I don't know what his commitments are. He's always so very busy."

"And you're always so very negative, Viola. Of course he'll want to come. He'll love to have the chance of a real *family* Christmas. Olivia said he can't wait to meet the boys – that he adores children. And isn't that just what Christmas is all about – children?"

Viola smiled to herself again – this time at her mother's ability to rewrite a convenient *raison-d'être* for Christmas.

"Well, I'll speak to him about it."

"Speak to him today, darling, please. I know what you're like. You'll only . . ."

"I can't do that. He's away in Brussels for a few days. But I'll mention it to him, when he gets back. Just a minute, Mother. There's someone at the door." This was not simply an excuse. "Look, I'll have to go. I'll call you during the week – love to everyone – 'bye."

Tom was at the door. Before she let him in, Viola made him promise he had no more snowballs secreted about his person. He swore there were not and was allowed to enter. What he did have in his hand was a pair of skating boots. He had found them in the attic. The old lady had forgotten whose they were – she thought they had probably been used by her grandniece years ago – but had been happy to let Tom take them.

He now turned them upside down and pretended to try and make out the size.

"Looks like a thirty-six to me. Does that sound right?"

"Sound right for what?" asked Viola.

"Right for you?"

Still Viola looked blank.

"I mean, is that your size? Would they fit you?"

"Yes, but . . ."

"I'll stop by about twelve-thirty. It's Sunday; I've got the day off, and *we're* going skating."

"But I don't know how," protested Viola.

"So I'll teach you."

Further protestations followed, but Tom was determined.

"All right, all right," she said finally. "But I warn you I shall be totally hopeless at it."

Tom picked her up at half past twelve – just as he had said he would. By now Viola could scarcely wait; not for the skating – that just seemed like a necessary evil – but for the opportunity to talk to Tom.

He could tell she was keyed up – more like she used to be, when they first met. To begin with he put it down to anxiety about learning how to skate. But he wanted that to be fun, wanted her to enjoy it. So he promised her he would not let her fall. It was when Viola – almost as soon as they were out of the front door – launched them into a heart-to-heart, that Tom realised it was for this, not the ice-skating, she had been summoning up her courage.

"Tom, can you understand the sort of racial fanaticism that made that man try to kill Professor Feinstein?"

"No, I sure as hell cannot."

"But can you understand *any* sort of racism? I mean, can you understand what makes some people act with such blatant, *physical* aggression towards other races – people they think are depriving them of what's theirs – jobs, housing, things like that."

"Sure. *That* I can understand. But I don't have to like it. It's called looking around for some other guy to pin your troubles on. It does nothing to solve the problem. It just makes for a whole lot of hate."

"You can understand what motivates those people though?"

"I don't give a shit what motivates them. I don't intend worrying my head, thinking up excuses for slime like that. They know what's right and what's wrong, just like you and me. Difference is, they choose to ignore it."

Viola was temporarily silenced. Not because of what Tom had said – she knew in her heart that he was right – but by how he had said it. Anger was a side of him she had never seen before.

Tom, too, was quiet for a moment. He was hoping his reaction would elicit further information from Viola.

"I guess those neo-Nazis make me madder than hell," he added. "They're no different from the Ku Klux Klan."

"Yes," Viola answered simply, but she offered nothing more.

They had now reached the Nymphenburg. They found a convenient bench, Tom rubbed the snow off it and sat her down.

"Allow me," he said, crouching in front of her and pulling off her boots. It was clear she was still deep in thought, so he took her sock-clad foot in his hand and squeezed it. She came to her senses and looked at him. He could see sadness had come into her eyes.

"Tom, do you *really* believe in love? That it's not just some romantic, unattainable dream?"

Tom wondered what had brought about the change of subject. "Well – I do believe in love, most certainly."

"Do you believe, though, that sex is an essential part of it?"

"You better believe it."

"So you don't think you could love a girl without – without having a good physical relationship with her."

"No, I don't – not completely."

"But what about the opposite? Could you have – could you enjoy – sex with someone you didn't necessarily love?"

"Show me the guy who couldn't. But I've got to tell you, there's a whole big difference between having sex and making love. Viola, listen to me, sex is something that happens just as much in your head, as it does in your heart, as it does in all the other obvious places. But if it doesn't feel good in *any one* of those, it's for sure you're never going to hit the top. I'm telling you – if it's not right up here," he put his hand to her forehead, "sex is never going to be great – not as great as it *can* be. It's too hard to separate how you feel from what you think."

"And has it ever all been right for you, Tom? Have you ever *really* been in love?"

"Well right now I'm getting pretty close."

He said no more – just busied himself lacing up the boots. When that was done, he sat down beside her and laced up his own. Then he pulled her to her feet and held her, while she struggled to find her balance.

"Don't be afraid, Viola. Trust me. I'm not going to let anything happen to you."

At that moment Viola came close to wishing it was Tom she was in love with – not Lutz.

There is no vulgar skating-rink in the elegant grounds of the Nymphenburg. But in freezing weather there is a considerable amount of ice. As the temperature plunges and the ice hardens, so the local population is irresistibly lured out onto it. On that particular Sunday, with the sky the colour of bluebells, the palace itself looked more beautiful than ever: its grand, white façade, now whiter than white under a frosting of snow – the crystals of which sparkled like tinsel in the sun's glare. On the canal, stretching close up to the forecourt, skaters were gathered, like splashes of colour – paint-box bright – gliding to and fro across a pristine canvas. It all looked so pretty,

166

Viola would have been content simply to sit and watch. But that was not Tom's style. Why should he want to watch life, when he could be part of it? So he took her onto the ice.

Viola found that she loved skating. She had not thought she would, but she did. To her amazement, it did not seem too difficult and so quickly did her confidence grow, she was soon prepared to let go of Tom. But she was under no illusions. The speed with which she acquired the rudiments of the technique, she put firmly down to his teaching rather than any innate ability of her own. And Tom was a good teacher. He was patient, gave clear instructions and encouraged perseverance. But above all he was there to catch her before she could fall. When they finally came off the ice, she might have felt exhausted, but she could not remember when she had enjoyed herself so much.

As they walked back to the crescent, Tom realised he had to know how things stood.

"So has that guy asked you to marry him yet?"

"Yes."

"And?" He paused for a reply. When none was forthcoming he pressed harder. "Well? Have you given him the green light?"

"No, not yet – he's only *just* asked me."

Why did she feel so sad?

"I tell you, there's no way you'd catch *me* driving up to Brussels for the weekend – work or no work – if I'd just asked a girl like *you* to marry me. How can he take off like that – without some sort of answer?"

Viola too attempted a laugh – to act as light-hearted as Tom.

"Why, what would you do?"

It was the phrasing of her question, acting like a cue, which made him remember some lines he had learned from *Twelfth Night*. He had read it only recently, for the first time, since Viola had told him she was named after one of its characters. It seemed to him the words had been written for this moment – just for him to say to her.

"Oh, I guess I'd *'Make me a willow cabin at your gate'*; somewhere I could *'Write loyal cantons of contemned love'*, and *'Cry out "VIOLA!"'*

167

– So,' he concluded, *"you should pity me.'"*

"'You might do much,'" Viola answered spontaneously – using the rejoinder Shakespeare had already prepared four hundred years before.

But it was another response – the response she gave him with her eyes – that was Tom's real reward. For a few seconds there was a spark that joined her eyes with his. Then Viola let out a short, embarrassed laugh.

"You've got it wrong though, Tom. Viola *makes* that speech – it's not said *to* her."

Tom grinned back and pretended to berate her. "Viola, allow me *some* poetic licence, please. I'm only a humble sports reporter. It's the right play, okay?" He paused for a moment. "Anyhow, maybe there's a bit of *that* Viola in me. And I *don't* mean I'm a woman dressed up as a man."

"Oh, then what *do* you mean? That you're really one person pretending to be another?"

Chapter Twenty-One

Viola always went into the University on a Monday morning, mainly to pick up her mail; not personal post – all her friends knew the address of her flat – but business letters. She had preferred not to give people like Professor Bryce her home address. For though he was a kindly man and Viola liked him well enough, she knew if she made herself too accessible, he would have had her running around museums, libraries, churches all over Bavaria, doing research for him. As it was, whenever he wrote, there was always at least one request for some obscure item of information; always of such supposed academic importance that its unearthing could only be entrusted to her.

There was a letter from Professor Bryce that Monday morning. She put it down and picked up another; it had a London postmark, though it did not announce its origins any more precisely than that – simply her name, the address and the word "private", type-written on a plain white envelope. The contents of the envelope, however, took her completely by surprise. It was a letter from none other than Hilly herself.

"Dearest little Flower," it began.

"Running the risk of sounding melodramatic, I'm sending this note to your uni. address (not your flat) because it's super-confidential. I don't want to take a chance on anyone else seeing it. I don't want to phone either – just in case you're not alone when I do. Also you'll need time to think about what I've got to say.

"It's late. I've just got back from a media junket at the Savoy, where I got into conversation with a producer from the BBC – a spectacular hunk (married, alas – but that's beside the point). What is to the point is that we happened to get talking about the BNP and its – for want of a more appropriate word – 'twins' all over Europe. Apparently the BBC's been working for some time on what's supposed to be a revealing new documentary due out sometime soon – shortly after this week's EU conference on the repatriation (for that read 'enforced repatriation') of non-ethnic community nationals. Anyway there have been two journalists out in the field – undercover – for more than a year. One as a common or garden member of the BNP – but the other one has managed to wangle himself into the upper echelons of Far Right European politics. It appears there's quite a little hierarchy. The very top, I gather, can best be described as a kind of Mensa for European Fascists.

"Now this might sound like a digression, but it's not. The timing of the broadcast of this documentary is crucial. As I said it depends on the outcome of the Foreign Ministers' talks in Brussels. That in itself is newsworthy – because if they agree to pander to the Right, then we're talking about Fortress Europe. And we're not just talking about it – but actually creating it. (Only think of the repercussions, Flower – repatriation on a biblical scale – the rescinding of passports. Just imagine what that would mean to the Third World.) Now then, the reason for waiting for the official communiqué is this – that that's exactly what the Far Right is doing – i.e. waiting to see if they're going to get their way. If they do – all right. If they don't – then they intend stepping up their terrorist activities to an unprecedented level. In other words their aim will be, quite literally, to force governments into changing their minds.

"At last I'm coming to the relevant bit, but I had to put it in context first. Well, according to this hunk from the Beeb, it's this Fascist Intelligentsia that takes the policy decisions – then passes them over to others for implementation. Sounds bloody well-organised and that's exactly what's so frightening about it. It's also apparently known that the 'Brains' meet on a fairly regular basis to plan strategy and the journalist-cum-mole has now got a pretty impressive list of their names.

"Well, tonight this producer bloke reeled off a string of them to me – none of which meant a thing of course – until he mentioned that one of Germany's top men is called Peter Lessel. Now I'm immediately on the edge of my seat. I ask him where this German is based and when he says Munich, I can tell you, Flower, my heart misses a beat!

"Look, I could lose my job for telling you this, and I'm probably barking up the wrong tree anyway. For all I know there may be hundreds of Lessels in Munich. But after what's been happening over there – especially after what's been happening to you – this whole story's given me the jitters.

"I think the time has come for you either to get the Hell out of there (altogether my favoured option) – or go to the police (which I've been telling you to do anyway) – or to find out if your Lessel has got any connection with this outfit. But if you plan on doing that, be very, very careful – this is serious stuff. Whatever it is you decide, do something! Don't just bury your head in the sand. Be proactive for once in your life – not reactive.

"Take care, all love, Hilly.

"PS. Having re-read this, I now think we need to talk a.s.a.p. I'm going to the old ancestral home for the weekend (my parents are at their place in Bermuda au moment). Taking your student, the handsome Haydn, with me – took him to this affair at the Savoy tonight actually, but neglected him shamefully. I expect I'll find a way to make it up to him! If you don't reach me there, phone me at work. Both nos. follow in case you haven't got them to hand.

"PPS. Keep a cool head."

After a letter like that, asking Viola to keep a cool head was like asking Hilly to give up sex for Lent. All the vague, niggling doubts she had had about Peter Lessel, which she had put down to his homosexuality, suddenly came into perspective. But could he really be the sort who would be involved in such distasteful politics? On the other hand, there had to be some considerable basis to the reporter's claims.

As the implications began to sink in, so Viola began to panic; although the form her panic took would not have been apparent to the casual observer. She carefully refolded Hilly's letter and put it back in its envelope. Next she picked up the communication from Professor Bryce again, opened it and read it through. She took out her Filofax and made a note of his latest request – that she visit the Heilig-Geist Kirche in Rosenheim and send him a detailed report on the wall paintings there as soon as possible. Then she gathered up her things and went.

As she was leaving the university building she bumped into Rupert Servranckz, coming in. She stopped to talk to him. When he asked for her help with a private viewing of the Alte Pinakothek he was organising later in the week for a party of important businessmen, she agreed, took out her diary once more and jotted down the arrangements.

Servranckz might – had he been a more perceptive man – have noticed a change in Viola's manner. He would have detected that her actions and her replies were almost mechanical. For Viola was simply going through the motions; functioning by means of conditioned responses. Inside, she was in turmoil.

Saying goodbye to Dr Servranckz, she walked along to the Alte Pinakothek and proceeded through its galleries until she arrived at the famous Dürer portrait. Here she stopped to admire the charismatic, Christ-like face. Professor Feinstein, and others too, had criticised Dürer for choosing to depict himself in such a hallowed light. But it had been common enough practice at the time – Viola would not condemn him for it. Besides, as an artist recognised for his greatness in his own time, Dürer had truly believed himself not only to have been inspired by God, but to have been superior among men. He was a genius and he knew it. And when she peered into that face – as she now did – and when she contemplated the extent of his talent, Viola could not find it in herself to dispute his reasoning.

Yet the significance of the face went deeper into Viola's

consciousness, where it became indistinguishable from that of Lutz; for could not the same also be said of him? – that he was beautiful, clever, talented – that he was superior among men? Was that not what she had always believed about him? Until recently, when she had found herself making involuntary comparisons with Tom Pajak.

She thought of how she used always to see people in black and white and contemplated how recent events had taught her how seldom that was the case. Take Peter Lessel, for instance – on the face of it, a man of charm, erudition and fair-mindedness, who would not otherwise have been a friend of Lutz. But now Hilly's phone call had confirmed her suspicion that there was something sinister about him. Indeed, if Hilly's contact was right, Peter Lessel was nothing less than a fully committed, militant Fascist, possibly even involved in organising some of the recent outrages.

That night in bed with Lutz, Viola wanted some questions answered before she could contemplate making love. She was confident that if Lutz read Hilly's letter, he would accept the unpalatable truth about his old friend. But Viola could not bring herself to show him. She felt he might consider it disloyal of her to have discussed with a third party the fundamental beliefs of one of his oldest friends. Nevertheless, the subject had to be broached.

She released herself from his arms so that she could look him in the eyes. "Lutz, darling. I must talk to you about Peter."

"What about him?"

"I'm worried; I heard a rumour that he's involved in the German neo-Fascist movement."

Lutz's eyes narrowed. "What sort of rumour? From whom?"

"A friend in London, as a matter of fact."

"In London?" said Lutz sharply, adding more slowly, "Who was that?"

"Just a friend – a journalist."

"Oh well," Lutz sounded relieved, "you know what journalists are. If they cannot find a story, they invent one."

"But she seemed so certain," persisted Viola.

"Look," Lutz continued with quiet impatience, "I am an international lawyer. I have financial interests all over the world. Do you think I would jeopardise my reputation by having friends like that?"

"No, no, of course I don't. But it's possible you simply don't know what Peter gets up to when he's not with you?"

"Schätzlein, I think I would have noticed if he held these so called extreme views."

"Why do you say 'so called'?" Viola asked, suddenly concerned about Lutz's attitude.

"I mean what you call in English 'alleged'."

"Oh, I see," Viola said with relief. "I thought for one horrible minute you might be sympathetic to those views yourself."

Lutz gave a short, disdainful laugh. "Come closer, Viola, we have far more important things to do than discuss fairy stories."

Lutz sent Viola a bouquet of red roses the following morning. The greeting enclosed with them read "Schätzlein, we must marry soon – I long to make you mine for ever and always."

Viola stared at them for a while after she received them, trying to work out what they meant. Last night, for the first time, she had realised her passion for Lutz was weakening – not because he did not excite her, nor because she no longer loved him. But, for no reason she could positively identify, something about his manner the previous night had made her stop and make comparisons; made her think that she would never have had these kinds of doubts with someone as straightforward as Tom Pajak.

Chapter Twenty-Two

When Lutz asked her down to Füssen again, Viola declined. She had a good reason not to go: she was already committed to helping Doctor Servranckz with his evening meeting, though she did not mention that to Lutz. She felt it more satisfactory simply to tell him she was not coming. Although it manifested itself no more than a second, she did not miss the flash of anger in his eyes.

But Lutz was accustomed to restraining his emotions, and he accepted her refusal with good grace. "You must come next time. I still have a few distant relations living near there, and I would like you to be with me when I tell them we are getting married."

Viola did not answer at once. He had not, after all, asked a question, although it became clear he was waiting for some kind of reaction.

"Perhaps we should wait until we've decided when," she hedged.

The evening of Dr Servranckz's private viewing started well enough for Viola. She went first to the hospital to see Professor Feinstein and was delighted to find him better than he had been. Now every visit she paid him provided her with further evidence of her old friend's slow but steady recovery. This time he was especially lively; a condition he put down – much to Viola's embarrassment – to a conviction that she looked more beautiful than ever.

As it happened Viola had made an effort to look her best that evening. Rupert Servranckz had left her in no doubt that the event was of considerable importance; and, after all they had been through together, Viola felt the least she could do was to play her part in trying to make it a success. So she had put on her special-occasion dress and experimented with her hair. Professor Feinstein commented on both, not only when she arrived at his bedside, but again when she kissed him on the cheek on parting.

Viola met Dr Servranckz for dinner along with what turned out to be a group of German banking supremos, in Munich for an informal get-together. From the way Servranckz had spoken and the endless telephone calls required to make the arrangements, Viola had expected to be confronted with an army of bankers. In the event, the whole party consisted of no more than eight, including herself and its organiser. The men – for Viola was the only woman among them – were passable companions, in spite of the fact that the conversation over dinner bore little relevance to her field of expertise. Once they arrived at the art gallery, that situation altered and she found herself being asked questions which left her in little doubt that she was in cultured, knowledgeable company.

The Alte Pinakothek is justifiably regarded as one of the world's half-dozen most important picture galleries. The superb collections – Dürers, Van Dycks, Breughels, Rubens and so on – are housed on two floors, with the bulk of the paintings being hung on the upper floor in a series of interconnecting galleries. It was to these that Dr Rupert Servranckz first led his party that evening. The museum had been closed to the public for several hours already. Only night security staff were on duty and these Servranckz had asked to make their presence as discreet as was proper, given the eminence of his guests.

They wandered at leisure through the seemingly deserted building, Viola offering general information as it seemed to her appropriate; expanding into more detail only when that was specifically sought. She had never been one to bombard with facts or to blind with scholarship. Rupert Servranckz suffered no such qualms. It was mainly his eagerness to exhibit his expertise that led to their being much later than planned in finishing their tour of the upper galleries. Viola guessed it was already well past ten o'clock – and when she glanced at her watch, she was not at all surprised to see that it was practically half past.

At that same moment, a massive explosion shook the whole building.

The deafening blast was made worse by a violent jolting directly beneath Viola's feet, hurling her to the ground. It felt as if a volcano were about to erupt through the floor of the galleries. All around her, the sounds of cracking masonry and timber rending apart confirmed that she had not imagined it. It took a second or so for the event to register, until, through a mist of terrified conjecture, she knew it was a bomb.

On either side of Viola, several of the men had also been flung to the floor and down onto the staircase. Masonry began to fall. It sent clouds of fine, grey, chalky dust flurrying up into the carcass of the building. As it floated back down, it settled on their hair, their skin, their clothing, filling their tracheae and their lungs with its powdery flotsam, so that they all began to splutter and cough uncontrollably against a background of thuds and bangs as whole chunks of the building crashed to the ground.

One stout old man, with thick-lensed spectacles, completely lost his equilibrium and, unable to save himself, tumbled down the steps – his head banging against one unyielding tread after another until he reached the bottom. Viola and others who were able scrambled down after him to help.

Viola could see at once that he was seriously hurt – although the only physical sign to suggest it was the trickle of deep crimson-coloured blood discharging from inside his ear, with no evidence of any external wounding. Security staff appeared to help the others to their feet. One, who seemed to have some knowledge of first-aid, insisted that the injured man be left where he had fallen until the emergency services arrived. They all obeyed. Viola bent down to pick up his glasses. Both lenses were shattered. Nevertheless, she carefully folded the arms together and placed them inside his breast pocket.

Viola was struck by the prevailing sense of calm. In spite of the frequent thud of falling débris, in spite of the choking atmosphere, no-one panicked. She herself felt strangely detached from what was happening – as if she were observing it through a glass screen.

Suddenly, the place was alive with people: firemen, doctors, police. The bankers were quickly ushered away towards the main door and thence to safety – but Servranckz refused to leave his precious pictures. And Viola, too, demanded she be allowed to join him in the salvage operation.

Viola's and Servranckz's labours were only just beginning. They were to continue throughout the night. They had no shortage of helpers either. Apart from the security staff on duty, other staff – having heard about the explosion on the late night news – had come flooding in to do their bit.

The bomb itself had been planted in the lift-shaft next to the restaurant. The adjoining gallery had been gutted. Not one of its great collection of late Gothic portraits had survived the blast. They were gone forever. When at last Viola was able to enter the room, she wept. She remembered vividly how it had looked when she had last been there with Professor Feinstein and the full, futile horror of the event hit her. Her tears flowed freely; but inside, the emotion that gripped her more than any other was anger.

People were scurrying about now like ants, clearing rubble, cleaning walk-ways, carrying to safety those items that had been salvaged. It seemed as if the whole city had turned out to help, and Viola was not at all surprised when Tom appeared, striding calmly through the chaos.

As he approached her, a man whom Viola had assumed was a policeman out of uniform, came up to him, and asked what he should do.

"How the hell should I know," Tom glowered at the man, who, momentarily affronted, glanced at Viola and backed away.

"Are you okay?" Tom asked her, "I didn't know you'd be here."

"I'm fine," Viola answered, though out of breath from her exertions.

"I suppose you're here for the story?"

"It's a big story," Tom excused himself.

"Well before you start, you can give me a hand with some of these." She nodded at a pile of smouldering picture frames.

When the damp, grey dawn finally arrived to swirl through the gaping windows, Viola was close to exhaustion – so was Rupert Servranckz. Both succeeded in persuading the other to go home and get some rest. Tom offered to take them, insisting they were both too tired to drive themselves. And so it was that, shortly before seven o'clock, they emerged from the main entrance of the Alte Pinakothek – grimy, sweaty and soot-stained – to be greeted by at least a dozen flash guns and cameras.

As they hit the cold air Tom slipped off his jacket and draped it over Viola's shivering shoulders. The press cameras whirred and clicked again – no doubt impressed by the image of pathos and drama this would generate on their front pages. The ENG's of half a dozen TV stations hummed as journalists surged forward to hear from the mouths of experts, just how bad the damage to the gallery and its pictures had been.

Although Rupert Servranckz was almost ready to collapse from fatigue, he rallied at the sight of so many reporters. Viola would have preferred to slink away, but there was no chance of that. So great was the curiosity of the media that morning, a dozen art experts would not have been enough to satisfy their needs. Besides, Viola had already caught their imagination – their cameras could not get enough of her. Journalists near enough fought one another to interview her. Their questions kept on coming, in one language after another, taxing her linguistic skills to the limit.

When the BBC's Morton Voller finally succeeded in getting near her, it would have been difficult to decide which one of them was the more relieved. Viola was so tired she was desperate just to speak in English. She even managed to smile at him.

"Are you okay? All this must have been a hell of an ordeal for you," he said in a kindly voice, before pushing the microphone into her face. "Can you say something for our British viewers?"

"By all means," she said, as if she meant it.

He turned around and nodded to his camera man. "I'm speaking now to the eminent English art historian, Dr Viola Addison. Dr Addison, I understand you were actually *inside* the Alte Pinakothek when the bomb exploded – may I just say, I'm glad to see that you're unhurt. Perhaps I could ask you to give us some idea of the extent of the damage in there."

"Well, I think it's mainly confined to the ground floor of the wing behind us. The rooms that took most of the blast are totally wrecked. The ones down the other side have suffered less. But I've been trying to save the paintings; I haven't really looked at the structure of the building."

"And in your expert opinion, how many pictures have been lost?"

Viola shook her head with uncertainty. "Several dozen must have been totally destroyed – major works of immense artistic and historic value. Dozens more have been very seriously damaged; they'll need a tremendous amount of restoration work if they're to be saved. It'll be a huge job."

"So, if all the other explosions have caused a similar level of damage as that done here in Munich, would I be right in saying that the sum total of affected pictures might well run into the hundreds? In other words this act of terrorism has dealt a substantial blow to the art world?"

Viola said nothing.

"You are aware, Dr Addison," added Voller, although he could tell by her expression she was not, "that there have been other explosions – simultaneous explosions – in other galleries across Europe?"

"No. I was not aware of that," she answered in a monotone.

"In the Museum of Ancient Art in Brussels, the Rijksmuseum in Amsterdam, the Musée d'Orsay in Paris, the Kunsthistorisches Museum in Vienna – even in our own National Gallery . . ."

As he reeled off the list, all at once Viola saw herself sitting at the dinner table in Füssen. She heard herself discussing these very places with the men around that table. What a curious reversal that now she should be hearing of their destruction.

She heard Morton Voller repeat the question. She heard herself answer it.

"No, I'm afraid I can tell you nothing about any other explosions."

She turned to go; but there was still one more reaction the interviewer needed from her.

"Dr Addison, I know you were a close friend of Professor Josef Feinstein. Could you give us your personal assessment of the contribution he made to the history of art during such a long lifetime of distinguished scholarship."

She did not hear the end of the request. That was drowned out by the impact of the words, "I know you *were* a close friend of Professor Josef Feinstein . . ." repeating themselves over and over again inside her head, until it made her dizzy. She began to sway. She looked across at Tom – a frightened, tortured look – begging him for help. Abruptly, the world went black as she fainted into his arms.

Chapter Twenty-Three

Viola had been to only one other funeral in her life. Until now, the only death to have touched her personally had been the loss of her grandmother. And, although she had been deeply moved by it, there had been something so serene about the old woman's passing that her funeral had been more a thanksgiving for her love than an occasion for sorrow.

What a contrast with today. Now an icy, intermittent rain joined a bitter wind to produce a mood of deep despair among the mourners, all painfully aware of the tragic circumstances that had almost certainly prompted Josef Feinstein to give up his fight for life.

While Tom, like Viola, was astonished at the number of mourners at the funeral, the other crowds were just what he had bargained for. He had reckoned on there being hordes of demonstrators out that day and he had been right. He knew only too well how the old man – first in illness, now in death – had been high-jacked by protesters of polarised persuasions, eager for a focus for their arguments. He wished that side of things could have been forgotten – for the duration of the ceremony at least. He wanted to mourn Feinstein the man – not Feinstein the Jew.

In the absence of any family to whom to offer condolences – for Josef had no living relatives – at the end of his interment, the assembly simply dispersed itself. Viola chose to linger at the grave-side. She wanted to be alone with her dear Professor just one last time. Tom understood. He walked a little way off and waited.

Viola stood beside Josef's grave in a kind of trance. The heavy

182

squalls, which had become more and more frequent throughout the morning, had turned now into a persistent rain. Tom could see she was getting drenched and after allowing her a short spell of meditation, he walked across to where she stood, put his arm around her waist and pulled her away.

"I can bring you back tomorrow, if you want," he said. "But we need to leave now. You're wet through."

"Yes," she replied, realising it suddenly. "So are you."

"Okay. Let's go, shall we?"

Viola turned to leave with him, but she said nothing.

"He was an old man, Viola. He'd come to the end of his life. Listen, you can't blame yourself. His death wasn't your fault. His heart gave out – that's all. It'll happen to you. It'll happen to me one of these days."

She looked up at him. Through her tears she saw only the blurred outlines of his face. But she needed to see him – to see his eyes – to know he meant what he was saying; that he was not saying it simply to comfort her. She found some more paper tissues in her pocket. She rubbed carelessly at her eyes with them until Tom stopped her and handed her his own handkerchief. As he did so he looked deep into her eyes, and saw the depth of her sadness.

He remembered his own grief when his father had died and he judged that what Viola was experiencing was at least as strong, despite the fact she had only known the old man for a matter of weeks. "Come on – stop taking it out on yourself," he murmured. "You had *nothing* to do with it. If anything the old guy lived longer than he should have done *because* of you." He meant what he said – every word of it. He was convinced, once and for all, that Viola's grief was real, that she could never have been involved in the shooting that had led to Feinstein's death.

When they arrived back at the crescent Frau Doktor Menne was hovering at the door. She had been concerned about their safety – as soon as she had learned about rioting in the city which had developed from the demonstrations at the cemetery.

"God in Heaven, where will it all end?" The old lady was clearly shaken by pictures she had seen on television. "I simply do not understand how it can be allowed to happen. Something must be done. Why is nothing being done to stop it?"

"Don't worry, Frau Doktor. The Police will get it sorted out in no time. But I'm afraid you'll have to excuse us. Our clothes – they're wringing wet. We need to get changed." He turned to Viola and lowered his voice right down, almost to a whisper. "Come on, I'll run you a bath. You'll feel better then."

"They will be showing the funeral on TV any minute now," the Frau Doktor said, still trying to entice them to stay and relieve her own anxiety about the tensions in the city. "It's nearly time for the News. Viola will want to see it." In a sudden lapse of memory, she had forgotten it was from this very event that her two tenants had just returned. She looked at Viola. "My dear, you will be interested, won't you? Ah, such crowds – so many people – and for a *Jew*." She realised her slip, looked a little flustered and added, "Although I know he was a very clever man – and of course a great friend of yours, Viola."

But Tom insisted that he and Viola go up and change. As soon as they were in Viola's flat, he turned on the television to catch the coverage of the riots – short clips of running battles between bottle throwing youths and police in space-age protective clothing; upturned, blazing vehicles blocking the roads; water cannons hosing the surge of rioters, irrespective of their opposing political stances – virulent racists; passionate liberals.

In contrast, the next piece showed Professor Feinstein's funeral. The reporter's voice reinforced the change of situation. The camera roved ponderously back and forth over the crowds of mourners – picking them out as best it could through the veil of rain – dwelling every now and then on this solemn face or that. Eventually it homed in on Viola, Tom and Rupert Servranckz.

Now, for Viola, sitting in her flat watching, this was the most harrowing moment of them all; observing her own grief; reliving her own sorrow; above all, suffering again those agonising feelings of remorse.

Yet no sooner had that image imprinted itself upon her consciousness, than it was superseded by another. That of a young man – short, blond, stockily built – standing some way behind her in the crowd. Though the cameras moved off him almost immediately, she felt the blood drain from her body. He was still following her.

Werner Fuchs had now appeared centre screen. The camera pulled back a second or two to draw attention to the sling he needed to protect his injured hand, then closed in again on his face as he issued assurances of a speedy conclusion to the rioting. His voice was calm. His manner was confident. But Tom saw beneath to the despair that they were all beginning to feel. Weeks had been spent on this investigation, and so far they had achieved nothing – had prevented none of the damage that was tearing Munich apart.

At that moment, a phone rang from somewhere inside Tom's wet jacket. He took it out, and pressed the answer button. It was Werner Fuchs himself, telling Tom to get himself back to the scene of the riots where he was needed. "Yes, boss," he answered. He put the phone back in his jacket. "Sorry, the paper wants me back to do some interviewing for a story. I've got to go." He got up to switch the TV off, then crouched down in front of her. "Now go and have that bath – and try to relax."

Fifteen minutes after Tom had let himself in later that night, he heard a knock on his front door. His heart gave a thump as he hurried to push files and photographs out of sight. "Who is it?" he called.

"It's me." Viola's voice sounded a long way off.

Tom pulled the office door to and walked through the flat to let her in. When he saw her, he tried to guess why she had come. Her whole manner displayed the uncertainty that precedes confession or the giving of confidences.

"Come in. Coffee?"

"Please," Viola mumbled, unconcerned one way or the other.

Tom waved her at a shabby armchair, while he went into the kitchen to make the coffee and allow her time to compose herself.

When he came back in, bearing two mugs, she was leaning forward with bright, decisive eyes. "I want to talk to you, Tom. I've got to tell someone what I think is going on, and you might have some suggestions."

Tom was fairly sure he knew what was coming. He opened his palms in a gesture of invitation and sat himself down on the bentwood chair opposite.

"You know what you were saying about it being like the Ku Klux Klan . . ." Viola began, " . . . all this – this mess? Do you suppose it's possible to be friends with someone who was involved? – I mean, to have known them well and not to know that they *were* involved?"

This was what Tom had been waiting for. This was no objective, hypothetical question. He had to tread carefully, though.

"Well there'd be no basis for friendship if you're talking about fundamentally opposed views, especially on an issue like race," answered Tom emphatically. "So, okay, even if you started out really liking someone like that, I reckon you'd pretty soon end up despising them. But what are we really talking about here?"

"I think I know one of the people responsible for organising all these bombings and rioting," she said quietly.

Tom looked staggered. "Who is it, for God's sake?"

"A man called Peter Lessel. Remember, the man I was talking to when we met before Professor Feinstein's reception?"

Tom nodded. "But what makes you think he's a neo-Fascist?"

"Well, I don't have any proof . . . " Tom's heart sank, " . . . but a friend of mine from London, a political journalist told me."

Tom wondered when. They had certainly not monitored any such phone conversation.

"She wrote to me," Viola went on, "to tell me that a colleague of hers had come up with his name as one of the leading lights of the German Far Right. And although he's never said anything specific to me that confirms it, his whole attitude seems to suggest it."

Tom looked at her intently. "Is that it?" He tried not to let the disappointment sound in his voice.

Viola nodded, embarrassed by how weak her statement must

have come across.

"You may be right." Tom said, "Maybe this guy is involved. But unless you've heard anything definite, or can pinpoint his movements in such a way as to implicate him in one or other of these disasters, you don't have a whole lot to tell."

"But I'm so sure of it. And I'd feel horribly guilty if they did something else, and I hadn't been to the police or someone and told them what little I do know."

"Then do it," Tom said firmly. "Go into the central police station, and ask to see the Chief." An official statement of suspicion from Viola was better than nothing. She had been seen with Lessel at the Hotel and at Füssen. Perhaps she had overheard something that might be useful to them.

Viola nodded. "I've met him; after the fire at the Alte Pinakothek."

"Fine. Let's check where the Polizeipräsidium is. It'll be marked on one of my street maps," said Tom, getting up to find one.

While he was rummaging through a drawer, he asked casually, "Didn't you say this man Lessel was a buddy of your boyfriend? That you didn't know him that well?" Now they had gone down this road, Tom wanted to press as hard as he could.

Viola nodded.

"So have you tackled him about it?" he asked. "About whether he suspects him?"

"Yes, but he doesn't know anything. Besides, people keep those sort of politics to themselves, don't they, unless they're with others of the same persuasion."

"And Lutz isn't?"

"Oh no!" Viola gasped, shocked that he should suggest it.

Tom backed off with a gesture of appeasement. "Viola, sorry."

"The trouble with Lutz is that, while he's a very clever man – exceptionally, as a matter of fact – he isn't all that interested in other people."

Tom detected the hint of bleakness in her voice. She looked awkward, as if she were being disloyal; and that very fact made Tom's heart soar.

Chapter Twenty-Four

The workload for everyone at the Polizeipräsidium seemed to have doubled and the place was humming with organised confusion, to the point where the left hand did not know what the right hand was doing. Tails had been put on Lessel, but he was proving much more elusive than Viola Addison, and there was still no further progress.

In addition, the drug's bust, which at one time had seemed ready to be put to bed, had run into trouble. Tom was beginning to think he would never see light at the end of the tunnel. In the early hours of one morning he had just drifted off to sleep with his head in his in-tray, when Heino came running through the station doors like an express train.

"Tom, had to tell you personally," he said breathlessly, "you're not going to believe this, but I've found a man who may be able to help us pin-point the boss of this Chinese gang. He's a small-time dealer but he says he'll identify the Chinaman and – wait for it – if we don't charge him, he'll also give us a lead into one of the Fascist groups."

"Fascists groups?" Tom woke up with a start. "Which one?"

"Just listen to me. I found this bloke stooging around outside the Ochsengarten, you know, that hang-out for gays who're into leather, over on Müllerstraße. Anyway, this character, Willi Weitz, did a fair bit of prostitution before he started dealing. And one of his clients was a certain Peter Lessel."

"And?"

"And Willi says he can tell us the names of Lessel's nearest and dearest – in the *Network*."

"You mean he'll testify he's even part of the Network? You're right, I don't believe it. Let's get the little bastard in before anyone else hears he's about to split."

Heino and Tom, in denim and leather respectively, sauntered up five flights of stairs, through smells of fried food and stale urine until they reached the battered front door of Weitz's apartment. Not for the first time, Tom asked himself why people bothered to risk living lives of crime when they clearly earned so little from it. He patted the slight bulge below his armpit. In addition to this precaution, a dozen officers were fanned out around the building, instinctively identifying gaps, back exits and bolt holes in case Willi had a change of mind. Taking a deep breath, Heino rapped on the cheap, plywood door.

"Who is it?" a rasping voice whispered through it.

"Timmermann," Heino replied. "We talked last night."

There was a rattle and a couple of thumps as chains and bolts were drawn. The door was opened slowly to reveal a short, greasy black-haired man in his mid-twenties. Sharp black eyes set in a ferret-like face looked Tom up and down, then he lifted one side of his mouth in a sharp, non-committal gesture of recognition at Heino.

"Okay. I'm coming. Put the cuffs on so if anyone sees they think I don't want to."

Tom nodded. "Struggle a bit too if you want, when we shove you in the car. It'll be fine by us." He smiled at Willi, who stared back without any sign of amusement.

Tom shrugged his shoulders and flipped his handcuffs from his hip pocket. He manacled the greasy, soiled little man to himself, and the trio set off back down the stinking stairway.

At that moment, three slugs chipped discs of concrete from the wall behind them. A split second later they heard the shots. Before another salvo could be loosed, they had all hit the floor and begun crawling along the chewing-gum spotted, urine damp surface of the passage. When they reached the cover of a corner, they paused an instant then dashed, zig-zag, Willi being tossed from side to side by Tom, to a revving car, its back doors open to receive them.

Seconds after, with a sharp squeal and a streak of rubber, the vehicle exited the dusty cul-de-sac where it had been waiting.

Ten minutes or so later, at the Polizeipräsidium, the driver opened the back doors to let out Heino, Tom and their guest.

Upstairs in an interview room smelling of old cigarette smoke, Tom nodded at Heino to start the questioning while he switched on the tape-recorder.

"Right, Willi. What do you want to tell us?"

"Before I tell you anything, what's the deal?"

"No, it doesn't work like that. You tell us, and if we like it, we overlook a few silly mistakes you've made."

"Bollocks!" growled Willi. "Stop fucking me around, Timmermann. How long have you been on the job, anyway? Three weeks? I've never seen you out before."

Tom did not wait for Heino to invite him to join the proceedings. "Listen, creep. If you want, tell us nothing, and we take you straight back home. We can pull you any day for dealing. Or you can talk – and we let bygones be bygones. You'll just have to trust us, okay? We don't welsh on deals like this, or no-one would ever do business with us, would they? And you know as well as I do that there are plenty of happy little snouts out there, plying their trade without any trouble from us whatsoever. But just remember this, next time you give my colleague crap like that, I'll loosen a couple of your teeth. Understand?"

Even fit, healthy, righteous people tended not to argue with Tom when he was in this kind of mood. Consumptive, five foot drug-dealers did not even consider it.

"All right, all right," muttered Willi. "But what I'm giving you is worth plenty, so just you make sure I get it, and protection if I need it."

"Sure," Tom said. "We don't like our snouts, but we do look after them. Now get on with it."

Willi sniffed, rattled a gobbet of phlegm into the back of his mouth and swallowed it.

"I told you about Lessel, used to come down the Ochsengarten a few years ago. I went with him a few times though he was a bit rough for me. Anyway, he stopped coming. He had a row with his boss." Heino and Tom exchanged glances. "I was there in his flat when it happened; he never told his boss I was there, in his bed, but this bloke says he couldn't come down the Ochsengarten again – he'd be risking the Network – that's what he called it. And I heard it since, from some of the heavy boys at the club. Anyway, this bloke says Lessel's exposing himself to blackmail, disease, the lot. Lessel goes a bit funny, and says what about if someone did try to blackmail him, and the other bloke says, if any one ever tries just to tell him and they'd have whoever it was killed. No messing about with the police."

At the word, Willi sniffed again, and paused in a ham-fisted gambit to build tension into his story.

"Come on," Tom pressed. "Never mind the drama, just give us the names."

"I'll tell you what you're dealing with first. Lessel's a big cheese in this Network – it's a Nazi group." He stopped, disappointed at the lack of reaction in his audience.

"We gathered that, Willi. You said he had a boss?"

"He's a very rich man, a lawyer, done a lot of work for a few of the menials in his organisation."

Tom's ears pricked up.

"Lawyer," he repeated impatiently. "What's his name, Willi?"

Willi extracted another moment's worth of suspense from his performance before he announced with a certain amount of triumph, "Lutz Ebenau."

"God!" Heino burst out. "Ebenau? That's incredible – I mean – Viola's boyfriend?"

"Calm down, for God's sake, Heino," Tom said. "It was always a

191

possibility." He turned back to Weitz. "Why do you say Ebenau's the boss?"

"Lessel told me, that night. After Ebenau had gone, he was well upset. He got himself pissed and was crying like a baby. I think he was in love with the bloke, worshipped him practically. Ebenau's a fucking good-looking bloke, and powerful too. But he's straight – at least I never heard he wasn't."

"Okay, Willi," Tom said, as evenly as he could. "If Ebenau is the boss of the Network, can you prove it?"

"No, that's your job. But I know he is. Why would Lessel bull-shit me about it? But he threatened to beat the shit out of me after. I reckon it was his boys took a shot at me on the way out the flats; and they'll be waiting when I get back. That's why you've got to protect me."

"All right, Willi. You can stay here tonight, then we'll take it from there. Tell the duty officer your favourite food and I'll make sure you get it. But first, just take us through the conversation you heard at Lessel's place, word by word."

A further hour's hard interrogation produced a workable statement about his encounter with Lessel. With a subdued, but certain sense of elation, Tom took it off to show Werner Fuchs while Heino carried on extracting details about the Chinaman.

Werner and Kurt Mohrfeld had been closeted together since they had arrived at work that morning, listening to the last tape Tom had taken from Viola's apartment. Tom had heard the original conversation, he had said, and was going straight out to pick up Heino's new snout.

"I don't know." Werner was shaking his head. "He doesn't actually commit himself to any direct involvement."

"But, Chief, we've never heard him talk to her like this before. She must have rattled him somehow before they came in."

"He's certainly showing himself in a new light; and she doesn't like it one little bit. Let's listen to it again."

The conversation had taken place the night before, after Lutz got back from work. Viola, who had been sitting up waiting to talk to him had, in the meanwhile, consumed most of a bottle of wine. Although by no means drunk, she was less restrained than normal. For the past few days she had been brooding on the two tragic losses in her life, and on the fact that all her instincts told her there was a connection with one of Lutz's oldest friends.

"Schätzlein," Lutz's voice was incredulous, "you cannot possibly believe Peter Lessel would have been involved in blowing up the Alte Pinakothek, especially knowing you were inside it?"

"I don't know what to believe any more."

Lutz sat at the small round breakfast table while Viola paced around the room, trying to retain the courage for confrontation.

"But what proof do you have?" he asked.

Viola ignored that. "And what worries me is, if I've got these suspicions about Peter, why haven't you got them too? And why won't you even condemn what's happened – what's happening – what these terrorists are doing . . . ?"

"I cannot condemn these terrorists, as you call them. I sympathise with their grievances. What other means have they of demonstrating their frustration at the government's weakness in dealing with the problem?"

"There *is* the ballot-box, Lutz." Viola looked at him, certain that he could not disown the intellectual correctness of democracy.

"Schätzlein," he answered with evident amusement, "you are being naïve if you put all your faith in the ballot-box."

"Lutz, I've never heard you talk like this before. Surely you believe in the democratic process – that governments should do what the people want?"

"But who are your so-called people? Do you think they have any idea what they really want, what is good for them?"

Viola stared at him in amazement. Here he was, openly revealing a side of himself she had only just begun to suspect existed. "And are you saying *you* know better? Because if you are, then you really don't believe in democracy."

"Does it not seem logical to you, as well as desirable, that in any civilised society, the superior intellect should carry more weight than the inferior?"

"Lutz, I refuse to get drawn into some abstract debate. What's happening here is terrorism."

Lutz shrugged. "These are simply people who want their voices to be heard, who want to reclaim possession of their country. They want non-ethnics to be returned to their country of origin, that is all. To me it seems a logical solution. No-one is proposing a repetition of anything like the atrocities committed by the Third Reich, for heaven's sake . . ."

Werner Fuchs leaned forward and clicked off the tape recorder. Schneider had just walked in to his office, to be followed a few seconds later by Silke Beckmeier, waving a sheet of paper with agitated excitement.

"What is it, Silke?" Werner growled.

"I've finally found a connection between Ebenau and all his pro bono clients."

Mohrfeld jerked his head up, and Schneider looked at her with more interest than usual.

"You don't say?" he said.

"Shut up, Schneider," Werner snapped. "What have you got, Silke?"

The policewoman slapped her sheet of paper on Fuchs's desk. "Every single case that Lutz Ebenau's office has defended free and gratis has been for men who are known as, or very likely are, members of The Network – neo-Fascists to a man. Though none of the cases has been for politically motivated crimes, as far as we can see."

Werner studied the names on the list and the sources of information condemning them. He nodded. "Good. It looks like Tom and Heino were right all along that we were focusing our attention on the wrong person. Pity they're not here. When are they due back?"

Schneider offered the information. "They're in questioning that guy they picked up. They should be through soon."

Werner nodded. "Right, we'll just listen to the rest of this while we're waiting for them." He switched the tape recorder back into life and the reasonable, mellifluous tones of Lutz Ebenau filled the room:

". . . Schätzlein," Lutz had now adopted a much more conciliatory tone, "I understand. Really I do. You are in a state of shock. This whole unfortunate episode with that Professor has unsettled you. But you will get over it soon enough. Then, for you and me, it will all be as it was before – only better – much better. We shall be married. We shall have a family."

"If only I could trust you, Lutz. But how can I? You promised me – ages ago – that you'd do something about that thug who was following me, but there he was again at Professor Feinstein's funeral. I actually saw him on the television."

"What? Viola – I did as I said. I had him checked out and dealt with, like I promised. I do not know why he appeared again."

Werner Fuchs paused the recording there – just briefly; as much as anything to air his frustration.

"Damn it! If he's involved, he's sure as hell not letting on to her."

"Maybe not," said Kurt Mohrfeld, "but he's beginning to show his true colours. She's going to be in trouble, though, if he thinks she's sussed him and is going to turn him in."

"No, he's too sure of himself for that; you can hear it in his voice. I only hope he hasn't found out he's being monitored. The performance he's giving is almost too good. We couldn't convict him for a thing he's said so far."

"Maybe," Tom Jablonski said, walking into the room, "but the guy we just picked up had it straight from Lessel; Lutz Ebenau is undisputed head of the Network – responsible for all major decisions."

Werner held out his hand for the statement, swapping it for Silke's list of Ebenau's clients.

"Take a look at what Silke's found."

While Werner absorbed Weitz's testimony, Tom read Silke's list through twice, nodding his head with a tight smile. "Good!" he nodded. "This will help. We couldn't convict him on Weitz's say so, or this, but at last we have a target. And with Viola's statement, too."

"Viola's?" Werner asked, handing Weitz's statement to Mohrfeld.

"Yes. She's coming in to see you, to tell you her suspicions about Lessel."

Mohrfeld was shaking his head as he read. "Lutz Ebenau? Head of the Network? It's amazing. And we never had a sniff before. So, he was friends with Lessel, but that didn't mean he was one of them; and he appeared for these heavies for nothing," Kurt pointed at the list in Tom's hand. "But that may mean no more than he's sympathetic. This Weitz – the drug dealer – how good is his information?"

Tom held up his hands. "We didn't prompt him – not once, you can listen to the interview tapes. He didn't have a clue what we wanted to hear. Okay, he knew we were after the Network for the bombings – everyone knows that. But he couldn't have just plucked Ebenau's name from the air."

Werner nodded; he looked depressed. "Tom's right. I blame myself. My God, maybe we could have nipped this whole thing in the bud if we'd taken a closer look at Ebenau at the start. As it is," he went on, "we can't put him inside for anything he's come out with so far. If it was an offence to rubbish the government – or to want to get rid of the immigrants – let's face it – we'd have half the population locked up by now."

"You'd have *me* in there for one," added Schneider.

Tom made no comment.

"What's that you said about her coming in, Tom?"

"She came up to see me, last night. Just to see me," Tom added quickly for Schneider's benefit. "Basically, she'd had a tip-off about Lessel through her friend, Hillary Farrell, in London. I've put someone onto the BBC to see if they've got anything we can use; hopefully, we're not too late. It would be just typical of a bloody journalist to find something out, go and broadcast it to the whole world and give

Lessel chance to make up some excuses, before we can pull him in."

"There's more," Schneider added. "We've been running checks on the people who were staying at Füssen the weekend Viola Addison was there. The guest list reads like a Who's Who in European Fascism."

"This has got to be it," sighed Werner as he leant over to offer Schneider and Mohrfeld his cigarette packet. "There's one thing that puzzles me though. From the change in Ebenau's voice, he was genuinely shocked when she told him Metzger was still around. Of course, it's obvious now that if Ebenau is the boss, Metzger would always have been working for him. He must have had him there to keep an eye on Viola for some reason or other. But he was telling her the truth when he said he'd pulled him off, I'm certain of it, and yet, Metzger was still following her." He paused and looked across at the others.

"Well according to Weitz," Tom began tentatively, "Lessel's been in love with Ebenau for years, and *we* know they've been friends since schooldays – probably did everything together then, you know how it is. Then at university Viola Addison turns up and cocks up their cosy set-up. Now, ten years on, Ebenau's off every night again with her. Ask yourselves – how would *you* feel?"

"I have to confess, that's an angle I hadn't thought of yet," admitted Werner, as he lit up another cigarette from the butt of his last. "You may have something there."

"There's something else," Tom said, suddenly struck with a new idea. "We were tipped off about Viola Addison being in Munich for the express purpose of harming Josef Feinstein, right? Let's go back to the snout's report. I bet it was fed him by Lessel or any one of his mates."

"Christ!" Werner exclaimed. "We swallowed that one whole. Still, at least we're getting somewhere now."

Tom sat fiddling around with his pen; staring intently, while he pushed its cap on and off with his thumb in a continuous, obsessive action.

Schneider put out his foot and nudged Tom's leg to get some sort of reaction out of him. He raised his voice a notch. "Are you with us, Jablonski?"

Tom looked up. "I was just thinking, if it is Lessel trying to scare her off, either because he's jealous or because he thinks she's taking Ebenau's mind off the job, whatever, what I'm wondering is this – first, how far is he prepared to go to do it – second, I doubt Viola's going to stay with Ebenau after this anyway, so how's he going to react if or when she calls their relationship off?"

"In that he seems fairly obsessed by her," butted in Mohrfeld, "I can't see him taking it too well."

"That's what's worrying me." Tom turned to Fuchs. "When she comes in to see you this afternoon, Chief, I'd like to use it as an opportunity to break cover. I think she needs to know who I am and that I'm there to protect her."

"Oh, is *that* the service you're hoping to provide her with?" Schneider grunted.

Werner ignored him.

"No Tom," he said. "There's no need for that – better she doesn't know. Besides I'm not sure how Ebenau *can* see her as a threat – after all, he hasn't told her anything to condemn himself. No, if there's any potential danger, I think it's more likely to be to you."

He picked up a copy of the *Münchner Merkur* from his desk. The front page was covered with pictures of the riots – with one exception. It was to this that Werner drew Tom's attention. It was a photograph, taken at Josef Feinstein's funeral – a blow-up of him comforting the grieving Viola.

"It's only going to be a matter of time before one of the heavies that works for the Network recognises you, Tom. If anything, I think you should move out of that apartment, get right away from Ms Addison. Tell her you've got to go back to the States or something."

The very idea of doing that made Tom feel cold inside. To his surprise he found himself with an unlikely ally.

"Werner's right," said Schneider, "but I *do* think Tom should stay in there. I think this could be the break we've been waiting for. With any luck Ebenau just might try something crazy enough to let us have him." He pointed to the newspaper. "I mean, for God's sake, wouldn't *that* be enough to make your average bloke come out of his corner fighting? And he'll have seen the two of them on the TV the other day – seen her fainting into Jablonski's arms outside the Alte Pinakothek. Did you see the look she gave Tom then – before she blacked out? "

Werner had seen the look. He remembered he had been struck by it at the time. It had displayed a familiarity between them which he had not liked at all; a familiarity that went way beyond the neighbourly. He paid closer attention to what Schneider was saying.

"So it's my hunch that if Viola leaves him, Ebenau's going to assume she's already got Tom here lined up to take his place in her bed. That's got to send him over the top. The thought of a Pole fucking *his* woman. They might spout all that crap about Europe standing united against the world – but what every good Nazi knows is, some Europeans are more equal than others – and when it comes to Poles, they're only a couple of steps up from the bottom of the heap." He leant across and punched Tom in the arm as if to reinforce this reference to his father's ancestry. Then he helped himself to another of Fuchs's cigarettes, before adding his conclusion. "It's the best chance we've got, Chief."

"All right, Schneider, you've convinced me. We'll give it a bit longer. Tom, didn't you say she's going back to England for Christmas?"

"Yes. Maybe next week. I think she's trying to bring it forward."

"So we'll give it till then. Right, let's move on."

"Chief," interrupted Tom, "I think Schneider has underlined for us that the risk to Viola is more than just a small one. I still maintain we should warn her."

"Don't even think about it, Jablonski. She chose to be with this man; we didn't ask her, and she doesn't sound like the kind of woman who likes having her judgement questioned. And frankly, if she blows him out now, she'll blow you with her. You want to stay on the case: then so must she, without knowing it. I'm sorry, but that's the way it's got to be." Werner paused for a moment. It was a favourite technique of his to blow hot then cold. "Besides, as you keep on insisting, you'll be there close at hand to protect her, won't you, Tom?

Chapter Twenty-Five

It was a relief to get out of Munich with someone like Tom. To Viola the city felt like a time-bomb, relentlessly ticking away, waiting to explode. Initially, however, the prospect of this outing had not filled her with delight. On the contrary, Rosenheim had always seemed a very long way to go for a ten minute visit to a church in order to satisfy one of Professor Bryce's whims. It was only when she had complained to Tom about it and he had told her he had a day off and would go with her, that she built up any enthusiasm for the trip. But most of all she felt she needed to get away from Lutz – to try and sort out her feelings about him.

The problem was that, despite his lack of condemnation of the Fascists' acts of terrorism and his apparent support for their racist ideas, she still could not bring herself to think ill of him. She was well aware that he had always been in the habit of playing the devil's advocate – a habit that was the product of a sharp, combative, lawyer's mind which relished a challenge. And while Viola was inclined to deplore his arrogance, that very same unshakeable self-confidence was, and always had been, a large part of his attraction for her. It would be just like him to be promoting views that were the exact opposite of his own, without giving her the remotest hint that was the case, simply to test the strength of her attachment. Whatever his motivation, she needed time to think.

Her conversation with Tom hardly touched upon Lutz or any of the recent events in Munich – Tom was determined to avoid all of

201

that. Having secured Fuchs's blessing to go with her on the trip –
"Come on, Chief – Metzger came after her at Linderhof. With all the
new info we've got, it's more than likely he'll try something again.
This would be the perfect opportunity" – he wanted to use the time
to get to know her as a person, not as a pawn in a much wider
game.

So they talked about themselves: Viola's interfering parents, in
whose opinion she could do little right; Tom's late family, in whose
eyes he could do no wrong. He flirted with her a good deal. She
even found herself flirting with him. It seemed impossible not to.
They dropped into Rosenheim only long enough to complete the
mission for Professor Bryce, then they drove cross-country the short
distance to the Chiemsee, and took the ferry over to Schloss
Herrenchiemsee.

"Of course," Viola explained, "Ludwig never had the same kind
of power as Louis XIV." They were wandering through the
extravagant, gilded Hall of Mirrors – a copy of Louis's at Versailles.
"But I imagine he thought that, being King, it should have been his
by right. But don't forget, this wasn't the only dream Ludwig had.
His head was full of them – heroic as well as glorious. And he knew
they were all fantasies."

"Yeah, but there are fantasies and fantasies – and I don't like the
sound of this particular one. I can handle the idea of him day-
dreaming about being a knight in shining armour – we all did that
since we were kids. But I tell you, for me, there's something weird
about a guy who wants to have power over anybody – even if it *is*
only in his imagination. Sounds to me like hankering after playing
God."

Viola did not reply. Instead she wandered across to the window
and looked down onto the garden beneath – down onto the fountains
of Fame and Fortune, protected now against the ravages of the
Bavarian Winter.

"That's what people like Peter Lessel and his friends are doing,
isn't it?" she said quietly, as Tom came up and stood alongside her.
"Dreaming of past glory. Wanting to recreate it – at any price. Craving

power. Trying to play God." She attempted to laugh. "What worries me is that Lutz may be like that too." She was silent for a moment. Tom waited. "I suppose I'm a romantic – a different sort. Look at me – ten years wasted while I wallowed in what may just turn out to be some pathetic, idealised piece of fiction."

She did not look him in the face as she spoke, but continued gazing out at the garden. Tom stood with his back to the window, so that at least he could watch her expression. It had been oddly impassive throughout.

"Forget him, Viola. He's not the man you thought he was." He hoped he had not over-stepped the mark.

"It's not as easy as that, Tom."

She swallowed hard, as though the words were sticking in her throat.

"Do you still love him?"

"I'm not sure. Part of me does, perhaps. I still find him extraordinary – in the real sense of the word."

Now she did turn her head to stare straight into his eyes. It was like being allowed to peer into her soul, as though all the impedimenta of convention, all the reticence born of self-protection, had been stripped away – leaving nothing to cloud his vision of her inner self.

"Maybe even ten years ago it was only a dream – I don't know. Looking back on it all, there was no great spiritual bond between us. I never felt *easy* in his company. The trouble is, when I'm with him there's an intensity of feeling I've never known with anyone else and it's exciting. I never felt it with John. However much I wanted to – however hard I tried – I just couldn't *desire* him the way I have Lutz. Perhaps it was because, with John, I never really got the feeling he desired me. Not that I'm blaming him. I think it just wasn't part of his make-up."

Tom was about to take her hand. He could feel his whole body shake, as he made the decision to tell her that desire was very much part of his make-up – that it had made him want her from the first moment he had laid eyes on her – that he loved her with a passion that far outstripped anything Ebenau or any other man could ever hope to feel.

He was on the point of declaring it all, when he was brought up short, like a man walking into a brick wall, by the sight of Volker Metzger lurking in the doorway. Metzger saw that he had been spotted, and disappeared round the corner, out of sight.

"Viola, there's something I have to do. Just wait there. Don't move until I come back. Promise?"

Puzzled, she nodded, and watched Tom as he walked, almost broke into a run, and disappeared through one of the doors from the Great Hall.

Tom caught a glimpse of Metzger's blond head bobbing through a knot of tourists outside the palace, and set off at a sprint. He reached the gang of chattering Japanese, but Metzger was nowhere to be seen. Furious at having missed his chance to get at him, and knowing it was a futile exercise, he searched down the three or four likely avenues of escape. But Metzger had outsmarted him, was probably smirking quietly to himself, watching Tom. "Shit," swore Tom, and walked back to Viola, thinking up an excuse for his disappearance.

However alert he stayed during the remainder of their visit to Herrenchiemsee, Tom saw nothing more of Metzger. Eventually he began to wonder if he had been mistaken – seeing ghosts, where none existed. Whether he had been real or not, the mere suspicion of their being followed was enough to kill the mood of confession he had begun to embark upon. Tom resigned himself to the fact that it was gone, at least for the time-being.

As it happened, a second chance did present itself as they drove back to Munich. For the first time in weeks Viola felt hungry. The fresh air and the exercise of exploring the island had brought back her appetite. So, when Tom invited her to have dinner with him, she accepted at once.

Tom took the next exit off the Autobahn and headed in the direction of Bad Aibling – and a charming, family run hotel he knew, which had just the kind of ambience he sought.

When they reached it, they found that a wedding reception had taken over virtually the whole place. It was early evening but well into the proceedings for the nuptial revellers. The commotion was audible from the car-park. They went in nevertheless, and found themselves alone in the restaurant – other than for an old couple who, evidently, had been so long together that they had run out of things to say and had lapsed into perpetual silence. If it had not been for the uproarious din issuing forth from the banqueting room on the other side of the hall, Viola and Tom might have found such circumstances inhibited their conversation – but as it was, they did not. It did preclude any serious talk between them though. There was simply too much background noise.

As they were finishing their dinner, the door from the hall swung open and a large, red-faced man burst through it and presented himself as the father of the bride. With a grand gesture of drunken munificence, he invited Tom, Viola and the elderly couple to come in and join the drinking and the fun.

The couple looked horrified and shook their heads. That was enough for Tom to accept the invitation on behalf of himself and Viola, and the next minute they were in the midst of a family wedding of completely unrestrained jollification.

In order to save themselves getting involved in long, convoluted explanations of their presence there, Tom asked Viola to dance.

Bolchester High School for Girls had prepared its pupils for polite society by teaching them traditional English country dancing. At Oxford Viola had tried to come to grips with something better suited to modern life, but – having never much liked making a fool of herself in public – had never really succeeded. Since leaving university she had taken considerable care to avoid any situation in which she might be asked to dance. The visit to the jazz club with Lutz had been totally, and deliberately, out of character. So, by this stage in her life, she had convinced herself, not only that she could not dance, but that she did not want to. Tom took no notice and led her onto the floor.

With Tom as a partner, the experience passed through stages – from the bearable, through to the agreeable, then on to the pleasurable. By the time she got onto this third stage, she had given up concentrating on what was happening and had simply given in to the beat of the music.

Then it all stopped. One of the local lads – put up to it by his friends no doubt – had tapped Tom on the shoulder to ask if he could dance with Viola. Before she had time to realise what had happened, Tom was handing her over. He whispered in her ear something about needing to keep the natives happy – and suddenly she was in the arms of this puny, lanky youth. He lurched and stumbled in such contrast to Tom's expert performance, that Viola could only laugh. Fortunately, the effort was proving too much for the young man's drink-curtailed stamina, and when Tom appeared in the corner of their vision, he stopped altogether. Tom muttered something in the lad's ear that made him grin and back away subserviently.

Now Tom and Viola stood facing one another. She could feel herself trembling, her breathing quickening, in expectation of being close to him again. He said nothing, but took hold of her hands and draped them around his neck. Next he pulled her to him and began to sway her back and forth to the rhythm of the music.

Viola had never denied that dancing must hold some major attraction. For any activity to have achieved such consistent, universal popularity, it had to have a great deal to recommend it. It was just that she had never succeeded in discovering what. Dance as art aside, of course, she did accept that it fulfilled the function of being pretty nearly the only form of sexual foreplay in which it is acceptable to indulge in polite society. That in itself, she had always assumed, was enough to guarantee its lasting appeal. Not that she had had any personal exposure to this benefit in order to back up her theory. Not, that is, until tonight. So tonight came as something of a revelation.

They danced slowly – at times barely moving – and so close together they could hear each other's hearts beating. With Tom's head resting against hers, Viola could feel his breath on her neck. She closed her eyes, wanting nothing else to inhibit the sensuality of this new sensation. He brushed his face against her cheek and held it there – holding her on the peak of the thrill that just the touch of his skin against her skin had sent shuddering throughout her.

By now she was scarcely aware of the music. She was conscious only of Tom's hands caressing her – of Tom's body pressing hard against hers. He pulled her hips up to meet his – so that her feet almost left the ground. She hung onto his neck, tighter than ever – yet secure in the knowledge that he would not let her fall. Had she been in any doubt before as to his intentions, there could be none left now. She could feel how much he desired her. All she had to do – she knew it – was look up at him and he would kiss her. So she looked up – and they kissed.

Just how long that kiss lasted, neither of them knew. It was only the sound of the wedding guests' clapping and cheering that made them realise the music had stopped. Not only that – but that it was they who were receiving the applause. Tom acknowledged the ovation with a knowing smile – even winked at the lads at the bar in response to their whistles of approval. But Viola's embarrassment was too great for anything like that. She could not wait to get off the floor. Tom knew it and as the band struck up again, he took hold of her hand and led her back to their table.

Tom decided it was time for them to leave. He wished they were already back in Munich – in her flat. He knew he could have her tonight, if he wanted. And he wanted it – Fuchs, Schneider, even his job meant nothing compared with how much he wanted it. They had almost reached the entrance hall when the figure of a man ambled into the doorway. He seemed to fill the space, to dominate it. But this was no ordinary man – not their host or any one of the wedding party. This was Volker Metzger.

Viola froze in the instant. Tom was about to take off after him again, but remembered just in time he was not even supposed to know who Metzger was. "Wasn't that one of the men in the line-up that night?" he said quickly.

"Yes, I don't want to go out there now, Tom. Something about him really scares me. I'm sure he's been following me."

"Stay there," Tom warned, taking off towards the doorway. By the time he got there, however, Metzger had vanished again. He looked left and right, but there was no sign of him. "Shit," he exclaimed for the second time that day. Next time, he vowed, he would get him.

Chapter Twenty-Six

As soon as they reached Frau Doktor Menne's house, Tom took Viola straight up to her flat, insisting that she needed sleep. It was the last thing he wanted for her or himself, but he had to report in. It was no longer merely possible, but probable that Metzger represented a real threat to Viola. It was vital that he be tracked down and watched.

He made Viola a cup of tea and suggested she went straight to bed. He did his best to reassure her that she was safe from being hounded, at least for the time-being. He wished he could have told her the precautions he was about to put into motion; he was already being torn apart with guilt about her position. He knew far better than she the risks she was running if she continued to see Ebenau. But professionally, there was no question that the right strategy was to keep her in contact with him for as long as possible.

Tom knew Heino was at the Polizeipräsidium – working the late shift that should have been his – and asked to be put straight through to his desk. Heino was not in a good mood, especially as he had at last plucked up the courage to ask Anke, one of their assistants, out to a concert that night and had had to cancel when Tom announced his little outing.

"Stop whining, Heino. You're not the only one to have his love-life messed about by the job. Now listen."

The silence down the other end of the line resonated with injured innocence. Tom took no notice. Instead he kept it strictly business and gave Heino a quick run-down on most of what had happened that day. Not everything – there are certain things a man, even a police officer on a case, chooses to keep to himself.

"So Heino, if Metzger can show up uninvited on Herrenchiemsee then track us down to that wedding – although how the hell he did that, God knows; I'd tucked my car right away around the back of that hotel – anyway if he's *that* keen to find us – her or me – then it's only a matter of time before he turns up round here. I want him found and I want him watched, okay? Not picked up – not yet."

"Right Tom, leave it with me. I'll get straight onto it." Heino sounded like his old self.

"Good man."

"I've got to come your way when I get off duty. I wanted to check up on . . ."

"Great. Sorry, Heino – got to go. She's making a call."

That Viola should be making a call did not come as any surprise to Tom. Whenever any sort of crisis occurred, she could be relied upon to try to get in touch with her friend in London. So confident was Tom that it would be Hillary Farrell's number Viola was dialling, that it came as a shock when he heard her start talking.

"Hello, Lutz. Sorry it's late, but I have to talk to you."

"That's fine; it is never too late to hear from you, Schätzlein. You are in a better mood now? Not seeing phantoms around every corner?"

"That's exactly what I'm seeing, Lutz. And I'm furious about it. If you thought it was just a question of paying somebody to warn him off, I'm afraid they've taken your money under false pretences."

"Now, listen to me. I give you my word, I was assured that this would stop."

"I wasn't just scared, Lutz, don't you understand? I was scared witless. It's horrible having some great thug following me around. You said you could do something about it. Well, if you love me as much as you say you do, then do it."

"Of course I love you. I have told you, I want to marry you."

"Well, you've got an odd way of showing it."

"What do you mean?"

"I mean I think you've told this yob to follow me; you're checking up on me."

There was a moment's silence before Ebenau spoke. "It is true that I do have friends whose loyalty I can trust and upon whose integrity I can depend. But let me give you just one word of warning. You should think twice about this American you have so readily taken into your bed. He may not, after all, be quite . . ."

"I haven't taken him into my bed, Lutz. He's a friend. Like you, this affair has shown me who my friends really are – whom *I* can trust – and depend on."

Viola put the phone down with a shaking hand. The conversation had not gone at all along the lines she had been planning in the car on the way home. Somehow, Lutz had managed to turn the whole thing back on her, to make her feel like the guilty party.

She went back into her bedroom, not expecting to be able to sleep. Instead she lay down and tried to wrestle with the turmoil inside her head. It seemed she had got her life hopelessly wrong and it was all her own doing. She had not drifted into this mess. She had worked hard to create it. She had no-one to blame but herself. Everyone who loved her had done their best to warn her.

And of the few friends she had in Munich, only Tom was left. Tom, whose needs and desires she had not even considered – so preoccupied had she been with herself. Yet now, when she did consider him, he aroused in her such feelings, her head began to spin with trying to sort them out. In the end she gave up the attempt. All that mattered was that she wanted to be with him – for him to hold her in his arms.

Upstairs, Tom could not sleep either. He could not get Viola out of his mind. It was clear to him that the time to get her out of Munich was way overdue. Whether Ebenau via Metzger – or Lessel via Metzger – meant her real harm, was impossible to know. But for no reason other than her peace of mind – which in his book was the best reason of all – it was imperative that he get her away.

211

They had made progress today, though. He was not just thinking that he had kissed her; he had tried all along to put personal considerations in second place. He was thinking of their conversation at Herrenchiemsee. She had talked so rationally then. He was sure, if only she could bring herself finally to leave Ebenau, she would soon get him out of her system – she was already more than half way there. She would need help. She would need time. The problem was, there was not much time left. If he and his colleagues got the breaks they wanted, it was conceivable that Ebenau would be charged in connection with one or other of the atrocities for which the Network were almost certainly responsible.

In the morning, whatever Werner said, he would see about getting her a flight back to England. Much as he hated the thought – from his own point of view – there was no alternative. He picked up the photographs of her and Ebenau he kept stashed away under his bed and shuffled through them.

A few minutes later, there was a gentle tap on his door – a tap so scarcely audible, he might never have heard it above the hammering of his heart, had he not been waiting, hoping, praying that it would come. He leapt to his feet. He started pulling on some clothes. His eyes fell upon the photographs and with a frantic scramble he gathered them together and stuffed them into an old copy of *Motorrad* magazine lying on the table beside his bed. Then he hurried to answer the door.

Viola he had expected; Viola in a silk dressing gown, her long, chestnut hair tumbling down her back, he was not prepared for.

"Viola, are you okay?" He did his best to sound controlled.

"Tom, I'm sorry to disturb you."

She had been disturbing him since they first met.

"I'm sure you were in bed."

"But not asleep."

"It's just, I'm really frightened."

She came into his flat, but walked straight past him – through into the bedroom – over to the window, so she could peer out of it down onto the crescent. She signalled that he should follow her and

212

look. When he did, he saw with irritation that it was only Heino – staring up at her window.

"That's the other one – the one I told you about in the car – the one who's followed me before. I can't believe Lutz is doing this to me."

Tom was on the verge of telling her who Heino really was. He hated this deception. "Agh, he doesn't look too scary to me. Just you wait here – I'll be right back."

Viola grabbed hold of his arm.

"No, Tom, *please* – I couldn't bear it if anything happened to you."

"Listen, nothing's going to happen to me. You just hang on, okay?"

Outside, Tom crept up on Heino, and took him by surprise. He dragged him back behind the hedge before he identified himself.

"Heino! What the hell are you doing here?" he grumbled.

"For Christ's sake, Tom; what's up with you? I told you I was coming round, to update you. I was just wondering if you were asleep, your lights are off. Listen, we've been building a really strong dossier around Ebenau. Still nothing to convict him, but enough circumstantial to get all the help we need from the banks, the tax people, all the official organisations who have any dealings with his office . . ."

"Great, but can't you fill me in with the details tomorrow? I'm in the throes of something else right now. And Heino," he paused, "this is the final straw – I'm sending you on a surveillance refresher course – you're bloody awful!"

Viola sat on a chair, waiting for what seemed inevitable – the sound of gunfire. She imagined Tom's body lying limp and lifeless on the pavement below – blood streaming from a wound that would be straight through his heart. Then suddenly he was standing in the doorway, grinning at her.

"It's okay. He's gone now. He was just some kid with the hots for you. You don't have to worry about him any longer. He won't be back. Listen, you're exhausted. Why don't you try and get some sleep."

"No, I can't sleep. I'm too scared."

"Don't be. Nothing's going to happen." He knew it sounded trite – but what else could he say? That he would move heaven and earth to protect her? That he would defend her to the death? "Look, sleep here tonight." He went over to his bed and threw back the duvet. He noticed a memo from Christian lying on the floor and did his best to kick it out of sight. "I'll take the couch next door." He pulled the covers over her. "Just call if you need me."

He left the door ajar, switched the radio on low and – with the object of lulling her to sleep – tuned it in to one of those all-night, soft-music stations. It used to work with him when he was a little boy. Though what he had loved the best, he now recalled, was when his grandmother would sit at his bedside and sing him lullabies in Polish or gently stroke his forehead with the palm of her hand. If he thought it would help her, he would do that tonight – sit at Viola's side, stroke her brow – just as gently – and simply be content with imagining how it would be to stroke all over her body – the most intimate parts of her body – with the palm of his hand and the tips of his fingers.

He stretched himself out on the couch. By chance the crack in the door separating them, aligned perfectly with the cushion he was using as a rest for his head, enabling him to see both that side of his bed on which Viola lay, as well as the window alongside it. Being an attic room, the roof sloped sharply either side so that, as the silver-white beams of moonlight purled their way across the ceiling, the glow reflected downwards onto the bed beneath – like shimmering, luminescent filigree.

At first Viola lay there motionless, but it was only a pretence of sleep. Before long she got up to look out of the window. Tom too got up and crossed over to the door to watch her. From where he stood, he could not see the moon, only its light as it shed an aura – magical and radiant – over her body. She gathered up her hair, held it for a moment high above her head, then let it tumble down, over

214

her shoulders, down her back to her waist, where it bounced up and down delighting in its freedom. She ran her hands through the tresses, combing them with her fingers; then she shook her head and allowed the hair to take flight around her body, while the moonlight spun through it, glinting gold and silver in the darkness. She loosened the tie around the gown and let it drop to the floor, revealing her underwear beneath.

Tom could hear his heart thundering. Surely she must hear it too – surely she must look around and see him. He longed that she would.

She started as he put his hands around her waist, but she did not pull away. Instead she leant against him and dropped her head back onto his chest. The heaviness of his breathing sent flurries of warm, seductive air fluttering across her – ruffling the wisps of hair which fringed her face. She let her head fall to one side, offering up her neck to the erotic potency of the sensation. Unable any longer to resist, Tom bent over and kissed it. He heard her catch her breath. He felt her shaking. And when he pulled her closer, so she could feel how he was shaking too, his hands slipped on the satin of her camisole and found themselves inside it, touching her skin.

Tom had needed nothing extra to arouse his passion – just the thought of making love to Viola was more than enough for that. But when he touched the skin of her body – soft and silken like the satin she was wearing – he felt such desire for her, it hurt him.

And as he continued to caress her body – daring to venture further bit by bit – he felt the same thrill she felt, pulsating back through the palms of his hands, as at last they found their way up to her breasts. He felt it through the tips of his fingers, as they brushed across her nipples. A sigh escaped her lips. The sound of it made him grow bolder. He wanted to gratify her every way he could.

Tom knew very well how to undress a woman. To him it was an intrinsic part of making love. But that was something new to Viola and so, when he pulled back to give himself the space that he required, she took it as a cue for her to turn around and face him. It was too soon for that. He stopped her – holding her shoulders firm in his huge hands.

With those hands he then gathered her hair together and swept it to one side to expose her shoulder and the thin strap of her camisole. Although there was no real need – it would have been a simple matter to pull the garment off over her head – he chose to untie the ribbons. As the bow fell apart, he felt her tremble. To heighten the sensation, he brushed his lips across the bareness of her skin.

She trembled more, as he lifted her hair to kiss behind her neck and make a path for himself across it to the other side. Once the second bow was loosened, her camisole – now bereft of its support – slithered across her skin and on down over her breasts. She expected him to take them in his hands again. In anticipation of the thrill it would give her, she held her breath. But he did not.

Another time she tried to turn around to face him. Another time she was frustrated. Instead, back and forth across her shoulders, he ran his fingertips – splaying them further and further apart, until his palms too were stroking the skin of her back. Using his thumbs, he searched out the tip of her backbone and with them carefully traced a path downwards along the length of her spine. When his hands came to her waist, he slid them down inside her knickers, still following the contours of her body – over her hips – onto her thighs – taking with them the last vestiges of her clothing which finally slipped and fell. Viola stepped out of them and kicked them to one side. Tom dropped onto his knees and back on his heels to kiss her buttocks. Now, he decided, was the time to turn her around.

With her hips in his hands, he swivelled her body to face him. She sighed aloud, stretched herself and – as part of the same instinctive action – arched her body back so far that her hair swept to and fro across the floor behind her. He gripped her hips tighter, enabling her to arch herself still further – allowing her pudenda to brush against his face. The scent of her filled his nostrils. He opened his mouth and the taste of her flowed around his tongue. So intoxicating was it, he reached deeper and deeper inside her, thirsting for more. She let out a sigh – louder than the one before – and then a scream

216

– the fragile scream of pleasure he had been waiting all this time to hear.

He got to his feet and lifted her high into the air above him. She tossed back her hair, so that he could look into her face and see her eyes. He lowered her slowly, pausing here and there to kiss her body – lingering longest as his lips drew level with her breasts. She closed her arms around his neck. She wrapped her legs around his waist. He eased her ever lower down his body – until the ultimate intimacy between them was only a hair's breadth away.

She pulled his head close to hers when he kept her waiting – so close her lips could skim across his ear.

"Tom," she whispered; he could hear the tremor in her voice, "sleep with me tonight?"

He whispered back, "I thought you'd never ask."

Chapter Twenty-Seven

Two hours later, in the misty, languorous frame of mind that denies inhibition between lovers, Tom found himself with an urgent desire to tell Viola the truth – because he hated lying to her; because he wanted her to be aware of the danger she was in from Lutz Ebenau, Peter Lessel and their henchmen.

The last thing he wanted was for her to leave Munich for London; but for her own safety, there was no question that it was the right thing to do. It was impossible to second guess the report Volker Metzger would have put in to whoever was his boss, although Tom did not doubt he had made much of his own presence with Viola.

Certainly, it was clear from what Lutz had said to her on the phone, that he had been informed of a growing closeness between them.

"Viola?" he whispered.

"Mmm?" she murmured sleepily.

"There's something I have to tell you."

"Mmm?"

"It's important. It's something I should've told you before."

"What is it?" she asked, a little more awake now.

"Look, before I tell you, I don't want you to worry. But I'm afraid it does mean you may have to leave Munich for a while."

Viola stirred, slid her back up the headboard until she was half sitting. Tom could just make out the profile of her face in the moonlight.

"It's about Lutz Ebenau," he said as calmly as he could.

"I thought it might be," she said with a break in her voice.

"I don't want to upset you. I know you've had a relationship with him for a long time. But I've got to warn you."

Viola jerked her head round. "Warn me?"

"Yeah. I'm afraid there are two people in your life who aren't quite what they seem. Lutz Ebenau," he paused, "and me."

"You? What are you, then?"

Tom gritted his teeth, hating, for duty's sake, to tell her yet another lie. "I'm not a sports reporter; I'm an investigative journalist. I've been running a series of in-depth pieces on the Neo-Fascist parties of Europe, specifically of Germany, given that I'm more or less a native speaker."

"What?" screeched Viola. "You mean you've been using me as part of your investigations?"

"Up to a point, yes."

"*Up to a point*. What do you mean?"

"Listen, Viola, everything's different now but to start with I was just following up a lead that you were over here to take out Professor Feinstein – for the Fascists. Okay, I now know that was total garbage, but you did have a connection with Lessel. And then, just recently, I've been taking a closer look at Lutz Ebenau."

"At Lutz? Why?"

Tom saw the look of alarm – alarm at something not entirely unanticipated. But he had to rein back a second, think about what it would do to her, even to her relationship with him, when he told her. He decided he would have to tell her now, whatever official policy back at HQ might be. He could not justify taking chances with anyone's life – most particularly not with the life of this woman.

"What I'm going to tell you I can't prove," he began, "but all my instincts – my journalistic instincts – tell me I'm right about it."

"What for God's sake?"

Tom took a deep breath. "Lutz Ebenau is almost certainly head of an organisation known as the Network – one of the most influential Fascist groups in Germany – in the whole of Europe. You probably met several of his national counterparts, down at Füssen, that weekend you told me about."

"You mean the male gathering, his friends from the big business schools?"

"Every single one of those men is known by their own police to have deep involvement in Far Right politics. We . . . I think that Ebenau and Lessel were responsible for ordering all the bombing, arson and rioting that's been going on in Munich over the last few months."

"The shootings, too?" Viola whispered.

"Yes, I'm afraid so."

Viola did not respond at once, then, still whispering, she said, "Josef, Ellie, both dead. And Lutz – Now you tell me, it all makes sense. In the last few weeks I have seen a side of him he's never shown me before." She let out a loud, desperate sob. "How could I have been such a fool. I was so obsessed with him – or what he was when I first knew him. He couldn't have been a Fascist then – I'm sure he couldn't. He always told me he supported what the Greens stood for." With the back of her hand she wiped away the tears that had welled up in her eyes. "Even when I saw the signs, I fooled myself they weren't real. Oh God, what have I done?"

"Viola, Viola," Tom murmured gently, guessing how she must feel inside. "None of this is your fault."

"But I should have guessed sooner. And I suppose it explains why that horrible man's been hanging about. Lutz must have organised it, to keep tabs on me. But Tom," she gasped suddenly. "Doesn't this mean you're in danger, too. I mean, not just because he'll be jealous, but because he might think you know too much?"

"Probably; that goes with the territory," Tom brushed it off. "But there's no way you should go on being exposed to this. You'd better start making arrangements to get home, as soon as you can. Though God knows," he added, "I'm going to miss you."

Tom had a broad smile on his face when he woke after a couple of hours' deep sleep. After the night he had just spent, it was hardly surprising. He was at that transitional stage which lies like a no-man's-land between sleep and wakefulness, in which it is difficult to distinguish fact from fiction – dreams from actuality.

An accelerated action-replay did nothing to settle the matter. It served only to re-awaken the urge to make love to Viola that had kept him going, almost non-stop, all night long. If, when he rolled over, Viola was not in his bed, then it had all been one long, erotic dream. If she was there, then he would slowly rouse every inch of that beautiful body of hers with hot, passionate kisses – from the tips of her toes upwards. He would not care how long it took. He would enjoy every second. After that he would make love to her again, so he could hear again how sweet it sounded when she cried his name – not Ebenau's – not anybody else's – but his. The very thought of it confirmed that last night had been no dream.

But when he opened his eyes, all he saw were the photographs of her and Ebenau, neatly arranged in a little pile in the middle of the pillow. The cold sweat of panic struck him.

He leapt out of bed, pulled on some trousers – the first pair that came to hand – and ran down to her flat. Half way down the stairs he sprang over the banisters to land directly outside her door. He knocked, gently at first – then progressively more loudly. There was no reply. He pulled out his skeleton keys and let himself in.

He knew she was gone the minute he walked through the door. He knew it before that – but now it was substantiated. There was that sense of emptiness and silence to the flat. It made him feel hollow inside. He looked into her bedroom. Her bed was made. Of course it would be – she had spent last night in his. He glanced around the room. Everything appeared to be in place. Her books still lay open on her desk. The photographs of her little nephews still stood on the table beside her bed. Her thick Arran sweater still hung over the back of the armchair. It all looked much as it always did; as though she had just popped out for a minute to get some rolls for breakfast, to post a letter, to fetch something from her car. But he was only fooling himself by even contemplating that – and he knew it.

His eyes continued their investigation of her bedroom, pausing when they reached her wardrobe. It was one of those large, old-fashioned types with drawers all down one side. Several of the drawers had been left open and their contents in a jumble – as though she had been rummaging through them in a hurry, looking for something. Underneath them, he noticed, on the floor – as if they had been thrown there – the satin camisole and knickers she had been wearing last night. He walked across and picked them up. In doing so, he untrapped the scent of her body locked inside them; it wafted up to meet his face. He stuffed the garments into his trouser pocket and carried on searching.

Her car would be gone. He was prepared for that. But years of training or habit – or perhaps simply hope – had programmed him to require proof, so he went back into the sitting-room, crossed over to the window and checked. He need not have bothered. It did nothing except underline the finality of it all. His mind flashed back to the neat pile of photographs on his bed and pain filled his heart.

He crouched down on his knees and buried his head in his hands. He held that position for several minutes – just long enough to conclude that capitulating to self-pity would get him nowhere. It would not get Viola back. It would not help him find her. But find her he would. He stood up and looked around the room for anything, however small, that might give him a clue as to where she might have gone. And there it was, staring him in the face, a letter lying on the table beside her sofa. He picked it up.

"Dearest Flower,

"No time for pleasantries. Where the bloody hell have you been? I've been trying to get you all day.

"1. You're booked onto Flight LH 4080 out of Munich for tomorrow i.e. your TODAY December 11th. at 13.05 (pick up ticket at airport). Be on it!

"2. Have made enquiries. There is NO Tom Pajak – repeat NO Tom Pajak – known to *The Houston Chronicle* – not as a sports reporter – not as a tea-boy – not in any bloody capacity whatsoever. So who the hell is he? Don't ask him. Just get out of there!

"3. LUTZ EBENAU IS PETER LESSEL'S BOSS! I've just had it from my contact at the BBC. I don't know how the hell you got yourself mixed up with this, but he is DANGEROUS. He and his merry men are about to go public i.e. enter the political arena in a big way. Not sure what's going to happen there – but you've got to get out.

"4. Get yourself along to the Police. Tell them everything about anything you know. You said yourself the Police Chief was nice to you. Ask him to be nice to you again and let you borrow one of his big, strong, handsome policemen to take you to the airport.

"5. I'm sending this by courier to make sure you get the plane info in time. See you this afternoon. No excuses.

"Love Hilly."

So that was where Viola would be. Not at the airport – it was not even ten-thirty – but at the Polizeipräsidium. He was convinced of it. He calmed down a little. After all, he knew how prepared Viola would be to do as her friend suggested and go to see Werner Fuchs.

She would be there now – telling Fuchs not only about Metzger following her to Herrenchiemsee and showing up at the wedding, but about the man hanging around outside her home last night – in other words, Heino – and about the bogus journalist, Tom Pajak, who had become her lover. All at once Tom's heart began to pump faster. He felt his hands grow clammy. Not because she would be telling the Chief about last night – despite his warnings, he was an understanding man, a forgiving man. But because she would not be telling the Chief at all – he would not be there – because today the Chief was in Bonn, attending a high level conference with the Interior Minister. All of which meant that Viola would be telling their story to someone else.

He left almost straight away. He would have left sooner than that, but Frau Doktor Menne waylaid him. She had seen Viola leaving in tears and wondered if he could throw any light upon the reason. He placated the old lady as best he could, but in the end had to be short with her in order to get away.

Just as Tom reached his floor of the Polizeipräsidium, he saw Schneider coming out of one of the interview rooms up the corridor. Schneider in turn spotted him and proceeded to make a gesture so explicitly obscene, Tom was left in no doubt he already knew about last night. Tom's heart sank. Of all the people Viola could have talked to, why, he asked himself, did it have to be Schneider? Mohrfeld would have been discreet. Heino would have been understanding. Silke would have been supportive. But Schneider – God only knew how he had handled it; probably demanding a run-down of how many times they had had sex – and in which positions.

Schneider slapped him on the back, as Tom drew level. "So, Jablonski, I knew you'd get your dick out in the end, you randy sod."

He slapped Tom on the back a second time. Tom tried to brush him off. Schneider persisted. "I don't know why you're acting so crabby. Jesus Christ, if I'd had a crack at *that* last night," Schneider pointed his thumb over his shoulder at the interview room behind him, "I'd have a bloody big grin all over my face today."

"She's still in there?" asked Tom, nodding at the door. "I need to see her."

Schneider bellowed with laughter. "I bet you do. Anyway, got to go and collect my winnings. I might have lost the couple of hundred marks I had on you pulling it off by the end of the Oktoberfest – but I had a thousand on you fucking her before Christmas. Such is my faith in you, Jablonski."

Tom did not reply – just pushed past Schneider, went into the room and shut the door behind him. Viola was sitting quietly, looking at an untouched cup of coffee on the table in front of her. She seemed so small – like a waif. He walked across and put his hand on her shoulder. She flinched and pulled away, then stared up at him with reddened, wounded eyes. When she spoke, it was in a voice so faint he could barely hear it.

"If you've all finished with me here, I'd like to go."

She stood up and walked across the room. Tom dithered around her. For the first time in his life – now, when it mattered most – he

224

simply did not know what to do. She opened the door and walked out. Tom hurried around her to block her path.

"Viola, we've got to talk."

"I don't want to, Tom – if Tom *is* your name, of course." There was an acerbic edge to her voice which cut him to the quick, and she kept on walking.

"Listen, Viola – everything about me's the same as it was before. It's only my job and surname are different. And they're not important. Hell, what's in a name? What's important is what's happened between us – what we mean to each other."

"And what's that, Tom? I'm so important to you – I mean so much to you – you couldn't tell me who you really are? How important to you does that make me?"

Tom noticed they were no longer alone in the corridor. Quite a little audience was gathering. He had no intention of sorting out his love life in public; he took hold of her arm and opened the first door they came to. She tried to shake him off, but he was not about to let her go and almost had to push her into the room.

Inside it he found Heino and Anke pretending to do some filing. The mere fact that it was Heino was bound to add to the insult, Tom realised, but there was nothing he could do about it.

"Heino, I think you'll find those files on my desk," he said curtly.

Heino took a moment to work out what was going on. He was alarmed to see that Viola did not appear to have come willingly with Tom. But it was clear his colleague was in difficulty of some kind and needed to be left alone with her. He took Anke by the wrist and led her from the room.

As soon as they went, Tom shut the door and leaned against it. Now Viola would just have to hear him out.

"So he was one of you all along." Viola sounded angry – and getting angrier by the minute. He understood. She had good reason. "How could you, Tom? You let me worry myself sick last night that man was going to kill you – when all the time you knew him."

"I wanted to tell you. But I couldn't. I'd had orders not to."

"*Orders!*" Viola no longer bothered herself with any attempt at self-control. She was shouting. "And I suppose it was in your *orders* to get me into bed? And what about those photographs I found? What were they for? To make sure there was no mistake – to make sure you *fucked* the right person?"

She had never in her life used that word before. It shocked them both.

"I *made love* to you, Viola, because I love you."

"You made love to me – if that's what you so nicely want to call it – because it was your *job*."

"No, that's not true."

"Tom, I deluded myself once. I'm not going to do it again. I may have acted like one, but I'm not a fool." She was shaking now – not with anger – but with hurt. "You've been using me all this time just to find out what I knew about Lutz and Peter Lessel. You were following orders, like you said. For you, I suppose last night was all in a day's work, wasn't it? Well, I can't tell you any more about Lutz than I already have, so I'm no more use to you. *Now* will you let me go?"

"No Viola, I can't. I've got to make you see, it wasn't like that at all. It wasn't some kind of *act*."

He caught hold of her shoulders. This time she did not try to pull away – but she did tremble; though from what emotion he could not be sure. He lowered his voice.

"Viola, I love you. You've got to believe me."

He looked into her eyes. They were so full of tears he could not make out their expression. But her voice, when she responded, sounded simply sad.

"Oh Tom, I don't know what to believe any more. *Please* – just let me go."

She pushed him away from the door and he watched her leave.

Chapter Twenty-Eight

Tom pulled himself together. What the hell was he thinking of – standing aside while Viola Addison walked out of his life? He ran out into the corridor and along to the service staircase. If he took that route he was pretty sure he could intercept her before she left the building. He passed Schneider on his way up.

"Losing your touch, Jablonski?" he taunted.

"Have you seen her?" asked Tom, not rising to the bait.

"She just left."

"Shit! D'you know where?"

"England. She gave me a couple of contact addresses when I interviewed her."

Tom thought of the plane ticket Hillary Farrell had organised. "Okay, Schneider – thanks."

He found Heino at his desk, and quickly put him in the picture, with instructions about what he wanted him to do.

"Right, now I'm off," he finished. "But remember, Heino – even if Viola's *not* at the apartment – you still need to pump the old lady for any info you can get."

"What shall I do if she *is* there? Bring her in – or what?"

"Just use your common sense. But stay with her," Tom called back over his shoulder. "Don't let her out of your sight – no matter what."

Sending Heino over to the crescent was simply a precaution. Tom did not think for one moment that Viola would go back to her flat – let alone that Frau Doktor Menne would be able to throw any light on her plans. No, Tom was convinced he would catch up with her at the airport.

When he got there, he did not bother sifting through the masses milling around the concourse, but got hold of a computer print-out of the passengers who had already checked in. He scanned through it. Good – he had beaten her to it. Now all he had to do was wait until she showed up.

On his way through the departure area, he noticed Ebenau's picture on the front page of the newspapers piled high on one of the kiosks. He bought a copy. Of course! Given the past few days' events, he had almost forgotten that today sentence was being passed on some of the hard-core thugs they had rounded up after the riots following Professor Feinstein's funeral. He skimmed the article. Well, at least he could rule Ebenau out of the current equation. He would hardly be in a position to get his clutches into Viola if he were tied up in court.

He glanced at his watch yet again and began to feel agitated. Even so, it was not until final calls came up for Flight LH 4080 that it entered his head Viola was not going to show.

His mobile rang. As soon as he heard the tone in Heino's voice, Tom knew something was wrong.

"She's not there then?"

"No," answered Tom. "And they're embarking now." He looked about him. "So where the hell is she?"

"They've got her, Tom."

"What d'you mean?"

"I think Lessel's got her . . ."

Tom felt his whole store of vital organs plummet to the pit of his stomach.

" . . . I went round to her flat – but I must have just missed her. I had a look around. She'd taken a few things – not much. And she'd packed those in a hurry, according to the old lady – while a man waited for her in a car outside. From the description she gave me of the car and its driver – it had to be Lessel."

"Jesus Christ!" Tom bit his lip. "Listen, Heino, I'm going to tell you what to do, and you'd better not screw it up."

Back at the Polizeipräsidium Heino followed Tom's instructions to the letter, first telling Schneider what had happened, then repeating it all to Mohrfeld. The order was significant. Heino knew only half the story and would inevitably leave gaps in relating it to Mohrfeld – whereas after his interview with Viola, there was nothing Schneider did not know.

"I think Tom's right," Schneider said, "Lessel will be acting on Ebenau's orders and have taken her to Füssen. There's about a ten per cent chance she got into that car knowing exactly what she was doing, and ninety per cent that he's tricked her. As soon as we get a trace on Lessel's car, I reckon we go with the odds and get a team of men over there. That woman's in danger, I can feel it."

Heino nodded. Mohrfeld looked doubtful. "If you and Tom are wrong, this department is going to be the laughing stock of Munich. More to the point, a lawsuit with Ebenau involved could cripple us. But I think I have to agree with you. We've been maintaining this investigation on gut instinct for too long to give up now." He sighed. "Shit! Werner's going to have my badge for authorising a stunt like this."

Over at the Law Courts, the media machine was making things difficult for Tom. Without going in heavy handed – an approach Tom had ruled out in advance – he could not get near Ebenau. Patience did not come naturally to Tom. It was something he had to work at. Nonetheless, even he realised the overwhelming necessity for it now. The last thing he could afford to do was rattle Ebenau – or Lessel, what with TV cameras and a clutch of journalists on hand to record the scene. So he hung back. He sidled over to a friend of his, there on duty to get the lowdown on the sentencing. It had been draconian.

He edged closer and relied on blending in with the reporters. What he heard was evidently the tail end of a prepared statement. There sounded to be nothing new in it. The departure from the norm came afterwards. Ebenau took questions.

"Acting, as it does, within a strict framework, the Law alone can only do so much," stated Ebenau in answer to a point raised by one of the journalists. "It serves either to punish – in its active capacity – or, to a lesser, passive extent, to deter. Of itself it has no other power. It cannot deal with the social issues which cause the offender to offend. *That* is a matter for government."

"So you put the blame for the recent riots squarely on the shoulders of politicians?"

"That is not what I said. I wish merely to point out that ultimately it is those in government who must bear responsibility for any civil unrest, including racial; certainly on the scale we have seen recently."

"As a result of your experience in dealing with the legal aftermath of such disturbances, do you believe statutory changes will be needed to stop this escalation in racial tension?"

"I do," responded Ebenau without a moment's hesitation. "Radical changes. Of course, they will only work if they reflect natural justice. If they are palliatives, simply to manipulate public opinion in favour of the interests of minority groups, for example – then they will do more harm than good. The German people will not be hood-winked. The Aryan intellect is too astute for that."

That single word was all it took. It meant Ebenau had decided to burn the bridges which, at least ostensibly, connected him with the Establishment. Tom guessed that this must be Phase One of the "going public", which Hilly had referred to in her note to Viola.

The journalists present also detected this dramatic new element in the racial debate and were caught between their desire to hear more and their urge to get back to their keyboards.

"It is time for firm measures – to undo the damage caused by years of liberal propaganda," Ebenau continued, liberated by the knowledge that his was no longer a covert fight. "We must take whatever steps are needed – however painful – to free ourselves from the guilt of a history that has been so flagrantly misrepresented."

The rhetoric stopped abruptly as Lutz's eyes alighted upon Tom's. They narrowed almost imperceptibly, then dropped down to his watch. When they looked up again, there was a certain smugness in them.

"Over the coming months," resumed Ebenau, "we shall doubtless have ample opportunity to pursue this debate. But for now, gentlemen, I must call it to a halt. I see I am already running late for my interview with *The Houston Chronicle*. Thank you and good afternoon."

"So, Mr *Pajak*," Lutz Ebenau gave the name deliberate, sarcastic stress, "What would you like to ask me on behalf of *The Houston Chronicle?*"

"On behalf of myself, I'd like to ask you what the hell you've done with Viola."

Ebenau's eyes narrowed again. His mouth stretched a fraction wider, into a knowing smile. "You talk as if she had been abducted."

"She was picked up by your friend Lessel, and hasn't been seen since."

Ebenau stared back at Tom, giving nothing away. "I am not responsible for what Peter Lessel does. He is his own man, and in any event, I see no reason why Viola should not have gone with him of her own accord."

"She wanted to be taken to the airport, but she never arrived."

"You were there to see her off? How very touching. If I see her again, I shall mention that to her."

Tom filled Schneider in back at the station.

"So did you get *anywhere* with him over Viola?"

"No. He's not going to tell us where she is – but I know she's in Füssen."

"So what *did* he say?"

"That Lessel's his own man. That he has no information on his movements *or* his whereabouts."

"Does he know you've been banging her?"

"He does."

"Okay. Look, they're bound to get a trace on Lessel's car soon.

And Mohrfeld's getting a team ready on standby. So don't worry. We'll find her."

Not worrying was easier said than done. It was possible as long as things were moving forward – but hanging around, waiting for something to break, it was not. Back at his desk, Tom put up his feet, cradled his neck in his hands and decided to use the lull in order to take stock of the situation – until Heino broke into his train of thought.

"Tom – we're on the move. They've tracked Lessel's car and confirmed there's a female passenger of the right description, plus two men in the rear."

Tom leapt up. His telephone started to ring while he was disentangling his jacket from the back of his chair. He looked down – it was an internal call. He swore under his breath, but picked up the receiver. He put it to his ear but covered the mouthpiece with his hand, so he could first grill Heino.

"So where are they?"

"Just north of Füssen."

"Any news of Ebenau yet?"

"He's heading south as well."

Tom removed his hand from the mouthpiece.

"Sorry, I didn't quite catch that."

"I've got a Ms Hillary Farrell on the line," the voice told him. "Says she's Dr Viola Addison's friend – the journalist from London. She insists on speaking to whoever's in charge of the case."

"Okay. Put her through."

"Miss Farrell? Tom Jablonski. How can I help?"

"I'm calling about Viola Addison. Your colleague tells me ·she came in to see you this morning."

"That's right."

"So you know what she's managed to get herself mixed up in?"

"We are fully aware of the situation, yes."

"And did you know she was supposed to be flying home to London today?"

"There was mention of it," Tom said, deliberately low key. He could not see any benefit in telling Hilly Farrell that he was as worried as hell.

"Well, she wasn't on the plane. That's why I'm phoning. Look, something must have happened to her – otherwise she'd have let me know by now what's going on."

"Don't worry, Miss Farrell. We know exactly where she is."

Tom heard her sigh in relief.

"Then *now* you need to give her protection – *and* persuade her to come home. You've met her – you've seen for yourself what a dreamer she is. She just doesn't realise the danger she's in."

"Miss Farrell, I assure you, your friend's safety is uppermost in my mind." Tom paused. He could see Schneider and Heino indicating that he should wind up the conversation. "I shall be dealing with the matter myself – just as soon as I've taken your call."

"Then I'd better let you go. But please, when you speak to her, tell her to give me a ring – as soon as she can – so I know she's all right."

"I'll do that."

Out of the corner of his eye Tom could see Schneider still signalling for him to get a move on.

"What was your name again?"

"Tom Jablonski."

The minute Tom put down the receiver, Schneider bellowed at him clear across the room.

"Pull your finger out, Jablonski. I've got a helicopter wearing its bloody rotor blades out, waiting to take us to Füssen. What the hell are you pratting about at?"

"Okay. Let's move."

Chapter Twenty-Nine

Viola lay on the crisp, white cotton-covered duvet in what had become her bedroom in the house in Füssen, trying to control the fear that permeated her whole being. She wondered what stroke of madness had let her be taken in by Peter Lessel. Perhaps some shred of doubt that Hilly and Tom were wrong?

And now she was a prisoner in what amounted to an armed fortress. Cold-eyed, gun-flaunting men strutted around in the grounds or laughed in the servants' quarters of the house. Even the man who had followed her was there and Peter Lessel had taken great pleasure in introducing him to her so that she knew his name, Volker Metzger.

She heard a key turn in the lock of the door, and then a creak as it was pushed slowly open. Clenching her fists, she told herself she must not, at any cost, let Lutz see how scared she really was.

"Lutz, why have you brought me here?" she demanded.

"I hope Peter reassured you."

"No, Peter just lied to me – laid on the charm." She shook her head in anger at her own stupidity. "I must have been mad, allowing myself to be taken in by him; by his saying he realised that it was in my best interests to get back to England right away. Then the *bastard* locked me in his car and two of your heavies jumped into the back seat. All done with your connivance, no doubt."

Lutz made a face to suggest it was beneath his dignity to reply.

"I suppose it was you who told him to rant on about my having fallen under evil influences," Viola said, "about my needing peace and solitude to sort myself out. Did you tell him to say that?"

"Schätzlein," he tried to hold her, but she pulled herself away, "Schätzlein, please, consider your situation logically. If you do, then you must reach the conclusion that your present behaviour makes no sense. Why would you be prepared to throw away the very love you have kept alive for so many years? Think back to our reunion. We both agreed then, there was no alteration, no diminution in our feelings. You said yourself – our love had transcended all its difficulties."

"But things have happened since then – things that have made me feel differently. And Lutz, we've been through all of this. Why can't you understand, I've *changed*."

"It is not *you* who have changed, but others who are trying to change you. No wonder your emotions are in a state of turmoil – that you have become blinded to your inner self. *They* have blinded you."

She sighed. "I suppose you're talking about Tom?" Viola marked the tightening of his jaw at the mention of the name.

"*And* the Jew. His influence over you was insidious."

She slumped onto the window seat. What hope had she of getting through to a mind – a heart – as bigoted as this?

"Well, for whatever reason, Lutz – it's now over between us. Please just accept that."

"I cannot. And once you have had time to reconsider – away from all such corrupting influences – you will not believe it either."

"What are you saying? That you are going to keep me here – against my will?"

"It is for your own protection. You will thank me for it as soon as you are well again. And here you *will* be restored to health. *I* shall restore you. We shall walk. We shall discuss. We shall . . ."

He pulled her to her feet and took her in his arms. This time she did not try to pull away. She was too scared for that. She remembered once telling Tom how she thought Lutz would never allow anyone to stand between him and his dream. Now, through tear-filled eyes, she saw the frightening consequences of that prediction.

"You need to rest. You must have lots of rest. And you must trust me, Schätzlein. I know this is best for you – for both of us."

Viola half expected to hear the click of the lock as he shut the door behind him. But one glance out of the window told her there was no real need for that. She turned around and surveyed the room. It seemed far smaller than when she had last been there – no bigger than a prison cell – and dominated by its bed. She gazed at it. She pictured herself on it – naked – spread-eagled – Lutz on top of her – Lutz inside her. The image made her feel nauseous.

She looked away – out of the window and upwards. The light was almost gone now. But even without it she could tell it was about to snow. The sky was heavy with it – closing in on the house – trapping her. In the distance she could hear the muffled whirring of a helicopter. How she wished she were inside it – flying away from reality – off into oblivion.

The helicopter touched down only long enough to deposit its passengers. Conditions had worsened steadily all the way down from Munich and the pilot was anxious to get back to base, while he was still able.

"You're right, Tom," grunted Schneider, as he tried to straighten his stiffened joints. "I must be mad. No fifty-year-old in his right mind plays these kind of games for a living."

Tom grinned and bundled him into one of the waiting vans. The rest of the squad piled in after them. Once the last man was inside and the door shut, Schneider stopped his grumbling and settled them down to business.

"All right – it seems we've got no choice. We'll have to storm the place. The local boys have tried the soft option, but Ebenau's denying he's got her."

"Have we had a confirmed sighting of her here yet?" Tom asked.

"She was seen being driven in through the gates, and other than Lessel no-one's been out since," Heino contributed.

"Right," Schneider said, asserting his authority. "There's no point pissing about. We've got to get you lot *in* there and we've got to get her *out*. Now give us the set up." He indicated to one of his surveillance team to take over from him.

"Okay, this is what we know. The perimeter fence is wired. It's also high. And – just to add to your challenge and amusement –it's being patrolled by what appears to be a private army. The only way in, as far as we can tell – *and* without giving the game away – is over the top of the fence."

"Is that possible?" asked Tom.

"Round the back it is. There are overhanging trees. But it's not going to be a cinch. It'll take nerve."

"Okay, so once we're in," he continued, "do we know anything about the lay-out of the place?"

Here another of the regular undercover team followed on and produced a rough outline drawing of the interior. He passed it around so that everyone could take a look.

"Don't get too excited," he warned. "I've no idea how accurate this is. It's cobbled together from odds and sods I've managed to get from the local window cleaner." He grinned across at Tom. "There's a limit to what you can work into the conversation over a beer in the local Gaststätte."

They peered at the plan for several minutes.

"I take it the house is wired, too," commented Tom, thinking aloud, "so once we're inside the garden, we need to hang fire until we see which door they're using." He looked up. "Are there dogs?"

"No. Our guess is Ebenau doesn't think he needs them."

"Good," said Tom. "Right – when are we going in?"

"Over the fence around midnight?" proposed Schneider. "Do whatever's got to be done. Then we can make it back to civilisation for breakfast."

"Other than for the men on watch, how many people are we going to find when we get in there?" This was the first time Heino had spoken.

"When *we* get in there, Timmermann?" countered Tom. "*You* are going to be out here – helping Schneider co-ordinate this little jaunt."

Schneider noticed the expression on Heino's face but ignored it as he pushed on.

"There's just Ebenau, Addison, a dotty, old housekeeper, and a couple of maids; that's what we've been told."

By midnight, Tom had relented over Heino's joining the main force. Schneider had put in a good word for him. While agreeing with Tom that he was probably not ready for it, how else, Schneider had pointed out, was he ever going to learn? So Heino went along.

Access to the garden went without a hitch. For Tom and his team, the entry, via tree and ropes, presented no problems. It took Heino longer to lower himself down, he was so anxious not to swing against the fence and trigger the alarm. But by that time, the nearest of the guards had already been immobilised and taken out of play, so some of the pressure was off.

It was snowing heavily by now. A mixed blessing – what made it hard for guard to spot intruder worked both ways. But once inside, the squad would have the advantage of surprise.

One by one, the patrol guards were silently struck down, concussed and trussed with their mouths taped. The building was encircled. The garden taken, the infiltrators settled down to wait until a way into the house could be identified and the signal came to move in. Not a man there was unaware of the danger, if that push came too soon. Tom decided to keep Heino with him.

"Presumably the only guards left are the ones we can see in the kitchen," whispered Tom. "Given there's no other light on downstairs."

"Some might be upstairs asleep," suggested Heino.

"According to Schneider, they never stay on site. No, I suspect that's it. How many d'you reckon it is?"

"Six at most."

"Yeah; we should be able to handle that," Tom said with quiet confidence. "We all go in together. These guys take care of Ebenau's merry men while you and I dash upstairs and get Viola."

"How d'you know which room she's in?"

"I don't. I'm hoping something'll happen soon to give me a clue."

"Well, we're pretty sure there are only three people on the first floor. The maids are in the attic rooms. The housekeeper's supposed to be ancient, so the chances are it's not *her* burning the midnight oil . . ."

"Hmm." Tom was not convinced of the logic of that.

" . . . Just *suppose* I'm right. That leaves two rooms and two people – presumably the evil Ebenau's in one and Viola's in the other. But how we can work out which is which, I don't know."

It was worked out for them. Even before Tom had chance to reply, one of the upstairs rooms was plunged into darkness. A few minutes later the shadow of a man appeared behind the curtains of the other and a few minutes after that, the silhouette of Viola – her hair loose behind her back – stood facing him.

"Okay. That's it," breathed Tom. "We're on our way."

Viola had kept her light on, not so much because she knew she would not sleep; but because – for the first time in her life – she felt afraid of the dark. And there had seemed only darkness ahead of her – whichever way forward she looked. Lutz was never going to set her free. His actions today went to prove that. They simply reinforced the intransigence of his position and the hopelessness of her own. The one crumb of comfort – and it was only a speck – was that it appeared he was not expecting to share her bed. Yet no sooner had she seized upon that slight cause for consolation, than a knock on the door took even that away.

"I noticed your light was still on. It *is* difficult to sleep, I know."

His tone had been conciliatory. Viola took heart.

"How could you expect me to sleep, Lutz, when I'm nothing more than your prisoner?"

"You are not my prisoner, any more than I am yours, Schätzlein. We can neither of us escape a love that is stronger than both of us."

"But I'm *not* in love with you, Lutz. You are not the man I thought you were."

At that, his whole demeanour changed abruptly. He grabbed her by the shoulders and began to shake until her head lolled back and forth – so much out of control, she feared her neck would break.

Suddenly her vision blurred and she yelled out in pain and terror.

To silence her, or in some manic attempt to make her better, Lutz suddenly leaned down and pressed his lips hard onto hers, forcing his tongue down inside her mouth. His nose, his cheek crushed her nostrils, blocking the only other passage to air she had. She struggled to free herself but – striving for oxygen – she did not struggle long. She ceased to fight. He slackened his hold – and she breathed again.

"Lutz!" she gasped, "you can't *make* someone love you."

As soon as she spoke the words, she thought what a fool she had been. She knew it when he forced his hand up between her legs – so high that, even through the cotton of her nightdress, the jabbing of his fingers hurt her. She cried out loud. To smother the sound, he put the palm of his hand over her mouth and held it there. She tried to grip his fingers – to prise them open – but she could not make them budge.

No longer conscious of what she was doing – only aware that this was a battle not just for her body, but also for her soul – she grabbed hold of his wrist with both her hands and sunk her nails deep into his skin. She dug harder and harder – until it was not she groaning in agony, but Ebenau. He pulled away and stared down in disbelief at the blood oozing out of his wrists.

Here was her chance. Viola edged a step or two backwards – then darted for the door. The bid was futile. She got no further than a couple of paces before she was stopped with a jolt. She heard the screech of fibre rent from fibre. She felt her nightdress ripped away as Ebenau's hands grabbed out and seized it.

Now Viola stood naked and motionless in front of him – stripped not only of her clothing, but of her courage too. Ebenau crossed over to the door, propped himself against it and with her nightdress dabbed at the blood leaching from his wounded wrist. But he did not look at it. His eyes were fixed on her – on her body. Viola could feel her heart beating inside her. It thumped so fast, she thought it would explode. She wished it would. That way at least, she would be free.

He walked towards her. She backed away. He drew closer. She

wanted to speak to him – to plead with him – but when she opened her mouth, no sound came out. He reached out, gave her an almost gentle push and back she fell – onto the bed. She tried to pull herself up, but he shoved her backwards – hard this time – and harder again the next. Then he stood over her, staring down into her face. Whatever the look was in his eyes, it filled her whole being with dread. He removed that look for a moment – just long enough for him to tear strips of fabric off her nightdress. He caught hold of her hands, bound the strips around her wrists and tied them to the bed.

It seemed like an eternity before he thrust himself inside her; though the air she expelled, when finally he did, acted to free her vocal chords and she let out a terrified scream. The deeper, the harder, the faster he bored into her, the louder the screams grew. She did not care if her lungs burst – anything was better than feeling him come inside her.

The six guards resting in the kitchen did not have time even to pick up their weapons as the men from the Munich task force entered the room at four different points. They were experienced enough to know that a gun at the head was not worth gambling against. There was no resistance as each of them was handcuffed and taped.

Tom had just found his way into the hall when he heard Viola's screams. Only in his dreams had he heard cries like these before. So full of horror, they seared through into his brain. He chased the sound up the stairs and along the landing.

In a matter of seconds he burst the door to the room wide open. From then on Tom acted solely upon reflex. He hurled himself across the room. With one hand he caught hold of Ebenau's shoulder, with the other he snatched a handful of his hair. Then he jerked his head right back and kept on tugging at it – in a frenzy to set Viola free. Their bodies snapped apart – and when they did, semen spewed out of Ebenau, spraying a trail across her stomach.

Viola shrieked in disgust.

"Heino," shouted Tom. "Get her out of here."

The command brought the hitherto stunned Heino to his senses. He took out his knife and cut Viola loose. She began to grapple with the sheets on the bed beneath her and, hysterical by now, rubbed at her stomach as hard as she could – desperate to cleanse the pollution from her body. Heino fussed around, wondering what to do next – until Tom yelled at him again.

"For Christ's sake, Timmermann. Get her out."

Now Heino acted. When she would not let go of the bedding, he wrapped her in it and put her arms around his neck. He picked her up and carried her from the room.

Once Tom had got Ebenau trussed up, he crouched down and allowed himself to draw breath. He said nothing to Ebenau – or Ebenau to him – each man realising the pointlessness of further confrontation – or else too drained for it. Tom thought of Viola and wondered how much she had been hurt. He thought of her screams, of the fright in her eyes. He could kill Ebenau for raping her – for tying her down to rape her. He could kill him for putting her through this whole ordeal.

And he could do it now. Ebenau was his prisoner – unarmed, unguarded, powerless. No-one would know. He could say it had been in self-defence. None of the guys in the squad would question it. Tom knew that in his position they would be contemplating the same themselves. In his current frame of mind he could even justify it. He would be doing Society a favour. He knew of course, it was not Society he was thinking of.

He stared across at Ebenau, kneeling next to him on the floor. He looked at his eyes – at the contempt in them. Just then he picked up a sudden shift in their expression. It lasted no longer than an instant. But that was all it needed to put Tom back on full alert. He registered the click of a revolver catch behind him. He homed in on the sound and, in that selfsame second, propelled himself round towards it. He was already close to the ground. It was an easy matter to bring the man down by his ankles – like a trip-tackle in football he had done a thousand times in high school.

At the shock of the unexpected, the gun went off in Metzger's hand. He had no time to aim it; the bullet found its own target. And Ebenau slumped onto the floor.

Viola was free at last, was the only thought that flashed through Tom's mind. It did not enter his head that the fluke which had just eliminated Ebenau, could as easily have done for him. But allowing himself the luxury of even that thought was madness – and he knew it. There was a job still to be done. He might have disarmed Metzger in the scuffle, but he was a long way short of giving in.

Metzger rammed his knee into Tom's groin. Tom bent double in an involuntary spasm to minimise the pain. Metzger seized the moment, slithered out of his grip, jumped to his feet and was off. His advantage was quickly eroded. Metzger might have been strong – but when it came to speed, Jablonski had the edge. By the time he had thundered along the landing and down the stairs, Tom was already closing hard.

Outside, the snow had stopped falling. Almost to order – as Tom followed through the same side door at the back of the building – a gap opened up in the clouds and a watery moon cast its spotlight directly onto the fleeing Metzger. Tom gave chase.

They raced uphill all the way until the road curved sharply to the left. Then – as Metzger rounded the bend – Tom lost him from view. At this spot, just below Füssen, the clear green waters of the river Lech are pent up against a weir before they confront the confines of a deep, natural gorge. A slender footbridge straddles the chasm at the very point where the river waters gush into it.

Tom looked across and, aided by the moonlight, scoured the steeply rising ground for any sign of movement – however slight. There was none, but that did not signify anything. Metzger could have taken up position behind a tree, a bush, a rocky outcrop. But he was over there – Tom was sure of it.

He knew how wrong he was a moment later when a pair of hands grasped him from behind and tightened around his neck. Tom's first thought was that it was all over. But when the strangler began to chuckle and mouth obscenities in his ear, Tom knew he was in with a chance of survival. He understood the mentality of the likes of Volker Metzger – and what fun would there be for him in a quick end?

Metzger loosened his grip on Tom's neck and yanked his arms high behind his back. He marched him out onto the bridge. Half way across he stopped and forced Tom's head out over the edge, taunting him by threatening to throw him over the top.

Tom saw his break. He secured himself, as best he could, at the waist and ankles, by pressing them hard against the railings of the bridge. He jerked his whole torso suddenly forward, with enough force to lift Metzger's feet clear off the ground. With the balance of power abruptly in his favour – and before his attacker had any time to react – Tom jerked again, this time so violently he lifted Metzger onto his back and up into the air. One more heave flung him, head over heels, off the bridge and screaming down into the rocky, foaming chasm.

By the time Tom got back to Ebenau's stronghold, Viola was gone. Schneider told him he had sent her back to Munich with Heino and the rest of the task force. Tom interrupted Schneider's discussions with the local police only long enough to tell them about Metzger, then he went back into the house.

Upstairs, in what had been Viola's room, he gazed down at Ebenau – at the blood on his shattered chest. He could not stop himself from bending down to touch it. It was still sticky and warm, like any other man's.

Chapter Thirty

Henry Melhuish made a dazzling Star of Bethlehem. For the first time in her life, Viola was conscious of an overwhelming craving for motherhood. Her youngest nephew was a cherubic three and three-quarter year old. But he was a demon in angel's clothing; a dare-devil, eager to perform any kind of mischief his fertile little brain could devise. Viola adored him for this exuberance and now realised that she wanted a little Henry of her own.

The performance was judged a total triumph by all his relations, and the grandparents proposed that the whole party dine out in Henry's favourite pasta restaurant to celebrate.

"Well, young Henry," Rory said. "What does it feel like to be a famous actor?"

Henry did not respond. His mouth was too occupied, struggling with wayward strands of spaghetti. He merely grinned.

"You'll be so famous now," teased the elder of his two brothers, "people will be coming up to you in the street, asking for your autograph."

"Talking of famous people – I see, little sister, your friend Peter Lessel is about to enter the realms of political stardom. I was reading a very interesting article about him in *The Times* on my way home this evening. Looks like it's Herr Lessel's intention to become Führer of the Fourth Reich. Just as well you pulled out of the Fatherland when you did."

"Viola should never have gone there in the first place. It was a ridiculous idea from the start. Goodness knows, we all warned her against it."

Margaret Addison retained her annoying habit of speaking about Viola as though she were not there. The brief respite from her mother's nagging, which Henry's enchanting performance had afforded, was now clearly over. How Viola wished her family in general and her mother in particular would have the good grace to avoid any reference to her time in Germany – at least until she had had time to come to terms with the whole sorry mess. It was wishful thinking.

"Well, I liked Peter," declared Olivia. She went no further. The focus of her attention had been switched to James and Edward, who had just launched themselves into a race – to see which of them could shovel the most pasta into his mouth at one go.

"*I* liked Peter," continued Rory, easily managing to ignore his sons' misdemeanours. "I liked Lutz too. And I fully admit, I agree with much of what Peter was saying that night at dinner – on the face of it that is. Where they and I would have parted company – and it's a pretty crucial difference – is *they* clearly believed the end justifies the means. Whereas *I* do not."

"But it's all over and done with now, thank Heaven," said Viola's father. He caught Viola's eye and gave her an understanding look. "So let's forget it, shall we?"

His wife bristled noticeably. The very last thing she intended was to allow Viola to forget it. Short of actually uttering the words, "I told you so", she was determined to do everything in her power to make her daughter feel suitably contrite. Charles Addison had a softer heart.

"We had a card from John Bowman this morning, Viola. Did your Mother tell you?" Of course she had – over and over again. "I'm glad he'll be back here for Christmas. He's such a nice chap."

Viola knew her father meant it kindly – even if it was his idea of a subtle form of brain-washing. Although quite how she was expected to respond, she was not at all sure. The boys' coughing and spluttering from the after-effects of their gormandising exploits – plus Henry's loud giggling at the spectacle they made – saved her from the necessity of any response at all. And when, after the brief fracas, Olivia started up the conversation again, she luckily approached things from a different angle still.

"Anyway, Viola's come out of the whole affair as quite a VIP herself," she announced, referring to Viola's television appearances, as well as the rash of newspaper articles about her since the Alte Pinakothek bombing and Professor Feinstein's death. Viola heaved a sigh of relief that the German Police had so far managed to keep under wraps her own involvement in the business down in Füssen.

"Yes indeed. And – if I'm not very much mistaken, little sister – a rather rich one into the bargain. Feinstein's leaving you that Dürer must have gone quite some way towards softening the blow of your other – what shall we say? – disappointments. It must be worth millions."

Viola's reaction was non-committal. She had already decided she could not keep the picture. In her eyes it was almost like blood money. She had resolved to sell it and give all the proceeds to the restoration funds of the art galleries afflicted by the bombings. It would be her means of atonement. She was sure Josef Feinstein would have approved.

Of the approval of her own family she was far less confident. Viola believed they would see such behaviour as conclusive proof of what they had long suspected: that she was at best eccentric, at worst deranged. As a consequence she had avoided discussing the matter and would continue to do so, at least for as long as it took to make the necessary legal arrangements.

When they left the restaurant Viola went home with the Melhuishes, under the pretext of helping Olivia to put the boys to bed. She sat in the back seat of the car, flanked by Edward and James and nursing the sleepy Henry. She hugged him tight. She rested her head against his. He smelt delicious. Tears of longing brimmed over from her eyes and rolled down her cheeks. Perhaps there were tears of regret there too, for she knew well enough that – had she married John – she could have been cradling children of her own by now. It was just as well she was going up to London tomorrow. The longer she stayed in Bolchester, the more every circumstance of her life would lure her into making a match of convenience rather than a marriage of love.

She discussed the matter with Hilly the following evening over a more civilised dinner which she had prepared herself. It was the first real chance they had had to talk.

"You know, Hilly, when you've felt that way about someone – when you've been so sure *everything* about him is right . . ."

"Everything *wasn't* right about him," interrupted Hilly. "Everything was *wrong*. You know that. And now forget him. There are plenty of other men around – thank God – the world's full of them. But not John. If he wasn't right before, he's not going to be right now. It would be marrying on the rebound."

Hilly was displaying an unprecedented degree of compassion. Viola recognised the fact and was grateful for it. But she knew Hilly could not possibly know how she felt. She doubted anyone could.

"It's having had it and lost it, that hurts."

"But tell me, Flower, what *did* you have? Think about it. You only had a dream. You were in love with a dream – an idea – a fantasy man. The real man turned out to be a shit."

"I know. You're right."

"Then you *can't* regret it."

"But I do. I can't stop thinking about him."

Suddenly Hilly's resources of sympathy dried up.

"I just don't understand you. You fall in love with a man. That I can understand – just about. But when you realise he's not the man you thought he was – why go *on* loving him? There's no sense in it. Anyway I refuse to believe you *could* love a man who stands for everything you abhor – racism, Fascism, terrorism, fanaticism."

"Hang on," Viola said abruptly. "Who do you think I'm talking about?"

"Lutz, of course – your reincarnated Hitler."

"Oh, Hilly, I don't regret that. The man raped me, for God's sake.

No; I'm talking about Tom."

"The Texan journalist?"

"And German policeman."

"Well, you hang on," Hilly said. "I don't *quite* get it. If you've gone and fallen in love with your Action Man from Texas, what are you doing back here? And why did you agree with me when I said he was a shit?" The penny quickly dropped. "Surely it can't be because he didn't tell you he was a cop. I mean what bloody use would it be – being undercover – if you're then going to go and blab about it?"

At last Viola told her about the night she had spent with Tom and about the morning after – about finding the photographs.

"Flower, Viola, I don't believe I'm hearing this. You're *that* pure and innocent. Are you trying to tell me if you had pictures of *him* all pumped up and ready for action, you wouldn't keep them by your bed – handy for indulging in a spot of auto-eroticism? There'd be something wrong with you if you didn't. And there'd be something wrong with him if he'd fed those pictures of you through the office shredder."

Viola fell silent – but Hilly soon put an end to that. Having whetted her appetite with the most titillating piece of news she had heard in years, Hilly was not about to sit around and watch Viola ruminate.

"Well, go on – tell all. Hold nothing back." She sprang to her feet. "Hang on a sec. This calls for champagne. *We* are going to celebrate."

It might have been because of the champagne that Viola slept so soundly that night. When she did wake up, it was to the sound of Hilly – never noted among her friends for the lightness of her step – getting ready to go to work. Viola snuggled further down under her bedclothes and pitied her. Though when she thought about Tom; when she thought about how she had run away from Tom, then she pitied herself far more. A few minutes later Hilly appeared with a mug of tea. Viola grunted her thanks.

"Drink up, Bed-Slug – or are you going back to sleep?"

Viola grunted again. Even Hilly, who over the years had heard Viola's whole repertoire of grunts, had trouble interpreting this one.

"Shall I draw the curtains – or shall I leave them closed? It's still dark outside."

Viola hauled herself out from beneath her duvet. She picked up the tea from her bedside table and took a sip.

"Hilly, how d'you expect me to make major decisions like that at this ungodly hour?"

Hilly took the decision for her and opened the curtains – in spite of the fact that the only light likely to come in would be from the street lamp directly outside the window. As she completed the task, so she let out a long, lascivious wolf-whistle. Viola laughed.

"What *are* you doing?"

Hilly did not turn around to look at her, though she did respond – after a fashion.

"*Very nice.*" She lapsed into a mock Southern drawl. "Why Miss Viola, I do declare – your *man* is here for you."

Viola put down her mug – she was shaking too much to hold it – and pulled herself up bolt upright.

"Hilly, what are you talking about?"

"Well put it this way, Flower, there's a guy out here who's just climbed out of a taxi and let himself in our gate. He's not one of *mine,* I'm sorry to say, because he's a real hunk – a definite ten out of ten for SQ. Nor is he one of *your* arty-farty, intellectual types." She swung around to face Viola and tapped her forehead with her forefinger. "So with the aid of my astonishingly high IQ and my highly developed powers of deduction, I've reached the conclusion he must be your playmate from Munich."

Viola leapt out of bed and ran across to the window. It was Tom.

He was sitting on the garden wall, underneath the lamp-post, with his legs stretched out onto the tiny lawn. He was using the light from above to read some papers, which meant that his head was bowed. Hence Viola could see only the top of his head – mainly his hair – which glistened as the street-light shone through the beads of rainwater which the drizzle had deposited over it. He stood up, rolled up the papers and stuffed them into a pocket of his leather jacket. He let out a long yawn and stretched.

Hilly made a salacious comment – the words scarcely registered with Viola, though the meaning did. It was the sort of reaction she would have expected from Hilly. Yet she knew well enough, any woman would appreciate a sight like Tom – especially the way he looked today.

He was wearing tight, black jeans that left little to the imagination and a jacket that delineated just how broad his shoulders were. But what was most striking about Tom was not the component parts which made up his body, but the manner of their combination into a whole. It created a physique charged with overt masculinity. As she looked down at him now, Viola marvelled that it had taken her so long to see it. How blind she had been.

She did not hear what Hilly said as she went downstairs.

"Hello, Tom," she said quietly, when she went out to meet him. She could feel herself trembling. She could even hear it in her voice as she spoke. "What are you doing here?"

He did not answer straight away, but allowed his eyes to wander around the pocket handkerchief of a front garden. When they looked back at her, they were smiling.

"Oh, just checking out where to put that willow cabin. I'm going to need some place to write those *'loyal cantons of contemned love'*."

He laughed. Yet she was conscious the laugh had a hesitant, uncertain ring to it; as if he were not confident he knew what its effect – or that of his remark – would be. She thought of her hysterical behaviour when they parted in the Polizeipräsidium – and again down in Füssen – and could hardly blame him for treading carefully. She smiled at him.

"So? Am I forgiven?" he asked – this time in earnest.

"There's nothing to forgive."

"Then marry me."

Hilly chose that very moment to leave for work. She came rushing out of the house like a tornado – greeting Tom in passing like a long lost friend. She shouted back a reminder to Viola about inviting him in for breakfast. It was just as well she did. Such a mundane thought had not even entered Viola's head.

251

They went indoors – into the kitchen. Tom took off his jacket and draped it over the back of a chair, while Viola put water on for coffee. He went across and stood beside her as they waited for it to boil. He did not attempt to touch her.

"Marry me, Viola?" he repeated. "You know I'm crazy about you."

"Tom, please don't . . ."

"Hey, look, if you're still freaked out about those pictures, I'm real sorry. I never meant you to see them."

"No, I don't care about the pictures. And I don't mind you didn't tell me you're a policeman either. I see now that you couldn't."

"Then marry me. We're made for each other."

"I can't."

"'I can't' isn't the same as 'I don't want to', is it?"

"No, it isn't." She paused.

"Then why can't you?"

"Because I can't go back.

"But you've got to. Okay – apart from me – what about Ludwig and his castles? What about your book? You've got to finish your sabbatical, don't you?"

"No, I can write my book here. I've done enough research. Besides, I'm missing my teaching."

"So you can do that in Munich. Rupert Servranckz would fall over himself to give you a job."

"Tom, I can't go back. Please don't ask me to. How could I live in Munich when every time I went out, I'd be looking over my shoulder to see if someone was following me – or every time I went into a restaurant, I'd be frightened of bumping into Peter Lessel?"

"Listen, if you don't go back, you're letting them win. Don't you see that?"

"Yes."

"Look, the only way you can come to terms with life – the good and the bad in it – is by meeting it head on." Now at last he touched her – touched her hand. He took hold of it. In his it felt so small and fragile. "Viola, I wish I could promise you there'd be no Lessel – no racists – no ugliness to bother you there. But I can't. This isn't a book. It's not a film. There's no script here for me to write them out of the story so it can all end happy ever after. This is for real. They're a fact of life – so we've just got to face them." He squeezed her hand and swept it against his lips. "You know it's ironic, isn't it? All my life I've thought of myself as an American – always planned on settling over there one of these days. And now – now you and I could just take off together and leave all this behind us – I can't bring myself to do it. When I look around and see what's happening – not only in Munich – not only in Germany – in France, in Russia – all over – the Far Right getting stronger, getting more support, more influence. You've seen them on TV – marching – flying banners – wearing uniforms – bullying innocent people. And I can't let them do that. I can't walk away from it – not without doing all I can to stop it. I owe it to Feinstein. Jesus! Twice in his life they terrorised that poor guy. I owe it to Ellie, who those sons-of-bitches gunned down in cold blood. I owe it to my boss, who's lost the use of his hand because of them. I owe it to *all* their victims – past and present – and future too, damn it."

"I understand, Tom. And I admire you for it – more than I can say. But I'm not strong like you."

"Sure you are – if you want to be." He laughed. He rested her hand on his arm and flexed his muscles. "Besides, I'm strong enough for two."

She tried to return his laughter. "Tom, when I'm with you, I don't feel afraid. But what about when you're *not* there? When you're away, undercover, for days – weeks on end. I'm not strong enough to cope with that. I know I'm not."

"But that's not the way it's going to be – I promise. My cover's blown now. How can I be on TV with a heroine like you one minute – or in the newspaper – and then go back on the streets the next? I can't. That's a part of my life that's over. Anyhow, Werner Fuchs wants me to head up the Anti-Terrorist Squad. So – not only do I get the job I want – I get to go home nights – all night – most every night." He leant down, kissed her neck and whispered. "Now all I've got to do, is get the girl. Marry me?"

With his aroma pervading the air around her – with his body closing in on hers – how could he expect her to answer him, when every movement he made deprived her of the breath to do so?

"Think about it," he murmured in her ear. "I'll wait – as long as it takes."

They kissed and when their lips parted – when their eyes joined – hers had a new dream in them – while his had a glint. He put his lips back to her ear, as if to tell her a secret that no-one else must hear.

"Only, while I'm waiting for your answer, Viola, d'you think you and I could go to bed?"

Viola laughed. Tom always knew how to make her laugh.

"Tom Pajak – No, Tom *Jablonski* – you're a louse. What am I going to do with you?"

He scooped her up in his arms and headed in the direction of the stairs.

"I can't wait to find out."